ONE MAN ESCAPED

SECOND EDITION

ONE MAN ESCAPED

SECOND EDITION

STEVEN F. MEEKER

LitPrime Solutions
21250 Hawthorne Blvd
Suite 500, Torrance, CA 90503
www.litprime.com
Phone: 1-800-981-9893

Published by LitPrime Solutions   05/24/2022

ISBN: 979-8-88703-009-8(sc)
ISBN: 979-8-88703-010-4(e)

Library of Congress Control Number: 2022909417

CONTENTS

READ THIS FIRST

Your Mission, if you accept it, is to find Alva C. Tenil Horr.

We've all heard from tales of famous criminals and how they ran from the law. Folk tales of Baby Face Nelson, Machine Gun Kelly, Bonnie & Clyde, John Dillinger, John Gotti, and Al Capone to mention just a few. But most likely you have not heard of Alva C. Tenil Horr. I will be honest, my dad's family knew him very well. All the great stories pretty much follow the same story lines. Things were once good, then something awful happened, and a great battle must be fought or a journey taken. A hero comes and sets things right. Not so in this mystery novel.

I want you to use your detective skills and track down Mr. Horr. I have given you tips in this historical fictional mystery novel on how to locate Alva C. ("Tenil") Horr. Try to put the clues together as you read. Then write down your best conclusion to this storyline, before you read the final chapter. **<u>Your tips are in Black Bold Letters and are underlined.</u>** You can visit bookspreferred.com and enter your best conclusion to this mystery novel. *Happy hunting!*

DEDICATION

This book is dedicated to my family members.

For Gail:
My wife, soulmate, and best friend without whom my accomplishments would be meaningless.

Also, thanks to:
Aaron, Nathan, Cecelia, Nancy, Dick, and to all friends who offered encouragement and support.

The dedications are the first place I look when I pick up a book... Because I love to see who's behind a writer. I'm captivated by the people who assist the author, to bring words to a page and meaning from circumstances that stop us in our tracks.

I have never maintained that I could really write a story. It's something that happened to me by accidents. But I figure one story every 100 years will be more than enough. Just saying.

What you are about to read is presented in the form of a story, but what is contained within the story is real.

This folktale has been handed down through generations by being told out loud. Every culture has its own folktales, but the stories often share certain characteristics.

Each character usually represents a specific trait or quality. The 200 characters in this story each represent a way of life that has been forgotten.

I have written this story so generations to come can read a true folktale.

If Horr had the brains of a turnip, this escape would have never happened; you would think. But as far as I'm concerned, Horr makes a turnip look bright. Maybe he had help from numerous folks in the township.

The first day I started looking for information about this murder, I pulled into a gas station in Danville Illinois. I saw a grim-looking man sitting in front of the store. He was filthy and spoke with a lisp as he described his painful life to me. I never got his name, but the image this man projected, give you an idea about Mr. Horr's life. Mr. Horr was tortured by memories. Outwardly, he was a man of success; he escaped. Inwardly, he was a flop and he knew it.

As few as 1 percent of families in Vermilion County Illinois accounted for half of all crime in 1900, and only 5 percent of families accounted for two-thirds of the crimes. But the significance of such astonishing statistics is revealed only when looking at the face of one man. Meet therefore Alva C. Tenil Horr.

In the first decade of his life, in the small town of Danville Illinois, Horr grew up as a member of respectable household. He willingly did household chores with his sister, briefly attended school, played with others his age, roamed the streets around home, and acquired a sense of the land that proved vital in later years. But the next ten years Horr's name would be well knowing throughout Danville.

1890: age 14, possession of firearms, remanded to Juvenile Hall where his rights as a youth were waived and remanded to the adult court as unfit for the services of the Juvenile court. Sentence suspended and placed on probation for one year.

1892: age 16, discharge firearm, sent to reform school for six months.

1897: age 21, stole a horse for a joyride. Charges dropped and his sister paid owner of horse to drop the charges.

1898: age 22, armed robbery with his closest friend. Sent to prison for two to five years. Released from prison after two years (1900). Friend was never apprehended.

By this time, Horr was a hardened criminal pitiless; unfeeling and unlikely to change. He was a gambler, wagering money that he often didn't have, and a notorious liar. Booze was his best friend. He often would drink to forget about the life he was living. A thief, liar, and a gambler. Horr was his own greatest enemy. But his best friends always helped him when he was in trouble.

Horr's life was saved by pure luck more times than not. Always causing trouble at Red's Saloon in South Vermilion County. Fortunate, indeed, but how did this one man escape?

Is this the man we are looking for?

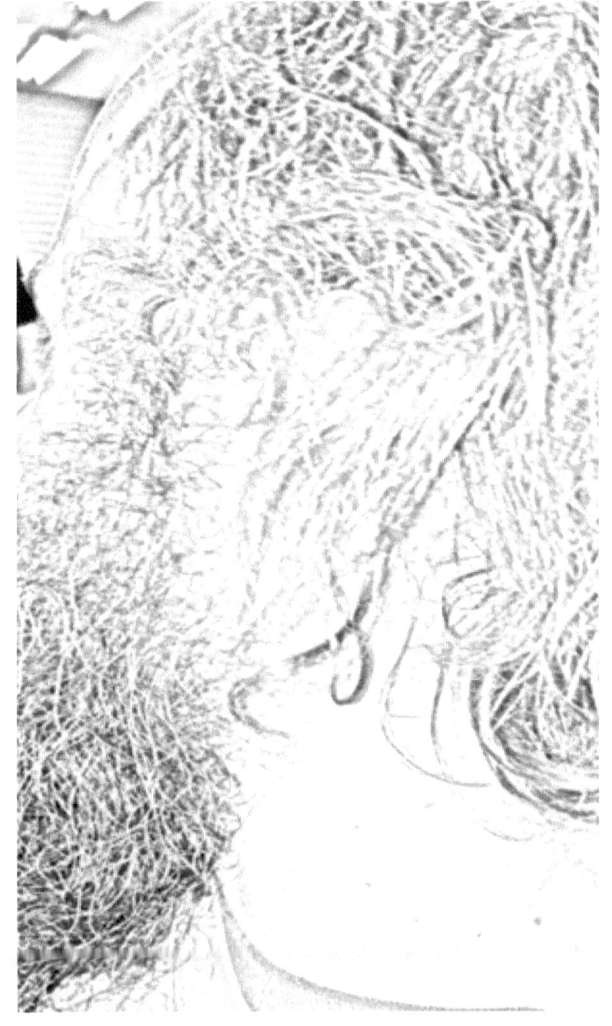

CHAPTER ONE

The Diamond Rings

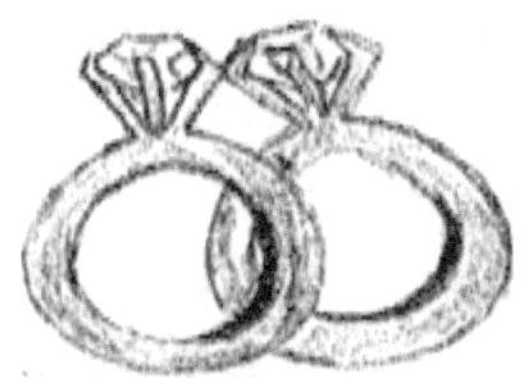

It was September 1, 1902. Twenty-years-old Ida Meeker, was about to become a wife. This five-foot-three, petite, young woman could have married any young man in the Danville area. But she had made up her mind that Alva was the right man for her. Her parents had mixed feelings about the man with whom she was about to get hitched. Her older brother, Frank, who always came to Ida's aid whenever she needed it, had introduced Alva Horr to his sister one afternoon at Barlow Park in Alvin, Illinois. Her absolute best childhood friend, Della, who knew everything about Ida, was helping Margaret, Ida's mother, decorate the Meeker home on Hampton Road in Danville for a celebration after Ida and Alva return from the office of the Justice of Peace that afternoon.

Margaret loved to cook, so preparing Ida's wedding meal was going to be a pleasure. She had a favorite pot that she cooked everything in. It was very valuable to her in a sentimental way because her grandmother gave it to her when she got married. She wouldn't let anyone touch it, unless she was in the kitchen with them. It aggravated Ida, who wanted to use it when her mother wasn't around. It only took one time for Ida to get caught using the pot! She never did it again.

When she located the pot, she started her work preparing the special wedding meal. She had a disheartened feeling about the whole day. So, to get her mind off of her uneasy feelings of Ida's marrying Alva she sang. Margaret loved to sing when she was down and especially songs that her husband Clark had made up. Her favorite tune when she was cooking was 'Bubble up'. Now, she didn't have a good singing voice, but that didn't matter; the joy she got from singing made her happy.

Ida's father, Clark, a large six-foot, two-hundred-pound man with big hands and a bigger heart never met a stranger; he would talk to anyone who would listen. He could play most any stringed instruments, but the piano was his favorite. Although playing cards with his wife and making up songs to play on the piano were great pastimes; his true passion was his devotion to his family. He would help anyone who wanted to help themselves. Clark wanted the best for his daughter, but he knew about Alva's troublesome background and the two years Alva had spent in prison for robbery as a **'Do-Pop'**.

Alva's parents, Allen and Maggie Horr, had given up on their son. They both were hard working folks who had five kids, three girls and two boys. Alva was the youngest boy and was in trouble with everyone in the Danville area. Allen could not control him. The fighting and stealing almost every day of his childhood took a toll on the relationship between Alva and his parents. **His older sister, Minnie, was the only family member, to help Alva when he needed support. The others turned their backs on him.**

Alva was neither a good kid, nor a smart kid. He could not read or write and loved sports, but disliked working. This caused conflict between Alva and his father. After serving his two years in prison and a short return to Danville, Alva disappeared for the next two years. When he returned, he had enough money to buy a café. When asked about his travels during those two years, Alva would never say. Alva and his friend Terrance J. **'Red'** Cutler were always together, and that's what concerned Clark. Red was the owner of a saloon on Lyons Road south of Danville, Illinois near Westville. Red was a bad apple in Clark's view. The Southern part of Vermilion County Illinois was rough, with every other structure a problematic saloon on Lyons Road, establishments had backroom card games, fights, and girls upstairs. With the Big Four Rail Yards nearby, the area was the least desirable in the county! What was Ida getting herself into?

Clark decided to have one last talk with his daughter. He wanted Ida to know she could back out of the wedding.

"This is my job today, that's what I am here for," Clark said to himself. He asked Ida to take a walk with him along the river near their house.

"Do you feel Alva is the right man for you? I don't want you to be unhappy; I want the best for you. Remember you can always talk to your mother and me any time. Our home is always open to you and Alva."

Ida convinced her father that Alva was right for her. They returned to the house and Ida started to get ready for the double-ring wedding ceremony. When Alva and Ida returned from the office of Allen Grant, Justice of the Peace, Margaret and Della had everything ready for the celebration. Clark entertained everyone with his music. He played the piano and the guitar making up one song after another.

After the farewell supper at the Meeker's, there were tears and long embraces. Just after dark Ida and Alva left. The next twelve years were difficult for Ida. She was always working while Alva was out having a good time. She had returned to her parent's house many times to stay because of being mistreated by her husband. Each time she returned back to Alva, with hope that he would change his ways.

Late Sunday, August 21, 1914, Alva came home. Before Ida could say anything, Alva started shouting,

"You better listen to me. Just listen to me! I need your diamond rings that you got back from the jewelry store. I need to pay **Adrianoplis** the Greek or the 'Italian', as I call him, the money I lost to him in a dice game last night. He has given me until the end of the month, or he will kill me! Do you understand? I need to hock them, again, for the money to pay Adrianoplis. He is with the **Black Hand Family**. He has threatened me with bodily harm and kidnapping. This is extortion, do you understand?"

Ida leaned back in her chair and fiddled impatiently with her hands. "Alva", she said once and for all, "I am not going to be part of your horrible schemes. I thought you told me that you always do well at dice. You said that your dice were rigged. Was that a lie also? This gambling must stop!" Someone is going to get killed. I am going to bed. By the way, my father dropped off a new pair of shoes for you today. Try them on they are a size six. See if they fit."

"Yes, I like these shoes. I have never seen a pair of shoes like these before." He stared at the soles, admiring the three grooves cut out in a 'V' shape pattern. As he examined the soles closer, he remarked, "A person wearing these shoes could leave a trail."

"Make sure you thank my father the next time you see him."

Surprisingly, under the circumstances, both Ida and Alva slept long and dreamlessly. But in the early morning, when the silence of night was replaced by the first shining of a new day, the rusty hands of the clock marked half passed five. Ida rose and went to the deserted drawing room. As she filled the wash pan with water, she could hear Alva moving around in the bedroom.

"Where's my bottle? Who took my bottle? Ida, where did you put my whiskey?"

Alva then walked into where Ida was wiping her face with a towel.

"For heaven's sake," she said, "Don't scare me like that!" Then she whirled around to face Alva, her eyes staring at Alva like a wild animal.

"Listen to me," said Alva, "I need those rings now!"

"Do you remember what I said last night?" Ida asked, "I'm not going to be any part of your schemes. Do you understand me? Look at me with your eyes; that way I know you are listening to me. Stop asking about the rings, do you understand?"

Alva started backing up, then stumbled, and fell onto the bed. "You're drunk," she said, adding, "I don't want any trouble from you."

Alva shrank back into the pillows.

Alva did not answer her at first. "Why-what do you mean?" he asked.

"I need to get to the café to open up," said Ida, "See you when you get there. Don't be late; I need your help."

Alva gazed around the room. "Yes, Ida, I will be along when I can."

"Please," Alva begged, "just tell me where the two rings are before you go."

Ida walked out of the house without saying a word.

Ida had just finished serving lunch to Matt Russell and Jack Hilman, her two best customers from Westville. They came into the café almost every day to talk with Alva. After they had finished eating and walked out of the café, Ida placed the "closed" sign on the door. She was looking forward to a quiet, restful afternoon before the dinner hour in her chair, located in the kitchen. About one o'clock, Alva came into the café with a look of anger on his face. He had been thrown out of a saloon on Van Buren Street. Alva propped himself against the wall in the kitchen and started asking questions about the diamond rings as soon as he saw Ida.

Ida said, "You will never get those rings! My father has them and he will never give them to you."

"I need them now! Your old man better give them to me or I…"

Just then, Ida turned, looked at him, and said, "You will never get the rings back, and I hope you sell this café. I cannot keep working twelve hours a day while you are out drinking and gambling with **<u>your corrupt, no-good friends!</u>** I will not be at home tonight; I will be at my parent's house until you sell this place."

At that point, Alva stepped toward Ida and started hitting her. "You better listen and listen good, you sorry-eyed monster!"

Ida had fallen to the floor by this time. Holding her hands over her face, "Stop! Stop! I cannot take this anymore."

Alva continued hitting and kicking her, as she crawled out into the dining area trying to get away. Alva reached into his coat pocket and took out his whiskey bottle and took a drink. The whiskey ran down the front of his mouth and onto his shirt.

At this time, the two employees, May and Nellie, who were in the basement ran up the steps and came to Ida's rescue. They pulled Alva off Ida and told him to leave the café.

Alva shouted, "I'll be back and you two better not be here, understand?" May, the café's cook, helped Ida to a chair in the dining room next to the pot belly stove. It was obvious that she was in great pain. "Do you want us to call the police?" May asked.

"No," Ida said, "Just call me a taxi." After a few minutes in the chair, Ida walked little by little to the cash box and pulled out money to pay the two employees, then went to the kitchen to get her purse and umbrella. By this time, the taxi was out on Hazel Street waiting for her. Ida handed the keys to May and asked her to lock the doors of the café. Ida walked slowly to the taxi and climbed in holding her purse tightly.

The taxi driver, seeing her face, asked, "Are you okay? Do you need a doctor?"

"No," said Ida. "I'll be fine."

May passed the keys to her while she was sitting in the taxi.

Ida then remembered that she had left her umbrella in the café. "May," Ida said, "Would you get my umbrella? It's in the kitchen."

May unlocked the door and went back inside to find the umbrella. When she returned with the umbrella, Ida took the keys and put them in her purse and placed the umbrella, next to her, telling May, "I feel better now that I have my umbrella. I feel safe now." Ida thanked May and Nellie. "But please don't come back until I call for you. It's not safe to be around Alva. I will be at my parents' house if you need to talk with me."

With that, Ida told the taxi driver to take her to West Williams Street just past the Sutherland Ford Bridge. "That is the Morin Addition area?" the taxi driver asked. As the taxi turned left on North Street,

Ida checked her purse for the two diamond rings, making sure they were in her possession.

"Are you Tenil Horr's wife?" the taxi driver asked.

Ida looked at him, and said, "Yes. How did you know his name was Tenil?"

"We are good friends, we play cards and dice games sometimes, I never win; he always ends up taking my money."

"What's your name?"

"Smith, James Smith, I own the **Smith Transfer Company at 21 East North Street.** Not only do I have taxies, but I transfer baggage and freight. If you have something to ship out of Danville, or you are shipping to Danville, I can help you. I can hold the item until you come to pick it up. We never open anything if the shipping label is marked 'Do not open' we have items in our storage that have been there for more than six years. This is my new vehicle, just got it. Do you like it?"

As he turned onto Logan Avenue, not giving Ida time to answer, Smith continued talking; "It's an 'Allen'. I went to Fostoria, Ohio and picked this vehicle up myself. It's the best vehicle I have ever owned."

"Do you own the grocery on East Main?" Ida asked.

"No, my wife, Emma, has that business she's from Chicago."

"Oh," said Ida, as she looked down at her feet, thinking, "I owe her money."

"Did you say West Williams Street?"

"Yes, turn left at the next street,"

When the taxi approached the bridge, Ida said, "Turn left at Hampton." And then she told the driver that she lived at the end of the dirt road.

"Do you know Frank and Charles Meeker?"

"Yes, they are my brothers."

"Those Meeker boys are dangerous; I would not want them looking for me. Your father must be Clark Meeker? What's your mother's name?"

"Margaret."

"I see your father in saloons sometimes," Smith replied. "He's always looking for Alva. He's a funny guy; he never meets a stranger. He talks to everyone. But I would not want to get into a fight with him. I heard that he bit a man's ear off one time. Is that true?"

"Maybe, I don't know. I think it was part of a man's nose. This is where my parents live. How much do I owe you?"

"Ten cents," Smith replied. Ida paid him and stepped out of the taxi. After getting out of the taxi, she walked very slowly to the porch and knocked on the door, but no one answered. She turned and sat down on the steps. She didn't know how to explain to her parents what had happened at the café. She thought, "I cannot keep coming back here every time Alva beats me, but this is the only place I feel safe." But how would she convince her father that she would finally file for divorce from Alva?

Ida had no doubt it was time to fight back. She told herself she didn't care anymore about trying to make a life with Alva. All she could think about was being beaten by Alva whenever he was drunk.

"What kind of life is this?" she asked herself. "I have no one to turn to but my parents. If I could stay with my parents, I would be much happier. I just have to convince my father that I mean what I say."

As Ida stood up from the porch steps, she could see her parents walking down the dirt road that led to the house. She could hear her father talking to her mother and laughing about some boring story, as he always did. She wiped the tears from her face, and waved to them. As her parents walked closer to her, she ran and gave both of them a hug.

"What are you doing here?" her mother asked. "I thought you were working at the café? Is everything okay?"

With that, Ida started crying and could not control her emotions.

Her mother asked, "What is it," Why are your eyes and your face swollen?"

"Did Alva do this to you," her father asked. "How did this happen?"

Half crying, she whimpered, "He did this to me and I never want to see him again. Can I stay here until I have things worked out?"

"Let me look at you," said her mother. "Let's go into the house and clean your face and we can talk about this."

Ida's father unlocked the front door.

Ida's mother took her into the room that serves as both a living and dining room and was used for sleeping as well on occasions.

"Let me look at you," her mother said, "over here in the light, by the piano."

Her father had picked up a towel and a wet wash cloth and handed it to his wife. In a stern voice, her father said, "When are you going to divorce this drunk? He has treated you this way too long. Are you going to put a stop to this crazy life style or do I need to? If you need the money to file the court papers for a divorce, I will find the money."

"Mom, Dad, there is nothing Alva and I share. It's not a good marriage; we're never together. I'm always working and he is always drunk and gambling away our money. I thought I could change him. I thought I could show him a better way of making a living. I thought the café would change things. But I now know after living with him for more than twelve years, it will never happen."

"Tomorrow," her father said, 'We will talk more about this. You need to rest tonight. You'll feel better tomorrow."

Her mother asked her, "Will you be okay here for a few hours? We will be down the road playing cards at the Bobaker's house. Maybe we should stay here."

"Please go, I just want to be alone for a while. Please go and have a nice visit with the neighbors."

"Well, before I go, I want you to eat something," her mother said.

Ida looked at her father and said, "Dad, I have something to give you." Ida went to her purse to get the diamond rings. "Here are the two rings that Alva gave me when we got married. I want you to keep these rings and promise me that you will never give them to him. Promise me that you will keep these rings for me." Ida gave the rings to her father and squeezed his hand.

He looked down at the rings and said, "Alva will never see these rings again."

With that, Ida sat down at the kitchen table to eat. As her mom kissed her goodbye, she told her "Have a good time tonight, I will be asleep when you get home."

It was getting dark and the August sunset gave Ida a peaceful relaxing feeling. She thought to herself, "This time I will change this crazy life I am living."

Ida had just finished cleaning her dishes when she thought she heard a clatter outside. She walked into the living room and listened, but did not hear any sound. "Maybe I am just over reacting." Then she heard the noise coming from the side of the house.

A voice yelled, "Are you in there? Are you in there?" It was Alva.

"Go away," Ida said with a firm voice. "Go away, please go away."

At that moment, Alva kicked the front door open and rushed into the house.

Ida started screaming frantically, "What are you doing? What are you doing?"

Alva reached into his hip pocket, pulled out his revolver, and grabbed Ida by the neck. Holding the *gun* to her head, Alva said, "Come with me now or I will kill you!"

She had no choice, "Okay, okay, just put the gun down."

Alva and Ida had a great deal of trouble during the last years of their twelve years of married life. On each occasion, Ida would leave Alva and go to her parents. On each previous separation, Ida always returned to Horr at the point of a gun.

CHAPTER TWO

Horr is Well Known

The noonday whistle had just blown. Horr had a look of stupidity on his red face.

"What was that?" Horr shouted.

"What do you want?" asked Frank, the bartender. "That whistle has blown everyday at the same time, you stooge. It tells the coal miners they have six more hours to work."

Horr looked up from the soiled, wooden table and said, "I thought I fired you two weeks ago?"

"Oh, I just came back to see if you were still drunk, you need to go home. Maybe you should get one of your friends to take you home. You're drunk!"

"You just think I'm drunk!" shouted Horr.

"Keep your voice down!"

"What friends?"

"You fool a lot of people but you don't fool me! Everybody knows you," Frank said. "You have friends in **Tilton,** Westville, Oakwood, Catlin, Grape Creek, Georgetown, even Danville. Do you want me to call your café and have your wife come get you?"

"Don't speak to me about my wife," Horr said, taking another drink of whiskey. "Frank, are you married?"

"How can you remember my name in the condition you're in?"

"I know everyone around these parts. I have more friends than I care to count. Are you married?" Horr asked again. "Frank answer me, stop looking out the window."

"No," said Frank.

"I was told you gave up drinking at your wife's request," "Yes."

"And you stopped smoking for the same reason?"

"I did," said Frank.

"And it was for her that you gave up dancing, card playing, and billiards?"

"Absolutely."

"Then why did you divorce her?"

"Well, after all these improvements, I realized I could do better," said Frank laughing.

Horr said, "I'll drink to that." And with that he downed all of the whiskey in his glass.

Then a voice came from near the front door, inquiring, "When are you going to pay me, Horr? You have until Saturday to come up with the money."

Horr stood up and turned to see who was talking. It was Adrianople, the Italian, who was as welcome as a monthly bill. "Damn it." said Horr. "Well, it could have been worst, "Horr thought. I owe Matt Russell and Jack Hilman both one hundred dollars."

"Frank, why didn't you warn me about that dumb Italian?"

Horr had been thinking about this gambling debt since he lost all his money, with no real prospect of paying the Italian. Horr knew if he could get Adrianople into a dice game, he could win the money back.

"Adrianople, will you give me a chance to win the $ 50.00 back?" asked Horr.

"No, I want my money by Saturday,"

"Adrianople, come with me. Let's go to Red's saloon, Red owes me money. Maybe I can give you some of the money today. Just come with me," Horr insisted.

With that, the two despicable men started out for Red's place, on Lyons road. "Hey, Adrianople, can I give you a suggestion?" Horr asked.

"What would that be?"

"You need to change your name; no one can pronounce it." "I like my name."

'Well, from now on, I'm going to call you, The Italian Wait! You need an American name. I got it, when we get to Red's place; he has an exchange book; just look at the names listed, and pick out one. That's all you need to do. That will be your new name."

"I know I **would change my name,** if I had a good reason to do so. I would just change one letter in my name. What would that letter be? I don't know, but I would think of a good name that would keep me safe from anyone looking for me, **something like Meeker."**

"That wouldn't be one letter. That would be completely different name. You are as stupid as they say you are. "

"I'm not stupid; I just can't speak very clearly sometimes"

As they entered the smoke-filled saloon, around the table was gathered as tough a gang as could be found in Vermilion County in August 1914. The game was fast and furious and the stakes were high. Suddenly, the dealer, Red, who was also the saloon owner, flung his cards down on the table and threatened to pull out his gun.

"Boys," he shouted, "This game ain't a straight one! Orville ain't playing the hand I dealt him."

That's when all hell broke loose. It was every man for himself. By the time the fighting was over, chairs were broken and two of the corrupt card players were being helped off the floor.

Horr walked over to where Red was standing and asked, "You okay?"

"Yeah," said Red, wiping his hands off with the bar towel. "Can you help me clean up this mess?"

"I would but I have a bad left hand," said Horr.

Red looked at him, "How long are you going to use that snake story and gunshot' for an excuse? You never seem to have a problem with that hand when you roll dice or shoot pool. Get over here and help me move these tables. You have most people thinking **you're soft and unable to stand hardship.** I know different."

"Okay, okay,"

As Horr walked over where Red was standing, "I have a question for you. Can I use the back room for a few hours?"

"Why?" Red asked.

"The Italian and I want to roll some dice."

"Who?"

"Adrianople."

"Oh, that no good, I-want-to-hear-myself-talk-dummy-mouth-piece. No wonder **his brother-in-Law sent him here** for me to school him," Red said with a disgusted look on his face. "Not that again. Remember last time?"

"I will give you half the money that I take from this dummy. Do you have the jagged dice?" Horr asked.

"Yes, but how are you going to get the dice into the game?" "Easy," said Horr, "I will tell the Italian that you have the

dice for the game. That way, he will think that you are a neutral party," said Horr laughing.

"Okay let's do it," said Red. "Remember I get half of the money."

"Can you loan me twenty?" said Horr. "You owe me that from the last card game, remember?"

"Okay, okay," said Red. "Here's the twenty."

"Well, just remember the deal we have, **I have given two years of my life for you.** Never forget that! Remember?" said Horr.

"I know," said Red. "But there will be **a day when my debt will be paid in full.**"

Horr walked back over to the bar and asked for a bottle of whiskey and two glasses. "Adrianople, will you give me a chance to even the score with you?" asked Horr.

"Well, maybe," replied Adrianople.

"What game do you want to play?" asked Horr pouring whiskey into the glasses. "I heard that you like craps. You beat me at that last time."

"Sometimes," Adrianople replied.

"Adrianople, maybe we could shoot some dice?" said Horr. "Okay, but I don't have dice, do you?"

"No, but let me ask Red if he has any dice." Horr, called Red over and asked, "Can we use your back room to roll dice?"

"No," replied Red, "Go somewhere else. I need to work back in that room today; I have a train load of chaps from Champaign coming to play cards."

"We only need it for an hour or so," said Horr.

Adrianople asked, "Do you have a new set of dice?"

"Okay, okay," said Red, "but just for an hour, let me get the dice."

"I need to see your money," said Horr.

"Don't worry about my money," said Adrianople. "I have three hundred on me and I can get more if I need to."

"Where?"

"Chicago."

"Okay, here are the dice that you guys can use," said Red.

"Remember, I need this room in about an hour from now, understand?"

"No problem, I will have Horr's money in short order." "Red, do you have any house rules?" asked Horr.

"Yeah! No cheating, understand? No cheating!" said Red. "Okay, get your money out, Adrianople," said Horr. "What are the stakes?"

"Ten a throw?"

"No," said Horr. "If I lose the first two tosses, I would be busted. How about, two dollars a toss?"

"Okay," said Adrianople.

"We need to set some rules, don't you agree, Adrianople?" "Yes, most definitely."

"I have just one rule. I insist that you use one hand and that the dice bounce off the wall, to be counted as a good toss. Do you agree?"

"Yes, I do."

"I will always use my left hand, that's my money hand. You must declare which hand you will toss the dice from," said Horr.

"I will use my right hand," said Adrianople.

"Any other rules?" asked Horr.

"Let's keep this simple," said Adrianople. "I will bet that you will toss a 4, 6, 8, or 10 before you throw a seven."

"I will take that bet, with one change, you can only pick one number, not four numbers," Horr replied.

"No way!"

"This is how it works; you can choose either the 6 or 8 being rolled before I throw a seven."

"Is this even money?" asked Adrianople.

"Yes."

"Are those all the rules?" asked Adrianople.

"Yes, let's keep this simple. One more question," said Horr, "Do you have socks on?"

"Why do you ask?" replied Adrianople.

"Do you remember which sock went on first?" asked Horr

"What kind of question is that? I always put my right leg sock on first; in order to ensure a day of good luck, all good Italians follow that rule."

Horr looked at him, with his devious blood shot eyes, "Are you sure?"

"Well, we will find out in due time."

With the rules set, the dice started flying. Horr was down to six dollars, he had lost eight times in a row. Adrianople was feeling good. "I tell you the socks don't let me down now."

Horr's face was pale and he was drenched in sweat. Thinking that Red had conned him he wondered, "Why would he do that, that phony SOB."

Just then, Red walked into the back room. "You two gents doing ok?" asked Red.

Horr looked at him with a grim troublesome face. "Thought you boys could use a drink; it's on the house." "By the way, let me see those dice. I need to inspect them." With that, Red looked the dice over, "They look fine to me, Adrianople, are you good with these dice?" asked Red.

"I'm good," replied Adrianople. "And my socks are good."

"How about you, Horr? You better be; they are the best dice in the house." Neither Adrianople nor Horr saw the switch that Red had made with the dice.

"I got to go, you gems have just thirty minutes and you are out of here."

"Okay, okay," said Horr.

After Red closed the door, Horr said, "Do you want to end this game?"

"What?" Adrianople said.

"You have taken all my money. I just have four dollars in my pocket."

"No, you have six dollars, that's how I count it," said Adrianople.

"Will you go double on the next throw?" asked Horr. "Well maybe you owe me $50.00,"

"The next throw double or nothing, okay?"

"I throw a seven we are even, or I owe you $100.00 is that the bet?"

"Yes, that's it."

When these two finished rolling dice, Adrianople was down $300.00 to Horr. Adrianople didn't know how he bombed.

"I think I know what happened; you put the left leg sock on first." said Horr.

"I need to go back to Chicago and talk to my older brother," said Adrianople. "Can you loan me train fair?"

"Yes, but you will owe me."

"I know, I will make good on the advance. The next time I'm in Danville, I will take you to Terre Haute and show you a good time. Deal?"

"Maybe, but I have no reason to go to Terre Haute."

"Well, my brother has a big business there and he can get us anything we need during our stay."

"What kind of business?"

"Mostly saloons and back room card games. He gave me the Danville area. Red and I will be looking after my brother's business here in Westville on Lyon's Road with all the saloons, and the Big Four Trains Yards; business is booming. That big turn table used to turn them train engines around is the reason my family backs the establishments here on Lyon Road. That's how Red got his start on Lyons Road. But my brother owes him for saving his life back in July in Chicago…"

"I know, I was in Chicago with Red when that detective got killed."

"Red can do anything, and my brother will back him. **All Red needed to do is say the word, and things happen.** That's how stuff works in my family. My brother sent me here to work with Red. You do know that 'Red's' not his real name?"

"I know everything about Red, I saved his life about three months ago when the Chicago police raided the Vice District. Red pulled a gun and someone was killed. I went to the police line-up, using Red's name, and no one could finger him."

"Do you know Red's real name, Alva?"

"I can hardly remember my name; I like to keep things simple, Red's good with me. See you next time." Horr turned and walked outside where the sun was starting to set. Red and Horr settled up before Horr returned home on 5ᵗʰ Avenue, where the August twilight faded into night. Horr had scammed Adrianople out of his last dollar. It was time to celebrate.

When Ida returned home from a night at her father's house, she found her husband sitting in an armchair, surrounded by empty whiskey bottles. Horr had the look of vacant stupidity. He wore neither vest nor shirt, his dingy trousers fit badly, his shirt was crumpled up on the floor in the corner, and his cheap hat was lying on the floor with a vile miserable odor, half full of vomit.

Ida tried to wake him, with no luck. She called Alva's sister, Minnie, to take him to the hospital. Horr arrived at Lake View Hospital on Logan Avenue in a stupor, unaware of whom or what had brought him there. He remained "unconscious" until 1 p.m. the next day.

Horr's one refuge in life was Ida. She kept the family business running. But Ida was finished. She appealed to her father- and mother-in-law, Allen and Maggie Horr.

At first, Horr's parents were pleased with their son's willingness to find a job and his cooking techniques. He had a wonderful wife, started a business with his own money, that he had saved working in different jobs, so they thought. Horr had many friends all over the area. But now, they were angry at his moodiness and irresponsibility with money. He drank excessively, always in need of money. Allen went to the hospital to encourage his son to get help. Horr refused help. After the hospital visit, Horr and his mother and father did not speak for about a year.

Is this the man you are looking for?

CHAPTER THREE

Home Sweet Home

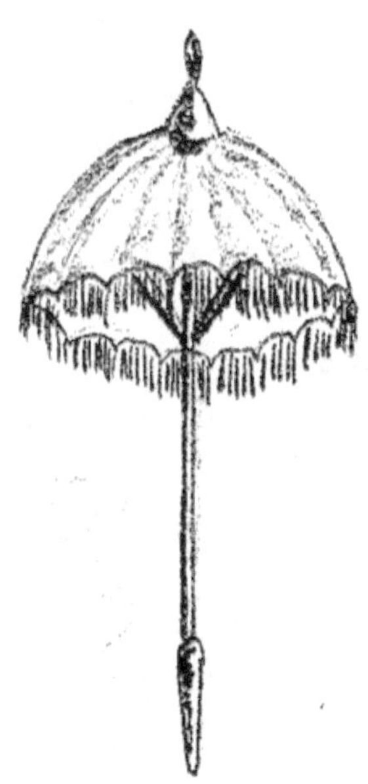

Horr decided it was time to sell the café, located in the Shreckrow block, on North Hazel Street. The cafe had been closed for two weeks due to Ida's refusing to open it. She was tired of Alva not helping. But the main reason for selling the café was that the pending divorce was forcing Alva to sell. Bert Lients had offered to buy the popular café from Horr. Bert requested afinancial audit because he didn't trust Horr. Horr was not in a position to say no and agreed to the audit but requested that Bert Lients pay for the review. Bert quarreled over the cost but finally agreed on a price.

Horr barely broke even with the proceeds from the sale. He was indebted to everyone. After paying his debts, Horr took the balance from the sale to his father's house. He wanted to show his parents that he was responsible, that he was not a business failure.

Horr's father, Allen, refused to talk at first but then he talked to his son. "Your dealings with the underworld have put your life in jeopardy. Your decisive behavior will only hurt innocent bystanders. These games you are playing conveniently can be categorized into three groups: 1) 'alcoholism', *(your* personal relationships and social standing revolve around alcohol), 2) 'now I got you,' (you are more interested in the fact that someone is completely at your mercy than having a good poker hand or making money), and 3) 'see what you made me do.' (You throw the burden of your decisions on someone else).

"Go on and play your games. Your mother and I are finished trying to understand you."

This sobering picture that Horr's father had painted made Horr very angry. "You can't stand being around me and I know why. You hate me because I have friends that will take care of me. **Friends that will help me whenever I need help!** You have no friends or life," yelled Horr.

For certain there was something that transcended between Horr and his father. The truth was that Horr was sensitive to criticism. Horr's, "I'll show them," opinion was the main cause of his problems. Thus, he attempted to maneuver himself into a superior position, not for the reputation or the material rewards but because it gave him power to exercise his revenge. Horr used every effort to gain prestige, not for the sake of craftsmanship or legitimate accomplishment (although those may play a secondary role), nor to inflict direct damage on his enemies, but so that they would be eaten with envy and with regret for not having treated him better.

His awareness of his father's anger made him think about their relationship. "Maybe, just maybe, he is deliberately trying to influence me, to get my life in order. Perhaps I'm better off without the help of my parents," Horr thought. Curiously enough, however, Horr didn't change his ways. He was more intense on setting the record straight with Ida. He wanted the rings back; that was his security.

Ida was not talking to her husband. Horr spent the next weeks walking the river bottoms locating a short cut from Logan Avenue to the river so he could watch the Meeker home where Ida was now staying full-time. She had moved all of her personal belongings out of the house on Fifth Street to her parent's home. Two weeks earlier, Ida had written her friend Della Hawes, who had been in Denver, Colorado the past year. In her letter, Ida went into detail about her failing marriage. She needed to talk to someone about her life and her relationship with Alva. She knew that Della would understand and that she would not be prejudiced since Della faced the same situation in her life a few years earlier. The one big difference was Della had two children. Ida had not seen her for over a year. She was Ida's most cherished friend before she moved to Denver. They used to, whenever possible, spend afternoons together, just talking.

Della was one of those people to whom Ida would tell her most private affairs. Della would always say what Ida needed to hear no matter what. That's why Ida trusted her opinion.

To Ida's surprise, Della had returned to Danville from Denver, Colorado to visit her parents. The morning after Della reached Danville on the train from St. Louis, they spent time catching up on each other's personal lives and remembering things they did when they were young and had not a worry. They both agreed that times had changed.

"Before I forget, I need to ask you about a town in Colorado. The name of the town is 'Meeker' have you heard of it?" asked Della.

"No," replied Ida. "But you can raise that question with my father when you see him.

"What about Ezra Meeker?" asked Della.

"No. Talk to my father that will give him something to think about. If anyone can tell you, if they are relatives he can."

"Remember," said Della, "the time when you're Uncle Moses came to visit with your parents?" They both started laughing.

"That crazy old man, he would argue with everyone," said Ida. "Remember that big old tomcat that hung around the outhouse?"

"That time the tomcat jumped at him, as quick as your uncle came out, I think he had to go back in the outhouse after that tomcat scared him." Della said, laughing.

"Those shameful piano lessons, which your father tried to give me, were depressing. That was a waste of time. All he could play was songs that he made up. He never played the same notes to any song ever. But I had a good time trying to learn to play. You know he needs to write down the lyrics of the songs he composes. I know he could sell them."

"My father doesn't care about that; he just likes to have a good time with people. Music makes him happy. No, dancing makes him happy."

"Remember we used to complain about having nothing to do. We'd walk uptown in those days and look at all the brick buildings like the new Court House on Main Street, and my favorite, the woman's clothing stores on Vermilion Street. On our way back home, we always walked by the Wolford Hotel and dream about staying at the hotel in a big room on the top floor someday," said Ida, laughing.

"Your mother would always ask us what trouble we got into," said Della. "Did you ever tell your mother about the time we went into the undertaker's place of work?" They both laughed.

"No," said Ida, "remember I had just turned nine and your birthday was coming up. We'd not seen a stiff. Remember Mr. Blythe the undertaker? We walked in and asked him if we could look around and you asked him if we could look at a stiff. Remember the look he gave us through those dirty glasses of his?" Then he said, "Young lady, we do not call the bodies of dead people, 'stiffs'. I refer to the body as the 'deceased person'. I received my three-day training for undertakers from Professor J. H. Clark, the father of embalming. Nowhere in that three-day school was the word 'stiff' used. If you have no business here, please leave." We ran out the front door like two scared rabbits.

"I remember the time we went to Alvin to have fun at Barlow Park that one summer. That's when your brother Frank introduced you to Alva," said Della. "Your brother had appointed himself as chairman of the blind date committee."

"That was the biggest mistake I have ever made in my life. That's when he had a job, and he saved his money. I thought we had a future together. But look at me now."

"You did have a great future with Alva. Remember the first job he took? I was at your house when Alva came home and told you about the job. Remember he went to the cafe that was advertising and nearly 50 applied. Out of the whole number, in a short time, the owner chose one, Alva, and sent all the rest away. And you asked how he got the job without a single recommendation with him and without any aid or support from his father. His father always told him he was incapable of doing anything. Alva could not read or write but was street smart, and still is today," said Della.

"Alva said you were mistaken; that he had a great many recommendations. He said it's not what's written down as much as your actions."

"Remember what Alva said about the old man that was interviewing him for the job, that he was watching everybody. Alva made sure that he wiped his feet when he came into the cafe and closed the door. When he was called to talk with the café owner, he took off his cap. He always looked at people when they were talking to him that way. They knew he was listening to what they were saying. That's why you thought you had a future with Alva. He was not book smart but street smart; he knew how to get around the city. He had friends everywhere; he was quick, knowing how to manipulate people and avoid bad situations. He has manipulated you since the first time you spoke to him. Young lady, you need to open your eyes and change your dealings with Alva."

"You are right, but I want to change the subject."

"I have a lot on my mind. Did you get my letter?"

"No," said Della.

"Well, I need to meet Alva at the office of Justice Henry Hall tomorrow. I don't know what to do. I know it's about the two rings that Alva wants back. I gave the rings to my father for safekeeping and told him not to ever give them to Alva. All he wants the rings for is to hock them, to pay for his gambling debts. The last time they were in hock, at the Main Street Jeweler Store I went and paid for them and took them home. When Alva found out that I had them, he demanded that I give them to him.

What do you think I should do?"

Della replied, "Did you get a court order to show at the meeting?"

"No," said Ida.

"Then I wouldn't go. This could be another plan of Alva's to get you away from your parent's home. He is street smart. I wouldn't go if it was me. Just keep away from Alva and you will be better off."

"I know."

"Every time he gets close to me, he threatens to kill me. We've had a great deal of trouble over the past years. The last time I was in court, Alva pleaded guilty to charges of disorderly conduct and paid his fine."

"What happened?"

'We had been separated for about six months and Alva was watching my parent's house. One afternoon my mom and dad walked into the city. Me and my sister, Alice, and her friend stayed home. Shortly after my parents left, Alva came to the house. We locked all the doors. That's when Alva kicked through the door and if my brother Frank hadn't come home, Alva would have shot me."

"How many times has he told you he would kill you?"

"I don't know, but he always has a gun, and if I say no to him, he tells me he'll kill me. What am I supposed to do?"

"Stay away from him, you can't trust him. I wouldn't go anywhere without your family being with you. That's your only protection, at this point. Do you understand Ida? Have you talked to the police about this?"

Ida looked Della straight in the eye, "What are they going to do? Alva would have to kill me before they would lock him up."

"You do have a lot on your mind, you need to relax and stay close to your parents. Your father and brothers will protect you."

"I know my father will not let anything happen to me. He keeps saying to me, 'That's my job, that's what I do!'"

"Where are your brothers and sisters? All nine of them are here in the Danville area. You have five brothers, right? Art, Charles, Frank, John, and Eli?" asked Della.

"Yes," Ida answered.

"And four sisters: Minney, Flora, Martha, and Alice?" continued Della.

"Yes," Ida again answered.

"They should all help your parents until this trouble is put right. Just one more foolish question. Why are you carrying an umbrella on a sunny day? Your bonnet keeps the sun out of your face."

"It's my protection. I feel safe with it in my hands," responded Ida.

"Okay, if that's what makes you happy," said Della.

"I want this umbrella with me everywhere I go. By the way, do you have any plans for Wednesday? My parents and I are going to Lincoln Park, for the Woodman Picnic. Can you bring your two children and join us?"

"That would be lots of fun and I know my children would enjoy that too."

"Just come over to my parent's house and we can walk to Lincoln Park."

"See you Wednesday morning."

CHAPTER FOUR

Battle on Williams Street

On Wednesday September 16, 1914, Della had traveled to Ida's mother and father's house in the Morin Addition just west of the city with her two children, Vertin and Helen, to enjoy the day at the Lincoln Park Woodman Picnic.

Ida was happy that Della came to join her and her parents to enjoy a fun day at the park. The weather could not have been better, not a cloud in the sky. The two kids were excited; Ida's father had a way with kids. He would get them all excited by telling them silly stories and getting them to laugh. He was a man who didn't know how to frown. His open smile made him popular with everyone, from kids to the old folks; he never met a stranger. That's what people liked about him, he made them smile. Clark taught himself to play both the piano and guitar. When asked by other musicians what music key he was playing a song in, Clark would reply, "The key of M." As a small child, Clark would play songs that he would make up. He didn't pretend to know much about anything. One thing he was always taking a crack at was finding water. He called himself a 'Dowser'; he had a forked (Y-shaped) branch that he cut down from a peach tree. Clark would walk slowly over the places where he suspected the water could be found. After a few minutes, the dowsing rod supposedly dipped and Clark would tell the person who he was helping to start digging for water! Very few times was he successful at locating water, but he like to see the expressions on people faces as they started to dig for water.

He did know that his family came first, no matter what.

Taking Ida and his wife to the Lincoln Park Woodman Picnic for fun was his job this day. He knew that Ida had a lot on her mind because he knew that Alva was bad for her. He didn't want to jump to any conclusions that Ida was safe, because he didn't trust Alva. At around 11 o'clock, they started walking to the park, Ida with her umbrella, her father hanging onto the picnic basket, and her mother carrying a blanket.

"What do they call this area?" asked Della.

"Hungry Hollow," said Clark.

"Why that name?" asked Della

'Well, the story I have been told…"

Just then Margaret interrupted;

"No, let me tell you. The name came about because the government starved the Kickapoo Indians. The government failed to help the Indians after they were told they would be helped during the winter months with food supplies. The road just past the river is called "Hungry Hollow Road."

"Heck all of us around these parts are hungry!" said Clark, "that's when I learned to eat skip-it."

"Skip-it, what's that?" said Della.

"It's good with eggs," replied Clark. "That's when you skip a meal."

"All the wild animals are gone, no more deer. The raccoons, possum, skunks, and squirrels are the only animals that you will find around here that you can eat," Clark said. "I prefer possum over raccoon any day that's when you learn to eat skip-it.

Clark replied, "I should put possum meat in a can and sell it. I would call it possum-in-a-can. A different white meat, it would be good with scrambled eggs."

I tell you, I would not want to be out in this hollow at night. The rattle snakes and spiders will cause big problems. Any man thinking he can camp out overnight should think gain. This time of year, the mosquitoes will carry you away. The last time I shot a Babbit,"

"What?" asked Ventin. The skinny twelve-year-old boy looked up at this six-foot, gray headed, seventy three year old man with a prized look on his face. "You mean a rabbit?"

Clark replied, "I can't get anything past you. You are a very smart boy. Tell me, can you count?"

"Yes," said Ventin.

"Can you tell me what one plus one equals?" asked Clark.

Ventin replied, "That's easy, two."

"Can you tell me what four plus four equals?"

"Seven."

"No, you better use your fingers and count."

"Okay one, two, three, four, five, six, seven, and eight." "Eight," said Ventin.

"Good job," said Clark. "I have a question, how many fingers do you have?"

"I have ten," said Ventin,

"How about you, Helen?"

"Ten."

Clark continued, "Can one of you tell me what six plus five equals?"

"Yes, I can," said Helen, "eleven."

"How about you, Ventin?" asked Clark,

"She said it equals eleven, and then she is correct," replied Ventin.

"Well then both of you have eleven fingers," said Clark.

Ida looked at her father and just smiled. She had fallen for this trick when she was a little girl. Ventin started counting his fingers.

"No, I have ten fingers."

Helen had a bogus look on her face.

Clark said, "Let me count your fingers. Ventin hold your hands out for me. I need to ask one more time, what is six plus five?"

"Eleven," said Ventin.

"Okay let me count your fingers," said Clark. He started counting with the left-hand fingers. "Ten, nine, eight, seven, and six," and he pointed to Ventin's right hand. "You have five fingers on your right hand, six plus five equal eleven."

Ventin looked down at his bony fingers; he could not believe what Mr. Meeker had just done. He counted his fingers again with the total of ten fingers. "Do that again, do it again," said Ventin.

"Let me count Helen's fingers."

"No, I have ten fingers. Ventin is weird; he probably does have eleven fingers," said Helen.

"Count my fingers again!" said Ventin

"Okay ten, nine, eight, seven, six, and five make eleven every time."

"How did you do that?" asked Ventin.

"Ventin, you are stupid!" said Helen.

When everyone was safely across the Sutherland Ford Bridge, Ida's father started telling more stories that Ida had heard a million times, not to mention her poor mother probably having heard the stories more than that. Clark knew that the kids would like it.

Then Ventin begged him to share another story with them.

"Okay," Clark said. "This is a story about a church. Do you go to church, Ventin?" said Clark.

"Yes, I go with my mother and sister most times," Ventin said.

"Fantastic I know that makes your mother happy".

"Okay."

"This is a story about a man who fell asleep during church. The preacher stopped in the middle of his sermon and asked a young boy sitting beside the man to wake him up. The boy said 'wake him yourself, you put him to sleep."

Clark's wife pleaded, "Please stop telling those stupid stories." Ida's father just laughed.

"Do you want to hear another story?" Clark asked.

"Yes, please tell us another one!"

"This is about a cemetery. Say we were walking by a cemetery, Ventin, could you tell me how many people are dead in that cemetery?"

"Yes," Ventin answered, "but, I would have to count them."

"Well, let's say the cemetery is a half-acre field. How many people are dead in that cemetery?" asked Clark.

"I don't know, maybe hundred or more," said Ventin.

"Well the truth is, I hope all of them are dead in that cemetery." Ventin didn't know what to say. "One more please, one more," said Ventin.

"Okay," said Clark. "Can you spell Bob for me, Helen?"

"Yes, b-o-b," replied Helen.

"No, that's not right," said Clark. "How about you, Ventin?" "Yes, I can, "b-o-b," replied Ventin.

"No, you both spelled it backward," said Clark.

"No, I spelled it right," said Helen. "b-o-b."

"You still spelled it backward," said Clark.

Ventin said, "I know, I know; Capital B-o-b, Helen you can't spell anything. Where did you go to school?"

"The same place you go to school."

"The reason I told you that story," said Clark. **<u>You need to pay attention to the questions asked of you.</u>** Think before you answer someone."

By this time, they had walked to Logan Avenue and turn left down the dirt path in front of the Children's Home.

"Ouch!" said Ida's father, "I didn't see that tree branch." "What tree?" said Ida.

"I thumped my crazy bone!"

'Well, just part your hair on the other side, and the knot will never show," said Ida's mother. Everyone started laughing at what Ida's mother said. She knew how to get her husband's goat. She just looked at him and smiled and stuck her tongue out at him.

"We make a good team, thank God for you, Margaret." By this time they were in front of the hospital.

"I just want you to know Della Clark will be talking to everyone. We need to find a place to set out our food. The kids can run and play while I do this. You two girls can walk around and see the sights. Remember, be back here in about thirty minutes. I should have everything ready to eat," said Margaret.

"We can help you get things ready."

"No, you two go and walk around."

As Margaret started fixing the sandwiches, she could hear her husband talking. She called him over to where she was preparing the food, and asked, "Would you lower your voice? Everyone can hear you."

"Well, those two old timers can't hear me. I was telling them about the time I bit off that crazy man's nose. They asked me to talk louder. I was just trying to make my point to those two jugheads."

"Anyway, it was not the whole nose, just the front corner on the left side of his nose. Every time you tell that story it gets transformed into a bigger story. Please do not sing that hen house song to those men! It's time to eat, can you find the kids, Clark? I will get Della and Ida."

Clark walked around the city park and fined the two kids playing at the swings. After lunch, it was time to watch the log rolling. Several men had signed up to participate in the contest. One after another was eliminated. Ida and Della were enjoying the day when Ida thought she saw Alva walking in the park. She told Della that she should find her kids and meet her at the vending booth. Ida walked over to where her mother and father were sitting and told her father about Alva. Clark stood up and looked around but did not see Alva. Ida's mother suggested that they find Della and her kids and stay together. Ida told her mother that Della was getting her kids and meeting her at the vending booth.

By that time, Clark had spotted Alva. Knowing that Ida would be very concerned about what Alva would do, he suggested that they stay together. Clark started walking around the park hoping that Alva would follow him. His thought was to keep Alva as far away from Ida as possible. After a few minutes, Alva was standing across from where Ida and her mother were standing. Ida's mother became concerned. She could see Alva was very angry. She didn't want anything to happen to Della's kids or to anyone. Alva became so obnoxious that the Meekers decided to leave. Margaret told everyone to help her pick up the food and to start walking together toward home.

As they started walking, Alva shadowed them, until they crossed Logan Avenue going south of the park. Alva waved down a taxi to pick him up. That was the last time the Meeker party saw him. Clark was not happy. He knew that Alva was wacky and unpredictable.

Clark suggested, "If we see Alva, do not say anything to him, not a word."

Della made sure her two children understood.

They had just walked past the Children's Home on Logan Avenue when they saw Alva pass them in the taxi. The taxi turned right onto Williams Street. Clark ran up to the corner and watched the car speed west out of sight around the Williams Street curve.

Horr said, "Do you know what to do?"

"Yep," said the taxi driver.

"Here's half of the money and you get the other half when you pick me up on Logan Avenue." As the others walked up to where Clark was standing, they all continued, crossing over Williams Street to the walk on the south side of the street.

Walking west toward the Sutherland Ford Bridge, Ida's mother said, "We will be all right; he's gone but we need to hurry home."

Just as she had uttered this, they saw the taxi coming toward them. It stopped in front of John Ridge's home, directly opposite of where they were standing on the south side of the street. Horr jumped out of the taxi and started toward Ida.

Clark told Horr to stay away from her. "She doesn't want anything to do with you".

Horr told Clark to stop talking and demanded the rings Horr yelled, "You, stupid old man."

He then reached into his hip pocket, pulled out a revolver and fired three shots at Clark. One of the slugs grazed the temple of Ida's father, just as he jumped behind a telephone pole.

Clark tried to get his pocket knife out of his front pocket to defend himself. While doing this, Horr fired two shots at Ida. All went wide. At the same time, the taxi driver turned his car around and drove off toward the bridge. Horr then aimed the gun at Ida's face and pulled the trigger. The revolver snapped but did not discharge. Horr ran east on Williams Street. Both Ida and her father followed.

"I have a knife in my hand, stop!" yelled Clark. Clark stopped and picked up a rock and threw it at Horr. It hit the back of his leg, but this did not slow him down.

While running, Horr reloaded the revolver. In front of the home of William Drucker, 1312 Williams Street, six houses east of the Ridge residence, Horr stopped and turned toward Ida and her father. Ida was in the lead. Horr aimed the revolver at her and fired but the bullet again went wild. When Ida reached Alva, she struck the revolver with her umbrella. The gun went off again.

Ida ran for the porch at Sarah Phillip's home, 1320 West Williams street, and tried to open the screen door. It was latched. Alva ran to where Ida was standing, pulled her off the porch and back into the street. Alva fired again at point blank range. Ida turned and struck Alva's arm once again with the umbrella. The bullet struck this time, puncturing Ida's heart. With exclamation, Ida's last words were "Oh my!" Ida sank to the street and died instantly.

Alva stepped back, turned and ran into the Drucker yard, jumped a short wooden fence, and ran to the dirt path located at the back of the house. Turning west toward a thicket, he disappeared in the river bottom. Ida's father chased, heaving rocks at him, until Alva went over a steep hill at the edge of the North Fork River. Ida's mother ran to where Ida's motionless body had fallen to the street. She dropped to Ida's side and started crying. "No, Please! No, please!" she screamed. Della ran to her side and tried to hold her, but Ida's mother stood up, and walked over and picked up the picnic blanket and covered her daughter.

A great crowd soon gathered. In fact, there were a number already on the scene, having been attracted by the first shot. Some were eye witnesses to the killing. Later the crowd reached enormous proportions and there were many who volunteered to assist in the search for Alva, although many drew the line at entering the thicket into which the man had disappeared. It was at this time that the **taxi driver returned to the scene** of the shooting. He later told police that he could not find another way back to the city.

The Danville city police were called to the scene of the shooting. Upon arriving at the scene, bystanders were yelling, "He went to the river." The city police notified the central desk informing them of the shooting. The central desk officer on duty then notified Chief Walker at his home, of the homicide. Chief Walker called for more police officers, who were sent to search the river bottoms, assisted by the volunteers. They were expecting to find Horr's body or Horr himself in the tall weeds and underbrush of the river bottoms.

Chief Walker directed detectives Vinson and White to interview bystanders. Walker started questioning Clark Meeker. Detective Smith was assigned to take a statement from the taxi driver, Theodore Vogt. When Detective Smith finished the interview, Vogt climbed into the taxi and drove to Logan Avenue, turned right and crossed the rail road tracks and turned into an alley, then stopped.

He waited about ten minutes, then Horr wet from crossing the river jumped into the backseat and covered himself with a blanket.

"Where's my money?" Vogt demanded!

"Here, take it, start driving. Remember, take me to the Hooton Cemetery and drop me off! Then you go home to Oakwood, and stay there until you hear from Red."

Corner Ralph Cole was also called to the scene by the central desk. After the corner completed his investigation, the body of Mrs. Ida Horr was removed to the Blyth Undertaking Establishment, at 304 N. Vermilion Street. A post mortem examination was performed, so that the bullet might be obtained for evidence at a trial, if one was necessary. Corner Cole announced that an inquest would be held at his office in the courthouse at four o'clock on Thursday, September 17.

After Chief Walker completed the interview with Clark Meeker, he tried to get a statement from Ida's mother, Margaret Meeker. She was not very cooperative with the chief. She was in shock and could not give a statement, as to exactly what happened. Clark asked that the interview with his wife be taken the following day. "She will be, in a better state of mind," said Clark. Margaret then left the scene of the murder, and went to the undertaker's.

Detective Smith had completed his investigation with the taxi driver and started interviewing Della. Della informed Detective Smith that he should talk with a lady wearing the big bonnet, who was standing across the street, on the walk. Detective Smith then approached the lady. "Do you have any information about this murder?" Detective Smith asked.

"Yes, I do," she replied.

"What is your name?"

"Mrs. Taylor, Mrs. William Taylor. I was an eyewitness to the shooting. I saw the man with the gun shoot the lady while she was running from him."

"Are you sure the lady was running away from the shooter?"

"No, the shooter was running at the lady, that's right, he was running at her." Her statement was exactly the same as what Ida's father had given to the chief of police. The only difference in the two stories was that Clark Meeker chased Horr into the thicket.

Chief Walker requested that if anyone could provide additional information about the shooting, they should come to the Danville Police Station, and give a written statement to the central desk. It was now after 8 p.m. and nightfall was setting in. Horr had not been seen since Meeker chased him over the hill at the rear of the Drucker home. Officers from the Sheriff's office and the city police surrounded the vicinity of Hungry Hollow, as far west as the Kelley farm. The Western Brick Works buildings were scoured, but no trace of Horr was found. One report to the police central desk said to have come from the search party was Horr had been surrounded in a grove of trees on the Kelley farm. This report was later denied. It was the general opinion that Horr fired the three shots into his own body. When heard by officers in a cornfield on the Stuebe farm in Hungry Hollow, but no such luck.

Chief Walker called off the search. While not totally abandoned during the night, Chief Walker advised everyone that the search would be resumed in the cornfield at daybreak.

CHAPTER FIVE

Follow Him

The next morning, September 17, Chief Walker held his normal 8 a.m. meeting with his staff. "Gentleman, we have a lot of work to do. The city has not had a murder on my guard. I want all of you to follow up on any leads that are reported. You have all been assigned a section of the city. When a lead has been reported to us from your area, make sure that you follow up. Now, I need for everyone to hear what we know, as of today. Joe, what do you have to report?"

"I interviewed the bystanders. Most of what I could gather from the bystanders they did not see the actual shooting or what led up to the murder. Most of them came to the scene after they heard the gunshots."

"What about you, Vinson, what do you have to report?"

"From what I was told by most of the witnesses, a gun was fired eight or ten times before the sound of the gun fire stopped. Everyone had a different number of gun shots."

"What about your report, Smithy?"

"I talked with the taxi driver. This may give us more information, listen to this. The taxi driver drove Horr to the scene of the murder. He stated he was driving through Lincoln Park when he was approached by Horr. Horr rushed into his taxi and told him to start driving. He drove Horr from the park downtown to a saloon, where Horr bought a half pint of whiskey. Then he stated he drove Horr back to the park. Horr told him he was looking for a woman. From his account, after they had passed the park, they turned onto Logan Avenue. He stated they went south, past the hospital, and passed a family walking on the west side of the street. He stated Horr looked at them, took another drink of whiskey then yelled, "You have something of mine, and I plan to get it!' The driver also alleged he did not know to who Horr was talking to. He said he was ordered to turn right onto Williams Street and drive past the bridge. At this point, Horr ordered him to turn around and go back, meeting the same party again. His statement reads, "Horr told me to stop, and he jumped out of the taxi walking toward the woman." Now listen to this quote, "I was not close enough to hear all that was said and the first indication I had of anything being wrong was when I saw Horr back away and pull a revolver from his hip pocket. He shot five times and from where I was sitting in the car it appeared that the shots were for the purpose of scaring the people more than to hit anyone. After he had fired five shots, I saw the man Horr had been talking to, advance toward him with what look to be a knife. Horr was reloading, as he ran away from my taxi. That's when I turned the taxi around and drove away."

"I think he knows more than he has told you," Chief Walker responded. "He stated twice 'five shots.' He may have known what type of gun Horr was carrying."

"What did Clark Meeker have to say?" asked Joe

"About the same as the others but let me read you the information I received. Here's his statement, 'Me and my wife, my daughter, Mrs. Della Hawes and her two children were returning to our home off West Williams Street, from Lincoln Park when the shooting occurred. Horr passed us on Logan in a taxi. We watched the taxi, as it turned on West Williams Street and disappeared. We walked to Williams Street and then turned west. The taxi cab came from the west this time. When the taxi was directly across from of us, and in front of the home of John Riggs, the taxi stopped. Horr sprang from the taxi and started towards Ida. I told him to go on about his business; go away. That's when Horr reached into his hip pocket, pulled out a revolver and fired three shots at me. He grazed my temple. I tried to get my knife from my pocket to defend myself. While doing this, he fired three shots at Ida. All went wide; he aimed the gun at her face and pulled the trigger again. The revolver snapped but did not fire. He ran east on Williams Street; Ida and I followed. I had the knife in my hand. While he was running, he reloaded his revolver. I think I threw rocks at him, but I do not remember. In front of the home of Drucker, Horr stopped and turned toward us. Ida was in the lead. He aimed the revolver at her and fired, but the bullet missed. She struck the revolver with her umbrella. The bullet went wide. He fired again and missed a second time. Ida ran away from her husband to the Philip's house. When she reached the porch, she tried to open the screen door, but it was latched. Horr ran to where his wife was and pulled her back into the street. That's when Horr fired at her point blank. I heard my daughter say something, but I could not understand it clearly. I think she said, "Oh my!" She then sank down to the street. Horr then ran and climbed a fence, and I followed him. I chased him down the dirt path behind the houses on Williams Street, throwing rocks at him. He plunged into the thicket and disappeared into the river bottoms."

"That's Meeker's statement," said Chief Walker.

"Okay," said Chief Walker, "let's get busy. We have a lot of work to do. I have a stack of reports to review from the bystanders. I want each of you to divide these reports and follow up with each one in your area of the city. Smith, you go to the coroner's meeting at 4 p.m. today. I will contact the state's attorney's office and fill him in on the homicide. Sheriff Shepard is leading the search for Mr. Horr in the county. Any questions?" asked Walker.

"Yes," said Joe, "what are your feelings towards finding the whereabouts of Horr?"

Walker replied, "If he is found, it will be in some field west of the city, or along the North Fork River. Those three shots heard by the officers last night near the Stuebe farm in Hungry Hollow will probably solve this case. Let's get to work on getting the reports written up."

"I have one last question, said detective Vinson, "Do you believe that the taxi driver was part of this scheme?"

"It's too early to make a judgment at this time. We need to follow him and see who his friends are. Maybe he can help us locate Horr, **if Horr is not found in the next day or two.** We need to keep a close eye on Mr. Taxi driver. By the way, what is his name?"

"Theodore Vogt," said Smithy.

"Follow him," said Walker.

Just then officer Dixon walked into the conference room. "Chief, I was just given this report: Horr has been spotted in a boxcar in Hillary."

"Who is the source?" Walker asked.

"It came from the central desk," replied Johnson, "Someone reported the information to them."

"What train?" asked the chief.

"It doesn't say," replied Johnson.

"Call the Sheriff's office inform them of this lead, they can follow up. I need all the information we have on Mr. Horr. Do we have the house on Fifth and Griffith in South Danville under watch?"

"Yes," said detective Smith.

"Chief, the central desk is getting more calls about seeing Horr," said Johnson.

"Dixon, keep a list of all the locations and send out an officer to follow up. I want to see a report at the end of the day on all sightings until we have captured Horr. Johnson, I have a question for you. Do you believe that Horr knows that he killed his wife?"

"Yes, I do, from the reports that I have glanced at, she was shot at close range. He saw her fall to the street. That's my personal opinion."

"I feel the same way. Johnson, what time are the newspaper people scheduled?"

"1 p.m."

"Make sure we have everything ready by 12:30 for me to review, before I talk to the reporters."

"Yes, sir."

"Yes, Joe?"

"I have the reason why Mr. Horr shot his wife. He shot her because she was a Horr."

Everyone laughed and walked out of the conference room.

By now, it was ten o'clock. "Here are the files we have on him," said Johnson.

"Lay them here," said the chief "I will look at them in a few minutes. If I remember previously, we took two pistols from Horr." The phone rang but Chief Walker didn't answer it. "Johnson, see who is calling; tell them I will call them back."

"It's the central desk; Horr has been captured."

"What?"

"They have captured Horr."

"That's what I thought you said great news. Get the location and make sure that we bring him in without any problems. When he gets here, I want to be at the booking. Also, call the newspaper and cancel the news meeting. Tell them we will reschedule the meeting, after we have interviewed Horr that it will be at 5 p.m. today. Vinson, follow up on the location. I need all the details. I know the state's attorney will be asking for a detailed report. Johnson, get the phone."

"Yes, sir. Hello, Chief Walker's office."

"Hi, this is Sheriff Shepard, is the chief in his office?" "Yes."

"I need to talk with him."

"Just a minute. Chief, the sheriff is on the phone."

Johnson handed the phone to the chief. "Good work, John. Your officers have saved me a lot of time."

"Hold on, Wesley, we do not have Horr. The man that was identified as Horr was not him. We are continuing our search." Chief Walker had a frustrated look on his face.

"Sorry, Wesley," said John.

"I have a meeting with the state's attorney's office today, I could use your support at that meeting. Can you join me?"

"What time do you need me?"

"I will meet you there in about forty minutes, is that okay?"

"Yes, I will see you there on the second floor of the courthouse in John Lawman's office."

"Johnson, that was a case of mistaken identification, Horr has not been arrested. Give that statement to the newspaper reporters and cancel the five o'clock meeting you set up with them. Tell them we have no further comments at this time. Also, get this report typed for me to take to the state's attorney's office; I will need it in about thirty minutes. Smithy, before you go to the coroner's inquest, follow up with the undertaker. Get a statement from him as to the cause of death."

"I better go now," said Smithy.

"Johnson has a date been set for the funeral? Follow up on that, and get back to me as soon as possible. Check with the Meeker family, and see what we can do to assist them. Joe, I need you to go see Mrs. Alice Taylor; she gave a written report and claimed she saw everything. Have her give you another statement. No, let's do this, bring her into the station, and question her. This way we can have all the detectives listen to her statement.

"Johnson, while I am at the state's attorney's office, read over the statements given by the bystanders, and stack them in the order in which we should interview them. I'm headed to the state's attorney's office. See you when I return. Do you have that report typed up?"

"Yes," replied Johnson.

"Read it to me, I want to make sure that I have covered what we know about Mr. Horr."

"Here's what you wanted.

Mr. Alva C. Horr and his wife Ida Horr have had a great deal of trouble during the last four years of their 11 years of married life. On several occasion, Mrs. Horr left her husband and went to her parent's home. About three weeks ago, she left him again. On each previous separation, according to Mr. Meeker, her father, Mrs. Horr always returned to her husband at the point of a gun. A separation of the couple about a year ago ended in the justice system. According to the evidence submitted at the time, Mrs. Horr had left him, and went to her father. Horr watched the Meeker home for three weeks. One afternoon, Mr. and Mrs. Meeker went to the city, while Mrs. Horr remained at home. Shortly after the Meekers departed, Horr went to the house. It was then that Horr kicked through one door, and if it wasn't for the timely arrival of Ida's brother, Frank, Horr would have shot his wife. Horr pleaded guilty to a charge of disorderly conduct and paid his fine."

"Thanks, good job. Let me have the report, I will see you after the meeting I have with the state's attorney's office."

For the next sixty days, leads came into the central office; some were of seeing Horr in two places at the same time.

Is this the man we are looking for?

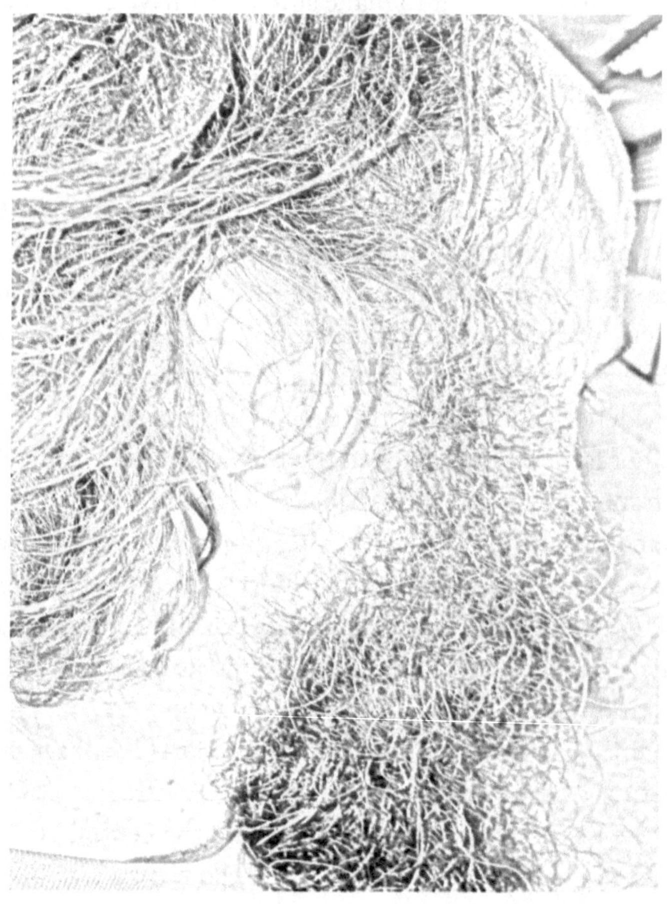

CHAPTER SIX

A Life to Remember

"Dead men tell no tales, but their obituaries often do."

Ida Meeker Horr departed this life September 16, 1914, by the hands of her husband. She was 32 years old, born October 10, 1882 in Bismark, Illinois. She was a lifelong resident of Vermilion County, Illinois. She attended grammar school, and worked as a cook until she became part owner of a café with her husband on North Hael Street. She was well known for her cooking; you never left her café hungry. Ida was always willing to give encouragement to her customers. Survivors are her parents Clark and Margaret Meeker, five brothers Arthur, Charles, Frank, John and Eli, four sisters Minnie, Flora, Martha, and Alice. As well as many aunts and uncles and their spouses; five nephews, and six nieces; all from the Vermilion County area. The body of the deceased will be at the Blythe Undertaking establishment 304 N. Vermilion St., on Saturday from 2 PM until 5 PM for visitation. Ida's funeral will be held Saturday at 1 PM at the First Union Mission Church on West Williams Street. Burial will follow at Farmer's Chapel Cemetery.

At Ida's visitation, there was a large attendance and many beautiful floral offerings. Ida's mother asked that everyone make their mark in the book located at the front of the parlor, so the Meeker family could remember each person who attended.

All of Ida's family members were at the viewing. It was said that the only time the family got together these days, was when someone passes. The parlor was filled with friends and neighbors, some familiar faces and some not so familiar. Most of the unfamiliar were Ida's Café customers. Matt Russell and Jack Hilman were both at the viewing talking to Ida's brothers, Frank and Charles, about Alva's sports betting. Information that Matt gave the two Meeker boys on the betting that Horr ran out of the café was a surprise to them. Horr's particular vice was his love of betting lines. Horr was addicted to most sports and placing a small wager was his entertainment. Both Jack and Matt confirmed that Ida did not know sports betting took place in the café. Matt's and Jack's main concern was getting two hundred dollars that Horr owed them. Matt and Jack threatened that they would get their money back.

Some other chatter in the parlor was about Ida's first-rate cooking. Everyone talked about her two best meals that were listed on the menu, her twelve o'clock meat pie and the sixo'clock meat pie she served. When customers ask Ida, "What is the difference?" she would look at you, smile, and say, "About six hours."

They all remarked on the sign that was hanging over the potbelly stove located in the back of the café. It read, "Be good and you'll be happy, but you won't get your name in the newspaper until you die." The newspaper writers from the Press Democrat and the Danville Commercial News were always wrangling over who gave her that quote. Ida would never take sides in this chitchat. One day, she would side with the boys from the Press Democrat and the next day with the boys from the Commercial News. The newspaper boys would go into her café just to see what side she would take that day.

Everyone had read the newspaper article about the shooting. The torment that her husband put her though must have been dreadful. Why did she stay with him? Some asked the question, "Why did this have to happen?" If we could read the secrets of her history, we would find out her sorrows and suffering. Did the police know about Ida's problems with her husband? Ida's father could not control himself, when these kinds of questions were brought up. This was an alarming state of affairs to Mr. Meeker. In his mind he had failed Ida. His sorrow and grief were enormous; if kept bottled up inside him, it would eat his heart away. The only solution to this selfish act by Horr was to bring him to "justice".

"That's my job now; locate Horr and bring him to the authorities," Clark told himself.

Services were held the next day at the First Union Mission Church on West Williams Street, not far from where Ida was shot. The church was packed. It was time for the family to be seated, and the service was opened with a song. Della was setting with Ida's family in the front pew of the church. Earlier that morning, Ida's mother had asked Della to say a few words. Charles, Ida's brother, his wife Ruth, baby girl, Margaret, and two young boys, Harold, and Don, were tired and cranky. Ida's mother was bent over with weeping and her shoulders shook as she cried. Ida's sisters tried to comfort their mother but it did not seem to help. Then the music ended.

Della stood up and walked slowly to the front of the church. Before she started reading, she said to herself, "This is for you Ida." With that she placed an umbrella next to Ida's body. "Now, you are safe in God's hands."

Della opened her bible and read the following from James chapter 1 verses 2-4, 12 God's words of life on suffering.

"Consider it pure joy my brothers whenever you face trials of many kinds, because you know that the testing of your faith develops perseverance.

Perseverance must finish its work so that you may be mature and complete not lacking anything. Blessed is the man who preserves under trial, because when he has stood the test, he will receive the crown of life that God has promised to those who love him."

Della then returned to where Ida's mother was seated and gave her a hug.

The service was short. Pastor George Woosley had not known Ida very well, but did share some words about life and criticism.

"No one cheers his own birth, and no one mourns his own death. We are here today to lift up Ida and her family. For a minute, think of something you enjoy, and you save up for months for the experience, and then splurge on it. I say to you, with tearful eyes, 'Be strong, rejoice in the life of Ida,' I say 'splurge your joyful thoughts.'" This is the moment that Ida would want you to boast of her life.

"Not knowing Ida as well as most of you, I do know she must have had a great personality. Personality is not an attribute that people possess in varying amounts. Rather, personality is what we are, a collection of all our many traits and attributes, the sum total which constitutes a unique individual unlike anyone else. Ida was unique; she always carried an umbrella when she was out and about the town. Now she has her umbrella to walk out and about in heaven."

The pastor closed the service with a reading from Colossian 3: 13.

'Bear with each other and forgive whatever grievances you may have against one another. Forgive as the lord forgave you."

After the church service was over, the Meeker boys carried the coffin out to the wagon and loaded their sister's body. Other family members and friends laid flowers around the wooden coffin. Then the team of horses towed the wooden wagon to Farmer's Chapel Cemetery. The grave side service was the last time family members would see Ida's face before the coffin was closed. When the body was lowered into the grave everyone held hands and sang.

"In the Garden" (1912)
Words and Music by C. Austin Miles, 1868-1946

  1. *I come to the garden alone, While the dew is still on the roses;*
    And the voice I hear, falling on my ear,

The Son of God discloses. And He walks with me, and He talks with me, And He tells me I am His own; And the joy we share as we tarry there None other has ever known.

  2. *He speaks, and the sound of His voice Is so sweet, the birds*
    hush their singing; And the melody that He gave to me within
    my heart is ringing.

And He walks with me, and He talks with me,
And He tells me I am His own; And the joy we share as we tarry there
None other has ever known.
 I'd stay in the garden with Him Tho the night around me be falling;
But he bids me go-- thru the voice of woe, His voice to me is calling.
And He walks with me, and He talks with me,
And He tells me I am His own;
And the joy we share as we tarry there
None other has ever known.

During the singing of the last verse, the family started walking away. Once all the wagons were loaded and the horses had walked back to Poland Road, everyone was talking about capturing Horr.

"Justice," Clark said. "That's my job today and every day until Horr is locked up." A silence fell upon everyone in the wagon. The Meeker boys sat silently. Ida's mother seemed to have a moment of complete understanding. Then she turned and gave her husband a look of approval. He had seen that expression before.

'Well, you know best, being their Pa," she said calmly.

'We will start early tomorrow; I know where to start looking for Horr's trail. I followed him after he jumped the fence and ran down the path into the thicket. I marked the spot where he entered the tall grass and weeds. I know what type of shoes he had on. I bought some the same day, from that traveling salesman. His soles have a 'V' shape groove cut into them. My soles have no pattern cut into the soles. He was wearing them when he ran into the thicket.

"Did you tell the police about his shoes?" asked Margaret.

"No," replied Clark, "but I will. I know that Horr is hiding nearby, I have something he wants."

"What would that be?" asked Frank,

"I have them in my pocket," said Clark.

Margaret looked at her husband and said, "Remember what Ida said, Clark?"

"I do," said Clark.

"Those dang things caused all this mess. Any way, we will tell you later. Frank, do not ask your Pa any more questions about what he has in his pocket. We will tell you all after Alva is behind bars. By the way, did you tell the police?" asked Margaret.

"No," said Clark, "that's not important now. My job is to find Horr. That's my job, that's what I will do. Everything I do from now on is for Ida until Horr is behind bars. Someday, I will sing a song about 'my job', but for now I need to look for Horr."

Clark did not consider the life he led as a farmer an exciting one, but family members and citizens of the Danville area who knew him thought so. When he would undertake a battle against someone, they better watch it! He was all business. His family all well remembered the time that he bit off part of the nose of that crazy old man that was stealing the eggs from the hen house. "Remember that song he would sing; who B the L on the H H D; I D K; BFIG who B the L on the H H D; BUT I'll FIND OUT; BEFORE I GO; WHO BROKE LOCK ON THE HEN HOUSE DOOR."

"From that point on, that crazy old man didn't give a hoot about eggs," said Frank.

The next day Clark was up bright and early hunting his daughter's murderer. He soon found footprints and traced them a considerable distance. The trail led directly to the river from the point where

Clark had marked the spot the day of the shooting, and then the trail turned upstream for about 100 yards. Clark walked along the river bank as the footprints were plainly visible for more than 200 yards. At this point, the footprints faded into the river water. Clark forged the stream, in nearly waist deep water. He followed the trail until he left the soft ground along the river and took to the pasture near the stream. Clark was going in a southeast direction when he lost the trail. He spent the greater part of the afternoon along the river, trying to pick up the trail again, with very little success. He knew that Horr used a trail, in order to get back to Danville without using the streets. That was the key in locating Horr. **"Find the trail back** to Danville **and I will find Horr,"** thought Clark.

LAST AVAILABLE PICTURE OF HORR
$200.00 REWARD

HAVE YOU SEEN THIS MAN?
ALVA C. "TENIL" HORR
WANTED FOR THE MURDER OF HIS WIFE

September 16, 1914

Fugitive's description: 36 years old looks younger, 5'6" tall, and weighs about 200 pounds when last seen but may be lighter now. Brown wavy hair, brown eyes, reddish complexion, left hand and wrist crippled from shotgun wound. Notify local police if you know his whereabouts. $200.00 reward paid upon the capture and arrest Alva C. Tenil Horr.

CHAPTER SEVEN

"Don't talk about yourself; it will be done when you leave"

The next few days passed in a blur. Police believed Horr jumped a ride on a Big Four Train to Urbana, Illinois, snatched a horse and buggy there and returned to Danville for the purpose of determining whether he had really killed his wife. Officers were divided as to Horr's whereabouts; some believed he was hiding in the woods and underbrush along the North Fork River. Others believed he was out of the community, completely.

Thursday afternoon, about 24 hours after the murder, Terrance (Red) Cutler, an acquaintance of Horr, who was tending bar at his saloon on Lyons Road, reported to the local police that Horr visited the saloon. Horr asked for some whiskey. He fingered his nervously revolver when he asked for it. While no threat was made, the bartender did not insist on payment. Red stated that Horr had told him he was going to grab a railer, a slang phrase about making a hurried departure on a train, and beat it. Red stated that Horr was without funds. He had only some diamonds he recently taken from his wife, and five dollars he had borrowed from a friend. No trace had been found of Horr since he left the saloon in Lyons on September 17, 1914.

Late Thursday night, the Danville police searched Horr's apartment on 5th street in South Danville but nothing was found which would assist in the man hunt. Business files confirming the sale of Horr's Café to Bert Lients, and the financial audit records were taken away by the authorities. A review of Horr's financial records might help the police in the investigation.

Sheriff Afusta Evans of Champaign County was notified to look for Horr. A description was telegraphed by an Urbana Big Four train employee to the sheriff's office. A railroad yard employee in that city had seen a stranger jump from a train. The jumper's clothing fit the description of that worn by Horr; he also reported the man had a crippled hand. These were included in the telegraphed description. Two railroad men, who claimed to have known Horr from the past, stated it was Horr beyond a doubt, when Horr asked them, "When is the next train due to leave town?" Horr stated that he cared not which direction the train was going, that he wanted to get out at once. But no train was leaving soon. Finding this out, he snatched a horse and buggy from East Main Street, a short distance from the rail road yard, and returned to Danville. The Twin City (Champaign and Urbana, Illinois) police confirmed that the horse and buggy were stolen from East Main Street.

After returning to Danville several people reported seeing a man answering Horr's description board the train at Lyon's Road, and the police investigated the stories, with no results. Chief Walker did not believe that Horr **left by train;** he still believed that Horr was hiding in the river bottom and late at night had made his way to Lyons Road. Walker did not believe that these people manufactured details, but believed the man who boarded the train was someone other than Horr.

At the Coroner's inquest, held late on Thursday afternoon, testimonies of eyewitnesses did not differ. Alva C. Horr was the unlawful murderer of his wife, Ida Horr, according to the coroner's jury, which heard the case.

Dr. E. L. Winslow, who held the post mortem examination of the body, testified that the bullet had struck the internal sternum slightly to the left side, passing the right side of her body, and through the right auricle of the heart. The bullet was located between the ninth and tenth ribs, 1 1/2 inches to the right of the vertical column in the muscle of the back.

Theodore Vogt, the taxi driver, testified he had no knowledge of Horr's plan. He said that Horr had approached him while his taxi was parked at Lincoln Park and asked him to take him, first one place and then another, to get a drink of whiskey. Vogt stated that Horr drank about a pint of liquor during the ride, but that he did not consider him intoxicated. He said that Horr directed his driving from Lincoln Park to Hazel Street and back to Williams Street. Then, they passed Mrs. Horr and her father and mother, Mr. and Mrs. Meeker, with whom she was walking.

"Horr did not make mention of Mrs. Horr or her companions as they passed," Vogt testified. He stated that when they passed the Meeker party, Horr paid more attention to Clark Meeker than anyone else. The driver of the taxi also said that the first indication that anything was wrong was when his passenger jumped from the moving taxi as they were returning east on Williams Street. He stated that the reason he started his taxi, turned around, and left the scene as soon as he saw Horr shoot at Ida was because he was afraid that he would be asked to help Horr escape and thus became an accomplice.

The testimony of Mr. and Mrs. Meeker, and that of Mrs. Della Hawes, who was with them at the time, revealed that Horr leaped from the moving taxi fired three shots at Clark Meeker and two at Ida. An umbrella was presented at the inquest, which revealed three dents caused by bullets from the revolver. The umbrella was used by Horr's wife in defense of herself and her father. As soon as the enraged man discovered his wife's intention, he turned on her and snapped the gun twice, but the gun failed to fire. He then stepped back in an attempt to reload the revolver. Two caliber shells were found upon the ground later. He then fired two more shots at his wife, the last one piercing her heart. She was dead before she hit the hard surface of the street.

Mr. Meeker testified that he was making every effort to defend himself with his pocket knife.

When Horr fled, he pursued him until exhausted, and then threw a rock at him. The murderer ran down the hill to the **east side of the river, disappearing** in the bottoms. Nothing definite has been heard of Horr since.

On Friday afternoon, the police learned from a call that Horr was walking west on Lyons Road. This tip looked promising. They expected to arrest Horr immediately. Sheriff Shepard, Chief Walker, Detectives Vutrick and Smith made a hurried trip to Lyons. Horr was not there. Later in the evening, they made inquiries around west Catlin, but learned nothing of his whereabouts.

Early Saturday morning, acting on another lead, an automobile loaded with officers left the city and spent the afternoon scouring the country to the south and west of Perrysville Road, believing Horr might be hiding in one of the old abandoned mines, surviving on food and drink that was being carried to him by friends.

It was pointed out by officers that Horr was unable to stand most hardships. He had no money. For years he had done no manual labor, and he was believed by officers to be depending on his friends for a certain amount of assistance. He would not do hard labor and that he would either be found among friends or with a class of people who lived by their wits, rather than by hard work.

The authorities in the nearby surrounding areas in Illinois and Indiana as far away as Terre Haute Indiana and Springfield, Illinois were given a detailed description of his appearance, habits, and dress of the wanted man. Officers believed that his arrest was only a matter of time and that the murder would not go on record as another unpunished crime with a sensational get away.

Monday afternoon, September 21, Illinois Governor Edward Dunne, at the request of state's attorney, John Lewman, offered a reward of $200 for the arrest of Alva C (Tinil) Horr.

It was now all but certain that he has made his escape from the Danville vicinity and was hiding out elsewhere. Though an extensive search had been conducted for five days, nothing had been seen or heard of Horr since the previous Thursday morning at Lyons Road.

Several pieces of mail were waiting for Horr at the local post office. The state attorney, John Lewman, requested that all Horr's mail be held for inspection.

Friends of Horr did not believe that the murder was premeditated. The fact, that previously he had given up weapons to avoid any trouble, was cited as proof of this. The only reason that Horr carried a gun was because he feared his wife's father. Horr often remarked that Clark Meeker did not like him and that he would not want to engage in a fight with Meeker. Meeker told Horr about the encounter in which he had bitten off a portion of the nose of his opponent, in a fight over eggs missing from the Meeker property.

Wednesday morning, September 23, Clark Meeker went out to hunt for Horr. He saw tracks in the mud along the river. The tracks stopped at the river edge north of the Ellsworth Park Dam. To satisfy those who held the belief that Horr had drowned himself in the North Fork River, part of the dam at Ellsworth Park was opened Tuesday evening to allow the water to flow out of Ellsworth Lake. The river bed was searched by officers from both the city and the sheriff's offices.

No trace of the body was found. The theory that Horr shot and killed himself was quickly fading away.

Clark Meeker was firm in his belief that Horr was **still alive.** Mr. Meeker denied that he has scoured the river bottoms with a Winchester rifle looking for Horr. He said he never owned such a rifle. He said that for his own protection, he did for several mornings perform a search of his property, and the adjacent wooded area for fear that Horr was lurking in the vicinity and might be bent on killing more members of the Meeker family.

Meeker was not afraid of Horr but he would not take any chances after the tragedy that took place the previous Thursday. When interviewed by the police, Meeker said that it was only by skillful dodging that he escaped the bullets Horr fired at him.

The next day Margaret asked Clark about the report in the newspaper. "Have you been talking to the reporters?" asked Margaret.

"No."

"Tell me what they are saying."

"That Alva is afraid of you and because of this fear, he will put up a plea of self-defense."

"That is untrue and does me a great injustice. I need to talk with the newspaper and get this story right."

After meeting with the paper, a new story was printed. To set the record straight, Mr. Meeker stated that he had never wanted trouble with his son-in-law, and evaded it whenever possible, and that on several occasions had swallowed his words and controlled his anger.

"Most importantly, I have tried to be friends with Alva. Many times, because of the treatment my daughter received at the hands of her husband, this had been hard to do. It seems to me that Horr has a vast number of friends. If some of those stories I am hearing are true, someone is trying to bolster up a self-defense plea in case he is arrested. They are trying to make it appear that Horr was afraid of me and my sons, and that it was because of us that he carried a gun. Horr loitered around in my neighborhood, slept out of doors many nights, and watched my house to see when I went away, so that he could break into my house, where my defenseless daughter was. This does not look like he feared me. Horr knew that I would not stand for any of his roughness at my house. Saturday, four days before the murder, my son and I were fishing along the North Fork River. My son heard a noise in the underbrush and upon parting the weeds and brush. He saw Horr, crouching back and pointing a revolver at him. He told my son at that time to get back or he would shoot.

"If he was afraid of me, why did he persist in staying in the neighborhood, spying on my actions? **I must have something that he wants.** My son called the police and asked that a warrant be issued against Horr. Afterward, Horr was taken by the police. The police called and informed us that Horr wanted to plead guilty to the charge of carrying concealed weapons. Whether he was ever fined or not, I do not know.

"Horr wears a size-six shoe, one size smaller than I wear. I know because I paid for his last pair of shoes. I paid for the shoes to know what to look for. Because of this, I have been able to track him. Many times, I have seen his tracks near my home when I have arisen in the morning. When my family was asleep, Horr would be present. Since the murder, I have come to the conclusion that he was in my neighborhood for no good, that he meant to kill me, as he has often threatened to do. When my daughter filed court papers for a divorce, she and I left my house together to visit her attorney Walter Gunn. Horr stated afterwards that he saw us leave and that he went into town by another way and waited for us to come out of Gunn's office. When he did not take the street, he missed the chance to kill us both. He even threatened to kill any attorney that might take the case of his wife, saying that he would not allow anyone to come between him and my daughter, although he made it impossible for her to live with him.

"At the time the divorce proceedings were dropped, he voluntarily took an oath that he would stop gambling, treat his wife as he should, and be a man. My daughter went back to live with him, only to be compelled to leave him again, when he became so abusive."

Saturday, September 26, ten days after the shooting, authorities were convinced that only luck would permit them to arrest him. Horr was ducking his old acquaintances. He was taking no chances by meeting his friends. The authorities were watching for him around the neighborhoods where old friends and acquaintances resided. Over half a dozen telegrams were sent to the Danville Police from other cities looking for the Ida's murderer. Unfortunately, in each incident, it is pointed out that Horr had not been seen. No person even remotely answering the description of Horr had been in those localities.

Since Horr left Lyons, two weeks prior, nothing had been seen or heard of him. The officers were absolutely without any tangible clues. Every possible rumor had been investigated, and yet the trail went no further than Lyons.

Ordinarily, a fugitive without funds **seeks out a friend** and asks for help. Ordinarily, a fugitive leaves some clues. By doing none of the things, Horr had shown that he was not an ordinary man, and that he could not be dealt with in the usual manner. It was now the belief of officers who have been handling the case that only a stroke of luck would enable them to arrest Horr and place him on trial for the murder of his wife.

The Danville Police widened the search for Horr. Circular Letters and telegrams were being sent out to police officers from coast-to-coast and from the Gulf Coast to the Canadian line. The country was being plastered with the circular bearing the photograph and description of the wanted man. Only by some officers recognizing the man from circulars, and with a bit of luck, would Horr be arrested.

September 28, Monday afternoon, the Sheriff's Department was advised once again that Horr was in Lyons. The caller did not give his name. Officers from the city police force and the Sheriff's Department were preparing to descent upon Lyons and Westville in hopes of routing out Horr. Just where the lead came from or where Horr might possibly be found was not known. Officers felt confident that the search for Horr over the past eleven days was about to end.

Officers had believed for the past few days that Horr was being hidden at Lyons, Westville, or Grape Creek by some of his friends and so certain were they in this belief that search warrants had been prepared, and raids at each site to learn if Horr was in hiding at any of these places were started Monday night.

The raids which ended near the twilight hour Tuesday morning did not produce any answers for the authorities.

On Tuesday, September 29, two days after seeing Horr at a residence in Oakwood, a young woman called the Sheriff's office. Officers searched every abandoned mine and other possible hiding places in the vicinity of Oakwood. Officers were again unsuccessful in their efforts to apprehend him.

From stories told by some of the residents of Oakwood, it seemed that there was a possibility that the man, who disturbed one or two families residing near the railroad Sunday night by raving and talking loudly, may have been Horr. If this was so, there was little doubt that the man was brooding over the murder of his wife until he had become insane.

One woman, who resided in Oakwood near the railroad tracks, heard the wild cry of some man apparently hiding in a boxcar along the track. Along with her husband, they both approached the boxcar and heard the man talking loudly about his wife. The man was said to have muttered several times something about having his wife where he wanted her now. Thinking that the man was unable to get out of the boxcar, her husband opened the door and the man jumped to the ground, and ran south and disappeared from the sight of his confused liberators. It seemed to be the opinion of many of the officers, judging from the description given by the lady who saw the strange man at the railroad in Oakwood, that Horr was insane and running wildly about the country, avoiding the public eye. The husband and wife, who released the man from the boxcar did not get a good look at him in the darkness. From what they could see, the description favored the missing man.

Police and county officers made a search for Horr near the Mission field area, on Thursday the 1st of October in both the afternoon and evening. Information reached the officers that a woman residing near the Pollywog Ponds, as they are called, had been badly frightened by a man believed to be Horr. She was going to the pump, not far from the barn to get a bucket of water. As she reached the barn, a man ran from the building. He collided with the woman, knocked her down, and fled. The description of the man given by the woman, matched with that given of Horr and the police believed it's possible that it was either Horr or a demented man whom they have been seeking for several days. So believable was the story, officers made a hurried trip to this location and a long search followed.

The search was barren. Everyplace where it was believed possible for the man to be concealed was searched, **<u>but no trace of Horr could be found.</u>** On Saturday morning, October 3, a posse of miners, fifty to a hundred scoured the hills, hollows and woods in the vicinity of Oakwood. This search was made due to reports received from Danville, the past few days that Horr, a raving maniac, was hiding in the vicinity of Oakwood. Several people living near Oakwood and at Mission field had declared a man answering the description of the murder had been seen. Officials investigated some of these reports. One ongoing investigation was the report of several frightened women. The man purposely collided with one woman residing near Gray's Crossing. Before he could harm the woman, she fled. Another ongoing investigation involved miners going to work at the mines at an early hour in the morning, shortly after sunrise having seen a man appearing much as Horr did. The stranger in the Mission field Hills area has thus far managed to elude them and has prevented them from getting a good look of his face. These Investigations have yielded no result.

Saturday afternoon, Clark and his wife Margaret were interviewed by the newspaper reporters. Both believed Horr was still hiding near the city, awaiting an opportunity to waylay other members of their family. Clark Meeker said he believed this. He stated that Horr was in the vicinity of the Meeker home the past Monday night and again on Friday. Meeker claimed he received word from a friend that Horr had stated he would get Charles and Frank before he was captured. Believing this to be true, and confident that Horr was lurking and hiding somewhere near, members of the Meeker family had mounted guard, day and night for the previous ten days. There was never a minute of the day or night when there was not one of the members of the family on guard, two most of the time. Their armament consisted of two Winchester rifles, one or two revolvers with considerable ammunition, and a pair of night glasses.

Clark's neighbor, Mrs. Rachael Bobaker, who had been in the city shopping, reported to the city central desk that she had seen Horr near the Sutherland Ford Bridge late Monday afternoon, just about dusk, when she was returning home. Horr fled, when she approached him. She knew Horr, she said, and claimed she could not have been mistaken. Members of the Meeker family investigated and were said to have found tracks leading into the underbrush along the river.

Additionally, Claude Cleland, a driver for a grocery wagon, called the central desk at police headquarters and reported he saw Horr

Thursday afternoon about four o'clock on McKinley Avenue. Horr emerged from the bushes along the North Fork River and walked along McKinley Avenue for a considerable distance before taking to the alleys and making it back to the River near the Sutherland Ford Bridge.

The strain of watching day and night, fearful every minute that some member of the family may be killed was proving to be too much for the Meekers. They decided to abandon their home on Hampton Road. Clark Meeker informed the city police about his decision to move his family.

The police meanwhile were looking for a rifle stolen from the cabin of W. Payne, former Danville Assistant Postmaster. Not many days prior to the murder, a Remington repeater, 32 gage rifle, was stolen from the Payne's cabin, located on the river just south of the Meeker home. It was reported that Horr spent much time in that immediate vicinity just prior to the killing. He was also known to have had a rifle. A grocer whose store Horr visited three days before the killing, thought the rifle was similar to the one that Payne had stolen. Horr, he said, explained the day he had the gun that he was hunting squirrels. No trace could be found of the gun Horr is said to have had, nor could the Danville Police Officers find any trace of the stolen rifle.

On Sunday October 4, the miners were also off from work. Again, they took the time to form a volunteer posse of miners. They searched the territory in the vicinity of the Mission field and the Pollywog ponds. A number of persons claimed to have seen a man answering the general description of Horr in that vicinity. The miners made an effort to roust the man.

Early Monday, October 5, a nineteen-year-old called the police, and claimed he talked with Horr on Sunday night. The boy was questioned by Detective Smith. "Was Horr in the vicinity of Clark Meeker's home again Sunday night?"

The 19-year-old youth, Hahn, claimed to have seen and talked to Horr. Detective Smith called George W. Woodworth and his bloodhounds to make a thorough search of the area. The woods and gullies were searched, but to no avail though only a short distance from the Meeker home was evidence that some person had been lying there for a great portion of Sunday night.

Young Hahn told Detective Smith he was walking alongside the Big Four track Sunday night. At a point just west of the arch bridge over the North Fork River, Hahn said that Horr jumped from the train. "He ran towards the spot where I was standing, and as he approached me. He asked, 'What are you doing here?' I replied that I was just loafing around. Horr ask me where do you live?' I said that I now live in the Bobaker house, next to the Meeker home."

According to the story told to Detective Smith, Horr, told the boy to advise the Meeker's that he "would get the old man, Charles, and Frank before another sunset." The boy told Detective Smith that following these words, Horr left the side of the track and headed toward the river bottom.

After being told of the threat, Frank Meeker, who worked in the city on the night shift, was notified not to come home until police protection was afforded him.

George Woodworth, of the bloodhound kennels, made certain that his dogs were at the disposal of the officers at any time for the purpose of trailing Horr. The dogs were taken to the scene in the police auto by detective Smith. Later Chief Walker, with detectives Vutrick and Vinson, assisted detective Smith in the search.

The hounds were given a discarded bit of Horr clothing, so they would take the scent on the trail.

The dogs took the trail at the railroad and followed it to a point about 100 yards from the Meeker home, straining at the leash all the way, baying often, as if on a hot trail. Leaving the Meeker home, they followed the trail westward for a considerable distance along the path. Beside the path was a place where some person evidently had been laying the greater part of the night. In the timbers, one of the dogs picked up a bit of paper, sniffed it wildly and bayed. The paper was a Chicago Daily, dated Sunday morning. Someone had lain nearly the whole night where the paper was found. From that point, the dogs worked rapidly, dodging in and about the trees, now on the path. They followed the trail to the railroad about a quarter of a mile west of the point where Horr reported had jumped from the train. There the trail was lost.

The young man who spoke with Horr Sunday night Hahn, was the son of Mrs. Bobaker the woman is who had seen Horr one afternoon during the past week when she was returning home from shopping. Both she and her son knew Horr quite well. They stated there was no possibility of their being mistaken, that the man they saw on the two occasions was undoubtedly Horr.

Friday, October 16, The Danville Police held a news conference. Chief Walker outlined what most residents of Vermilion County already knew. He stated, "Thirty days ago, Alva C. Horr fired the fatal shot that killed his wife, Ida Horr. Despite the efforts of police, sheriff's forces, and private detectives who would be interested in the capture of Horr, there has been no trace of him or his whereabouts. It was if the earth opened and swallowed him completely. Many individuals had claimed to have seen Horr, but in many cases the descriptions do not tally with the correct appearance of the man. There appears to be as little known about Horr now as there was immediately after he plunged into the thicket near where he shot his wife. There are many skeptical people who do not believe that Horr is far away. In fact, there were a number who thought that he was not far from the scene of the tragedy or that he was dead. We do not have any grounds to believe any of this to be true. If Horr is alive, he has performed a wonderful stunt and is managing to elude identification by his friends, as he was one of the best-known persons of the sporting world and has acquaintances all over the county. We are aware of the addresses of many of his acquaintances, and we have sent written request to many of them asking for information should Horr ever show up and ask for assistance. In almost every incident, a reply has been received, agreeing to do so. I am troubled to report that Clark Meeker and his family will move from their home in the Morin's Edition. They will no longer take a chance on the return of Horr. So certain are members of the Meeker family that Horr intends to return and wreak vengeance on some of them, that they will abandon the home. The police have arranged for a house in the northwest portion of the city for the Meekers to be relocated, in a day or two, so that they may have some rest. So insecure have they felt in their own home someone has been on guard constantly for the past couple of weeks and the members of the family are worn out."

Chief Walker added one additional piece of evidence, "A state warrant for the arrest of Horr on a charge of murder was issued by the State's Attorney's office yesterday. This was done merely as a precaution, and to aid in the event of a hasty arrest. Also Judge Morton W. Thompson dismissed the divorce suit filed by Ida Horr before her death."

At the end of the news meeting, Mr. Meeker thanked Chief Walker for all his hard work.

Once again, George Woodworth offered his bloodhounds services to the Meeker family. The offer was made with the provisions that the tracks be kept open until the arrival of the hounds. No compensation would be wanted from the Meeker family. Several police officers had volunteered to go with the hounds the instant the Meeker family notified Mr. Woodworth of the man's appearance.

The mysterious individual, who for several days terrorized the Oakwood community, was caught Tuesday morning, October 6. The man had terrorized women, men, and children of the western part of the county. The supposed Horr was none other than a demented resident of Catlin, and well-known character of the city. Miners made the "capture" shortly before daylight near the abandoned Gray Mine. The man was sent to his home at Catlin. The mystery has been solved!

Late Saturday night, Guy Farrell, who for the last several months has been employed in Mattoon, returned to Danville. He did not know of the murder until he arrived here. When he learned of it, Guy went to the Danville Police Department and spoke to Detective George Garrard. Guy recalled that he had met Horr in Mattoon one week ago. He stated that Horr asked him how long it had been since he was in Danville. Detective Garrard asked Guy for the address where he had met Horr. "We were outside the city of Mattoon in a farm house in a card game," replied Guy.

"Can you describe the person you played cards with?" asked Detective Garrard.

"Yes, his left hand was impaired."

"Did anyone at the table know this person?"

"No, we just wanted to take his money."

"How much money did he have?"

"He entered the game with something like 30 cents; he broke up the game by winning $35. He then disappeared." With almost conclusive evidence obtained from Guy Farrell it was decided that Horr was in the poker game at Mattoon on September 23, 1914.

Chief of Police Wesley Walker, Deputy Sheriff Harry Colt, Detectives George Garrard and Joe White went to Mattoon early Sunday morning. With assistance of the city police at Mattoon, who heartily co-operated with the Danville officers, a thorough search was made. A business man at Mattoon, who also was an alderman, when shown the picture of Horr, recalled that Horr had been in his place about the time that Farrell says he was in Mattoon. That was on September 23. No other trace of the murderer was found.

Horr was seen September 28th, Monday afternoon in Oakwood. He entered a barbershop and got a shave. Several minutes after he left the shop, someone recalled that the man just given the once over by the barber was Horr. Another search was started.

Since the evening of Horr murdering his wife on West Williams Street, Wednesday September 16, 1914 he had been spotted in many places:

Urbana, Wednesday evening just a few hours after the murder.

Lyons, Thursday morning September 17.

Near Meeker's home Saturday, September 19.

Mattoon, Wednesday, September 23.

Lyons, Saturday, September 26.

Oakwood, Sunday evening, September 27.

Visited Meeker home, Sunday night September 27.

Oakwood Barbershop Monday September 28th.

Grape Creek Road, Wednesday September 30.

Mission field, Friday, October 2.

McKinley Avenue, Danville, Saturday, October 3.

Near Meeker home, Sunday, October 4th.

Baldwin Street, Danville.

Bowman Ave., (Germantown) Danville.

South Danville.

Also in the North Fork River area.

Other places too numerous to mention.

Horr had covered a great deal of ground in a very small amount of time. Ida's murderer has been seen in various parts of Vermilion County, but he had not been seen twice in any one place. Two reports sent to the police, within five minutes time, had him in two different places at once. One said he was seen at Oakwood, the other said he was in the vicinity of Vermilion Heights. Efforts had been made to get to the bottom of every report. Two and three details of officers were out at all times to arrest the man believed to be Horr.

A woman living on Bowman Avenue confirmed Horr was standing within twenty yards of her house while she was telephoning the police. Deputy Sheriff Fay Fiedler and Chief of Police Walker investigated. They found that the man had "looked like" Horr.

One night surpassed any previous night since the murder for reports from people seeing Horr. In nearly every case, the person who reported the incident was confident that it was Horr.

Whether it is purely imagination or there was an individual in the city resembling Horr, the police were unable to determine.

One thing they were positive of, however, was that the individual could not be in two different places at the same time.

The story told by Guy Ferrell was substantiated by an official of the city of Mattoon. If he was in Mattoon, with the $35 he was said to have won in the poker game, he could have traveled many miles. At any rate, the Mattoon clue was really the only one that had, in any way, been substantiated.

It had been ten days and no one had reported seeing Horr in the area. Horr escaped, not from the police or the sheriff's office, but from the great eyes of Danville's curious public. More important was that the man "who looked like him" had not been captured. His escape from the curious public was considered remarkable, after the events of the previous Tuesday, during which Horr was reportedly seen at least 29 different times and in as many different places.

Now that all the bizarre clues had been run down by city detectives, and had been thoroughly investigated, the officers expected to resume the campaign where they left off two weeks ago, when the first report came from Mattoon. The climax was reached shortly before nine o'clock Tuesday night when someone called police headquarters and declared that Horr was standing outside the police station with a bundle under his arm.

The Mattoon phase of the search had by no means been abandoned, and will hereafter play a prominent part in the manhunt for Horr.

A month later on the morning of October 17, 1914, Horr was said to have been with friends in Lyons. A month after the shooting of his wife, despite a thorough search, almost nationwide, Horr was yet at liberty.

Since the day of the murder the police, sheriff's forces, and other interested in the search had received many tips as to his probable whereabouts, but few of these tips led to any clues that would have been of assistance in the end. In spite of the efforts made by the officers, they were at a dead end.

The search had progressed and certain results had been obtained, which would ultimately bring about the capture of the fugitive, although it was thought not to be for weeks. To say there had been no trace of Horr since he left the scene of the shooting, the police said, is ridiculous. While all the tips received were not high quality and the majority were soon eliminated, there were others that were good leads.

A few skeptics felt Horr was far away. Officers in charge of the search would not offer any opinions on this. Some officers believed he was not far from the scene of the shooting. In addition to those opinions, one city detective thought that the Meeker boys found

Horr just a few days after the murder, killed him, and carried his body out of the area.

However, if Horr was alive, and officers had every reason to believe he was, he had been remarkably lucky in eluding his friends and the scores of officers all over the country who were constantly on watch for him. The police thought that while he had been fortunate, thus far, something would soon occur that would alter whatever plans the murderer had laid for the future.

November 16, 1914, Ida Horr's murder happened two months ago. Have you an opinion as to the whereabouts of Alva C. Horr?

CHAPTER EIGHT

Time is Money,
especially a good time

The remaining months of 1914 passed slowly with no real news. The City of Danville Police Department and Vermilion County Sheriff Office received numerous tips, on a weekly and monthly basis. The tips were all recorded and each investigated by law enforcement officers, but Alva was elsewhere having a good time.

The night after the shooting was one of his hardest. The next morning, (September 17), when Smith and the Italian came to get Horr from behind the Hooton Cemetery, south of Danville, Horr's clothes were damp, and wet, he was cold, and hungry, but most of all thirsty. Horr's intense need for a drink over shadowed the mosquito bites that had infested his neck, face, arms and lower legs. Mosquitoes had buzzed his body all night long, leaving their calling card everywhere they could.

"Get in, lie down, and shut up," said Smith. I was told to take you to the West Montezuma Train station. You are to ask for Ferrell, he will take care of you. See that bag? It has new pants, shirts, socks, shoes, and a hat for you. **Make sure you wear this hat at all times.** This sack has the money Red sent with me. I do not know how much, but it looks like over two G's. That should keep you out of trouble for a long time."

Horr didn't want to hear about all these details; he wanted a drink. **'What do you think you are, a trustee,"** yelled Horr.

"Here, take this," said the Italian.

Without asking, Horr grabbed the bottle and swallowed the half empty pint of whisky, never taking a breath. Some of the whisky spilled out of his mouth dripping from his dirty beard to his neck. The whisky that covered his neck helped to stop the extreme pain of the irritating mosquito bites.

"Why so long getting here?" asked Horr.

'Well, if you didn't know, the police are looking for you for killing your wife."

"Good. They can look all they want. They will never find me. I bet old man Meeker is happy now. All he needed to do was to give me the rings and Ida would not have been killed. I should have killed Meeker before I jumped over the fence. That old man can run. He almost had me another twenty feet and he would have been on top of me. He hit me with rocks twice, but that didn't slow me down. That path I made from the bottoms up to Logan Avenue helped me more than you two jail birds will ever imagine. The cops can look all they want; they will never find how I got to Logan Avenue so fast. Old Man Meeker has walked by me so many times, when I was watching his house. They will need hound dogs to trace me out of the bottoms."

"Here's an onion sandwich, you better eat while you can." "Smith, where is Volt?"

"He's at home in Oakwood."

"Can we trust him to keep his mouth shut?"

"Red has his eyes on him; he will not say a word if he understands what Red will do if he attempts to talk."

"Where are you taking me?"

"To the train depot, at West Montezuma."

"Where's that?"

"South of here in Indiana, It's about 40 miles from Danville. I will drop you off just south of the train depot, and you will walk about a mile north to the depot building. Before we get there, you need to change your clothes. We will take Grape Creek Road. When we get to Perrysville's Road, we can stop and you can change your clothes."

By this time, Horr was feeling a lot better about his situation. "Is the Italian going with me?"

"No," replied Smith. "We're going to Terre Haute and we'll meet people from Chicago. All you need to do, Horr, is follow the directions that Ferrell gives you. Do not question his plans for your escape. Ferrell is a man of few words. The Italian, and I, know nothing about your escape plan. That's the way Red wants it. The less people who know about your escape, the better chances you have of getting away. When we drop you off, that will be the last time I will speak to you unless you fall victim to trouble. Red may send me to assist you. Do you understand? Ah… what, this better be a good plan. Do you understand, Horr? Answer me you…"

"Okay, okay!" Horr shouted.

"You will have a new name." said the Italian "Remember how you told me to change my name?"

"Yes."

"I will go by…"

"Stop," said Smith, "keep that to yourself. The only thing I know about your plans is the code word 'ESCAPE'."

When the three men reached the point where Horr could change his clothes, Smith pulled the car off the road and parked behind an abandoned saloon. Horr quickly changed his clothes, and the trio was on their way to the train depot.

"Do I keep my gun?" ask Horr.

"No," said Smith, "We will take it with us to Terre Haute. The gun will find a new owner back in Chicago when the Italian meets his brother. You better hand over the gun now before we forget. Here, take this shirt and wipe down the gun."

Amazingly, they had very little trouble finding the train depot. "We made good time, in this car it's just now noonday," said Smith.

"How do you know its noonday? I didn't hear a horn blow," said Horr.

"That's only in Lyons; where they sound a horn at noonday. That's for the coal miners. They know they have six more hours to work" said Smith.

"What's the name of this car?" asked Horr.

"It an Allen," said Smith, "It's the best car I have ever owned. Did you see how smooth we took that big hill in Newport? She's a Jim Dandy."

"Maybe, someday these cars will have clocks in them," said the Italian.

"Ha dumbbell, that's a dumb idea. Henry Ford would not put a clock in his cars; the machine would cost too much," said Smith.

The depot was just east of Highway 63 before you crossed the Wabash River to Montezuma, on State Road 36. Smith stopped the car at the bottom of the hill, and shook Horr's hand. The Italian told Horr to watch his back that every cop would be looking for him. Horr climbed out of the car with the hand bag and money, and never looked back. As Horr made his way down the side of the road, Smith yelled, "There is one more thing."

"What's that?"

"Red told me this area is called Snake Hollow. Watch out for the snakes, they are everywhere!"

Horr stopped in his tracks. "You're joking," yelled Horr. Goose bumps covered his arms.

Smith and the Italian drove off laughing, saying, "A B see ya."

As Horr walked he had one eye on the rails and the other watching for snakes. By the time he reached the train station, he was a nervous wreck. He could smell the smoke, as wind carried the smoke away from the tall red smoke stacks at the local brick plant. Up the tracks he could see a crew of Gandy-Dancers working on the rails.

But, Horr could not see anyone at the station. There were cars parked to the east and north sides of the building. One machine was parked on the south end of the building. The side door opened and two men stepped outside. It appeared they were looking for something; just then a voice called out, "Over here."

Horr turned and he could see a big, rough gent. He had the hat like the one that Horr was wearing. "You must be the package I'm looking for," said the tall gent.

"What's your name?" asked Horr.

"Don't ask so many questions. Just shut up. The next train is due in at one o'clock. Until then, see those two gents standing over there Sit in the back of their car and stay out of sight. Here's a ticket that will get you to E-ville."

"Where's that?"

"I said don't ask so many questions."

"Hey, leatherneck, I need to know all the details."

"When you get to E-Ville, get off the train and ask for Spinuzzi; he will have the same hat, as you do. Got it?"

Horr shook his head. Then the man turned and walked back to the brickyard.

The train was on schedule. Horr sat by himself in the sleeper car second from the diner's car, as the train pulled out of Montezuma. By the time the train pulled into Terre Haute, Horr had had a meal and had fallen asleep. When the passenger train stopped in Vincennes, Horr woke up and watched people board the train. He thought he recognized a gentleman from Danville stepping onto the train. This made him very nervous, thinking that he would have to deal with this man until he got to Evansville. Just then he noticed that the man was getting off the train.

The sun was still high in the sky as the train pulled out of the train station. Another hour and he would find out the next step in his escape. Staring out the window from the sleeper car, he could only think about how his life would change. Would he ever see his best friend Red again? "All my friends, the boys from Chicago, **That's my family now, they will take care of me, until I die.**"

As the train picked up speed and the phone poles passed the window one by one, Horr sat and stared out the window; he asked himself if he would ever see his parents, brothers, or his sisters again especially Minnie. She always helps me when I needed something. The reality of his actions and behavior were dominating his feelings. His self-image, accompanied with the events of the last twenty-four hours was eating at him. These meaningful images motivated Horr to start drinking. By the time the train rolled into Evansville, he had drunk enough to forget about his dilemma.

When the train came to a stop at the depot station, Horr opened his bag and checked his money. With the money securely in place, he walked out of the sleeper cabin and down the narrow hallway to the door leading off the train.

He didn't know what to expect next. As he stood on the train station platform, he didn't see anyone that had a hat like his. He walked inside and looked around, and setting in the far corner was a man wearing the hat Horr was looking for. As he approached the husky built man, he saw two other men with the same hat. Were all three together? Or were two of them decoys? Horr decided not to take a chance, and walked back outside to the front of the train station. When he looked around, he could see the husky gentleman walking toward him.

When the man walked by Horr, he said, "Follow me."

Horr turned and started walking, until they were across the street.

"Are you Spinuzzi?" asked Horr.

"Yes."

"What's next?"

"You are on your way to Louisville, Kentucky."

Just then, the two gentlemen that Horr saw in the train station pulled up in a model T Ford. "When you get to Louisville, you will be working on a horse farm south of the city. Until you hear from me, do not leave the horse ranch for any reason. Understand, Orr?"

"That's not my name."

Spinuzzi looked at him and said, "That's your name while you are in Louisville. Tonight, you will be at Billy's place. Make sure you get a bath and shave before you leave for Louisville tomorrow."

"Where's Billy's place located?"

"Don't ask so many questions these two will protect you while you are here in Evansville. Tomorrow, they will drive you to Louisville. That's all you need to know for now. When they drop you off at the horse ranch, look for Homer; he will have the same hat."

The next day, all three men started out for Louisville. Neither of the two men said a word to Horr. If any conversation, it was between the two riding in the front seat of the model T. Horr decided to sleep while the two men took turns driving.

Horr had never seen Louisville, but he knew about the local horseracing. As they crossed the bridge over the Ohio River into Kentucky, Horr began to get excited. He could gamble on the horses at the local racetracks. Horr was feeling really good about this plan.

Horr pondered the thought of getting the two gentlemen to take him to the race track. "Hey, do you guys play the ponies? Can we go by the racetrack and make a bet?"

"No," said the driver, "that's not the plan that Red has for you."

"Do you know Red?"

"Shut up, don't ask so many questions. Follow the instructions that Spinuzzi gave you, and you will live to see next year. Change any of the plans, and you will not see tomorrow. Understand, Orr. Understand?" asked the driver.

Horr leaned forward from the back seat. Curious, he asked, "If I change the plan what will happen?"

That's when the gentleman sitting in the passenger seat turned and pointed a gun at Horr's head. "Our orders are to take you to Homer. If you decide to change that plan, I will kill you. Understand? Sit back, shut up, and follow the plan. Understand?"

"Yes, yes I do."

When they arrived at the horse farm, Homer was waiting at the water pump. Horr just stared at this white haired, sixty-year-old man.

He had never seen such a tall man; his hands were twice the size of Horr's. This burly figure of a man with coal black eyes seemed to have come from some unknown, distant country. Horr grabbed his bag and climbed out of the model T. Horr looked up at this massive, overpowering man. "Are you Homer?"

Then the man with a big smile said in a slow manner, "Yesum-I-share-bees-tha-man. You boys get this jalopy out of here and don't come until I call for you, go-on-now-get. You must be the next man from Illinois. They sure have some bad boys from Chicago. Why I get all these muckamucks I don't know, but the money is good. Bring your bag and I will show you where you will be staying for the next month. Remember just this one thing, Orr; that is your name, isn't it?"

"Yes, **that's what they call me in these parts.**"

"Remember I'm in charge. If you choose not to follow my instructions, I will kill you, and bury you under the racetrack with all the other boys from Chicago that are missing. All I need is a call from Romma. He will tell me what to do with you. Understand?"

Horr shook his head, "Yes, I do."

As they walked to the stable barn, Homer introduced six horses to Horr. "You will be working in this stable until you leave."

"Is that part of the plan? I've never worked in a stable before."

"Yes, that's part of the plan. Before you leave here you will know how hard working on this horse ranch can be. Tomorrow, we start at 5 a.m. feeding the horses. After that we will clean the stables, and then you will walk the horses. That will be your job every day until you move from this ranch."

Horr was not happy; first of all, he was not used to physical labor. Secondly, he did not like the 5 a.m. wake up. And being around smelly horses all day was not something he would enjoy, but he knew that Homer would kill him if he didn't follow the plan.

The next two weeks were hard for Horr. Homer would come to the bunkhouse and wake him up each day. Horr had not worked this hard in his entire life. By the end of the day, Horr was so tired that all he wanted was sleep. He had not taken a drink of whiskey since the train ride. His hands were calloused from the shoveling of straw in the stables. His legs were sore from walking the horses around the mile racetrack. He had six horses that he worked each day. Homer made sure that each horse was treated the same. If Horr tried to take a shortcut, Homer would have him start over each time. By the end of the second week, Horr was feeling better about himself. Each day he had a job to do, and the responsibility to get the job done right. That meant a lot to him.

Homer had become a person that Horr trusted. When Homer said he would do something, he followed through. Horr had never been around a person like Homer.

The next morning, Homer told Horr that he could ride the horses around the track. Horr had never been on a horse. He had walked everywhere when he was a kid living in Danville. He explained to Homer that he had never ridden a horse, but was willing to try. Homer was happy with Horr's decision. After the stables were cleaned, it was time to saddle the horses. Homer explained how to load the saddle on the back of the horse. By the time the fourth horse was ready to be saddled, Horr had the job under control. At the end of the day, Horr had run the horses around the mile track without any problems. That night after riding all day, Horr's legs were sore, and the next morning, they were like two sticks of wood. He could not bend them, when Homer came to wake him. "You don't look at all well. Are you ill?"

"I do feel rather out of sorts," was all Horr could say. Horr looked like a man who was going to die.

"What's the matter with you? Are you in pain?"

"A little tired, but it's nothing."

Jokingly, Home replied, "What does your doctor say?"

"He calls it a pain in the, ask me no questions, and has ordered me to eat no red meat."

"Orr, no one can feel worse than the man who gets sick on his day off. I have some Corona Ointment for horses that you can rub on your legs; you just stay here in the barn. I will take care of the horses today."

"Will this ointment cause me problems after I use it say, next week or maybe six weeks from now?"

"No, just rub it on your legs. I have never had a horse complain."

"Do you think it would be okay if I just walked the horses from now on, no more riding?"

"No, you need to ride these horses. It will make a man out of you, and besides, you never know, you may be in the picture shows someday riding a horse." Both men just laughed. "Take the day off and get some rest. By the way, you are the only man so far to last this long. Most of the gents put up a fight by the second day. They never see the third day on this ranch."

Horr sat up from his bed. "Look here, old fellow, just tell me the exact truth."

"I have nothing to tell you, that I have not already told you. You have just two more weeks with me before I send you on your way. See you tomorrow morning."

Horr had all day to think. His mind wandered off in deep thought, "There's nothing wrong when you talk to yourself, but watch out when you start listening!" He was silent for a few moments to collect his thoughts, his eyes staring looking into space, thinking of the terrible drama which had wrecked his life.

The next two weeks passed without any problems. It was now the middle of October. Homer had done his job. Horr was ready to move on. It had been over a month since he had taken a drink. His mind was clear. Those long walks had a way of clearing his head and helped him think. That was why Homer made him walk the horses. The hard work had changed his outlook on life.

The morning of October 21, Homer informed Horr that he would be leaving.

"Just when I was getting used to that humpy mattress."

"Today, you will travel to Louisville and take a train to Atlanta. At the first train station in Atlanta, you will meet Levi. He will have on the hat. During your train ride, do not speak to anyone. Stay in your quarters and have food delivered to you. There will be many stops along the way before you get to Atlanta. Get all the sleep you can. You will need it. Remember, **talk to no one.** The police have pictures of you posted everywhere. Put on your happy face. At the train station in Louisville, talk to Sammy. He will tell you what to do."

The short ride to Louisville was uneventful. When the driver stopped at a flat grassy field next to the train depot, all Horr could see was circus tents; he didn't know what to think.

"Hey you two jail birds, what is this?"

"Get out and look for Sammy. He will have a hat on just like yours," said the driver of the model T.

Horr didn't know if the driver was on the level and started arguing with him, "This is not what Homer told me. He didn't say anything about a circus train."

"If you want to see the sunrise, get out of this car. Start looking for the hat as you were told. Got it?"

Just then a man, dressed as a clown, with a hat that Horr recognized, walked up to the car. "Hey gents." He tipped his hat, and pointed his finger at Horr, "You come with me." Horr gave the two jail birds in the front seat of the car a slap on the back of the heads. Both men jumped out of the car and started after him. Sammy stepped between them and stopped the fight. "Get back into your car and get out of here. You know what Red will do if I tell him about this." Both men took a wild swing at Horr and got back into the car.

"Do you know Red?" Horr asked.

Sammy looked at Horr and said, "That will be the last time you will talk to anyone but me on this circus train. Follow me, I will take you to your sleeping quarters; bring your bag."

"Do you have a stage name?"

"Yes, I go by the name Hoppy. I will be the only person that you will speak to until we get to Atlanta."

"Will that be tomorrow?"

"No, we have several stops before we get to Atlanta."

"What do you mean? I thought I would be in Atlanta by tomorrow."

"That's not the plan,"

"Where will we be traveling to before we get to Atlanta?"

Sammy reached into his hip pocket and pulled out the circus train schedule for the next month. "The schedule read: Louisville for two days, Middlesboro, Kentucky; Knoxville, Tennessee; Johnson City, Tennessee; Bristol, Tennessee; then to Norfolk, Virginia; Rocky Mount, North Carolina; Raleigh, North Carolina; Durham, North Carolina; Winston-Salem, North Carolina; Spartanburg, South Carolina; Greenville, South Carolina; Anderson, South Carolina; Columbus, South Carolina; Augusta, Georgia; and then to Atlanta, Georgia."

"What do I do until this freak show gets to Atlanta?"

Sammy walked toward Horr and grabbed him by the throat. "You are a guest on this circus train. This is not a freak show!" Horr pulled Sammy's hands from his neck and shook his head.

"My father has worked the three-ring traveling mud show all his life. I remember when he invented the end-loading process; that's the revolutionary way of putting circus wagons onto trains."

"What's your father's name?"

"Mr. Coup is what everyone called him."

"Where did he come up with the end-loading idea?" "Terre Haute, that's my home town."

"Terre Haute, Indiana?"

"Yes, Back in 1870's when Joshua Purdy Brown invented the big top circus tent, the circus trains could move quickly and easily anywhere in the country, requiring only a flat, grassy place near a railroad stop to set the tents. See where we are located, in a large flat grassy field next to the train tracks."

"You must be proud of your father."

"Yes, very much. He had a very hard life but he was always there for me whenever I needed him."

"That's what father's do, that's their job."

Horr thought to himself, "What a great story. This guy doesn't know how lucky he was to have a father; who helped his son get a start in life. If I had only had a father who cared about me, maybe I would have made something out of my life. My drinking bouts just covered up my hard feelings toward my father and mother. Look where that has got me, on a freak show train to nowhereville. Maybe I should listen to this guy, and see what he is all about."

"Horr, are you okay?"

"Yes. What do you want me to do, while I am on this train?"

"You will do as I tell you from now on. Do you understand?"

"I can't stay in this boxcar until we get to Atlanta."

"No, you will be dressed as a clown. I will bring you a trunk with items you can use to dress. None of the other clowns know your name or where you are going. Your job, while you are with the circus, is to walk around the big tent, wave and smile at the crowd. Do not talk to anyone. When you are not in the big tent, go to your quarters and stay. In each town we have policeman that help us with the crowds. While we were in Evansville, the police ask us if we had seen you. They had a picture, with your information, and a $200 reward. If someone working on this circus train fingers you for the person in the picture, these low-lifers will take the reward money. We have midgets, Siamese twins, giants, bearded ladies, animal trainers, clowns, drunks, cooks, beauty queens, x-cons, racketeer's, cheats, counterfeits and local chaps setting up the tents. That is not to mention one murderer and most of all, the Black Hand group".

"How do you know about the Black Hand group?"

"Why do you ask?"

"That's who Red works for, **I was told never to use that name.**"

"**I** just want you to understand who you are dealing with, that's all. Now do you understand? Stay to yourself, dressed as a clown. I will bring you your food. If you have any questions, talk to me, no one else. Do you understand?"

"Yes. If you get in trouble, Sammy, is there anyone else that I can trust?"

"Yes, the cook."

"What's his name?"

"Romma"

"Where will I find Romma?"

"He will be in car number six, that's where you'll find him when he's not cooking."

"I like this plan. I've never been a clown, what a great idea. So, I just dress up as a clown, and walk around, wave, and smile to everyone?"

"Yes."

"I will go get the trunk now and bring you some food. You will need to shave your face, clowns do not have beards. Only the bearded ladies in this circus crew have beards."

Horr could not believe how easy this would be. "Sammy, all I do is wave and smile?"

"Yes, wave and smile that's it; that's the plan. Stay here I will be back with the trunk and your food. You get those whiskers off your face."

When Sammy returned, Horr had shaved his face. "You do look like that wanted poster with your picture on it. How old are you?"

"Thirty-eight."

"You sure have a baby face for your age. We need to give you a name; I will call you Faces. I want you to have a different clown face at each town we stop in. That way no one will recognize you from town to town. We have two shows each day, one in the afternoon and one in the evening. When the show is over, come back to your quarters, and never talk to anyone. I will tell the circus crew that you are deaf and cannot hear, that you have a hard time talking, and prefer keeping to yourself." Horr smiled and shook his head up and down not saying a word. "Here's a list of things every clown should know. Read these notes; my father gave me this list from when he started clowning in the mud shows back in the day, when horse-drawn wagons, slogged ten miles each day through mud. Here's the list read it over."

Horr took the wrinkled, folded, aged, yellowed paper, and unfolded it, so he could read the hand written note:

Your hairpiece and costume should be lightweight and comfortable. You don't need to act like a clown. You just need to be a clown.

After Horr finished reading, he handed the note back Sammy and said, "That's good advice. Thanks."

Sammy lugged the trunk in front of Horr's feet. "You have very small feet for a man your size. You may need to cram some paper inside your oversized clown shoes so you can walk without tripping up. In this trunk, you will find oversized shoes, wacky accessories, face paints, and bright clashing costumes, some checks, some stripes that all mismatch. Put on your best robe, and you have faces. In the bottom of this trunk is a false bottom. Let me show you how to open the false bottom lid. You pull the false bottom from the center of the trunk like this."

"Can I try pulling the false bottom out?" asked Horr.

"Yes, you try it; just let me put the bottom back in place," responded Sammy.

Horr bent down, stared into the trunk, and said, "You cannot see any false bottom." Then he reached into the trunk and pulled the false bottom lid out.

"If you every need to hide anything from someone, use a trunk with a false bottom. No one will ever guess that you have a trunk with a false bottom. Oh, one last thing," advised Sammy, "if you have valuables that you want to keep safe and out of the hands of the circus crew, let me know now. Like I told you, we have all kinds of characters on this circus train. Trust no one!"

Horr gave this some thought, "Was Sammy trying to con him, or was he on the level?" Horr told Sammy that he had no valuables.

"Fine, just remember this conversation. If you lose any of your personal items, that's your business, understand? If you change your mind, let me know. The next show will be at seven tonight. Make sure you have your new face on, wave and smile to the crowd. I'll check on you after the show," stated Sammy. After Sammy left, Horr decided to hide his personal belongings and money.

For some reason he did not trust Sammy. "Why did Sammy ask me about my personal items?" he wondered. Did he know I was carrying a large sum of money? I need to set a trap! I will leave five dollars out and hide the rest, which should answer my suspicions about Sammy." Horr positioned all his money in the bottom of each clown shoes, leaving five dollars out in plain sight. "That was good advice Sammy gave me," thought Horr.

During the seven o'clock show, Horr followed Sammy's directions. He walked around in the big top, waving and smiling. The crowd loved him, and by the end of the show, Horr had walked around the big top countless times. After the show, he returned to his sleeping quarters. He was anxious to see if his five dollars was missing. When he entered the room to look for the five dollars, his hunch was right. The entire sleeping quarters were in disarray. Someone had ransacked it.

Horr had guessed right, Sammy could not be trusted. At the end of about an hour, Horr had cleaned up his sleeping quarters. Nothing was going to get better here; to Horr, that much was plain. At this a panic set in, consuming Horr's thinking: "Do I stay here, or do I find another way to Atlanta? I have money to buy a train ticket to Atlanta, but how will I find Levi? Do I stay here, and lose all my money? Maybe I should question Sammy about the money?"

Wise enough not to utter his thoughts, he decided to wait until Sammy came to his sleeping quarters. It was now after 11 p.m.; Sammy had not stopped in to check on him. Was Sammy going to finger him?   Was he going to notify the police and collect the $200 reward? Horr was getting nervous; he knew that something was not right. If Sammy was on the level and was concerned about his safety, he would've been here by now. A few minutes later, there was a knock at the door. Horr could not see who it was. Should he say something, or just wait until they left?

The pounding on the door got louder, "Are you in there, Horr? Open the door, it's Sammy, open the door." His voice was so empty, he sounded like a desperate man.

"You have a key to the door," Horr shouted back. "Why don't you unlock it and come in?"

"Open the door, please open the door."

When Horr opened the door, he found Sammy lying on the steps in front of the door. When Horr bent over to check on Sammy, someone punched him in the back. Horr fell on top of Sammy, and rolled to the ground in front of the steps. That's when Horr saw the handgun that Sammy had in his right hand. Without thinking,

Horr grabbed the gun and fired two shots in the air. The attacker immediately took off running into the darkness.

Horr knew that he had to get Sammy into his sleeping quarters before anyone could see them. He only had a few minutes, before someone would be investigating the gunshots. With all of his strength, he helped Sammy into the sleeping quarters and locked the door behind them.

Sammy was barely alive; he had been beaten severely. Who would have done this? Sammy opened his eyes and reached for Horr's arm. Horr leaned over to see what he wanted. In a very weak voice Sammy whispered, "See Romma, and go back to Homer tonight." Without saying another word Sammy closed his eyes and his hand dropped to the floor.

Horr knew that he needed to find Romma, and let him know about Sammy. "Will there be someone outside looking for me?" wondered Horr. "How will I get to Romma's sleeping car without anyone seeing me? Do I wait here until early morning, or go right now? Would Romma open the door in the middle of the night?"

Horr decided to wait until early morning when he thought his chances would be better for Romma to open the door and talk to him. The next morning Horr took all his personal things and went to see Romma to explain what had happened the night before. Without questioning Horr about the details, Romma told Horr to stay in his sleeping quarters until he returned.

"This is going to cost you big bucks," said Romma. Romma locked the door behind him and walked away from the rail road cars. When he got to the train station, he placed a call to Homer. "Send someone to get Orr immediately; we will be in car number six. How long will it be until you get here?" asked Romma.

"My two cohorts can be there in about thirty minutes or sooner," replied Homer.

Romma returned to the sleeping car where Horr was held up. Romma informed Horr that he would be going back to Homer's location shortly.

Nervous, Horr asked Romma, "Do you have any whiskey that I can take with me on my trip back to Homer's ranch?"

"Before I give you the whiskey," said Romma, "we need to settle a little financial issue."

"What issue would that be?"

"Time is money, especially the good time you are going to have with this bottle of whiskey."

"How much do you want for the whiskey?"

Romma turned and walked toward him, and said, "You have a reward of $200 over your head. I figure this bottle of whiskey is worth $200. You have until the two gentlemen pick you up to come up with the $200. I will go get you some breakfast and when I return I want to see the $200." Without saying another word, Romma left the sleeping quarters.

When Romma returned with breakfast, Horr had the $200 ready for him. "Where's my whiskey? He boldly asked

Is this the man you are looking for?

CHAPTER NINE

Cops and Robbers

The ride back to Homer's ranch was immediate. Romma had made one phone call, and the wheels of the Black Hand started turning. Two men were at the train station within five minutes. Horr carted his bag to the model T and jumped into the back seat.

"Do I know you two jail birds?" asked Horr. "I know... I know just shut up, and don't ask so many questions." The two men in the front seat didn't say a word to Horr.

Horr knew that Homer would have many questions. "How would Red react to the trouble Horr witnessed? Who was the man that killed Sammy?" Horr rubbed his face and took a deep breath. It was a cool October morning as they made their way out of the city. Horr looked over his left shoulder, out the side of the model T. He saw two other Model T's following, very closely. "Hey you two jail birds, do you see the two following us?" asked Horr.

"Sit back. There's a first time for everything," the driver said, smiling.

"It's if there is some kind of connection between the three drivers," Horr thought to himself. "They know each other; they are following us to Homer's horse ranch." As hard as Horr tried, he could not pretend or ignore the two other cars.

"Do you know them?" asked Horr.

"Yes," replied the driver, "they are bringing some Chicago men to see Homer."

"Why?" asked Horr.

The driver looked over his right shoulder and said, "Homer gets all the Chicago boys that need some help in adjusting their attitude. You are the only person in the last year that I have taken back to Homer."

"What's that mean; I have a good attitude?" asked Horr.

"If I were in your shoes," responded the driver, "I'd have a real good reason for going back to the horse ranch. Those Chicago boys behind us will cause you trouble, if you hang with them. My advice to you, find some way to get away from this ranch as soon as you can."

"If I had any guts," stated Horr, "I'd get out of here now." Then Horr asked the driver, "How many men are coming to see Homer?"

"I think four this time," said the passenger in the front seat. He continued to advise Horr, "That's not your business; keep to your own business, asked no questions about the others. Homer will deal with them."

Horr thought for a minute, "That sounds like good advice. Thanks for the tip.

When the three cars turned onto the dirt road leading to the ranch stables, Horr started looking for Homer. He was not standing in front of the water pump, like the last time. Then he spotted Homer walking from the racetrack. Horr could see Homer was carrying a shovel in his right hand. He didn't have his hat on. When Homer approached the three cars, he walked by Horr, without saying a word.

Homer walked directly to the third car, dropped the shovel and pulled the man out of the back seat by his neck. "What's your name?" Homer asked.

The tall skinny, dark haired man, with a huge nose just looked at Homer and spat at him. Horr knew this dummy didn't have much time left. Horr was going to witness what Homer's real job was. Horr was wise enough not to utter his thoughts.

Homer reached down with one hand to the ground where this indefensible, apathetic young man was lying. Homer picked him off the ground. "I said, what's your name? I want to get the right person in that hole over there. So, if you have a name, I suggest that you start talking."

Then he reached into his back pocket and pulled out a folded piece of paper and a picture. In a very angry voice, Homer exclaimed, "Look at this! Did you write this note? Look at this picture-that my family!"

Then Homer pushed him away and walked over to the other car. He looked in the back seat and found three men tied up. The one setting in the middle was missing part of his lower left ear. He also had a very long cut below his ear that needed some medical attention. The man setting to his left had blood all over his clothes. "Untie these three men," ordered Homer.

That's when Horr saw Homer looking over at him.

Horr said nothing. At this point, Horr was overtaken by panic. He fearfully thought, "What should I do? Should I say something, or keep quiet?" He took a deep breath, closed his eyes, and pulled his hands down over his face.

Just then the side door of the Model T opened. "You need to go inside the stable barn and wait for me," said Homer with a smile on his face. Horr climbed out of the Model T with his bag and never looked back as he walked to the stable barn.

"You two go back to the train yard and find the Hoe-boy and let him know what to do when you bring Horr to the train yard tomorrow. Make sure he understands the plan that he is a decoy. Remember tell him to walk, not run. Be back here to pick up Horr at 4 a.m." Homer then turned and walked back to the other cars.

When Homer finished his business with the other four men, it was after 2 p.m. He walked to the stable barn to check on Horr. Horr was setting on the edge of his bunk, with his head hanging down, his hands covered the sweat running down from his forehead. He was nervous thinking about what Homer would say about Sammy. "How will I explain all that has happened?" Horr thought.

When Horr looked up, he saw Homer standing in the doorway. "Got a lot on your mind?" asked Homer, seeing Horr's head buried in his sweaty hands.

"Wh-what?" asked Horr with a surprised look on his face.

"I just finished my work and that took all my energy," said Homer.

Horr wondered, "Should I ask what work or should I keep my thoughts to myself?" Horr remembering that he had just been told to not ask questions.

Before Horr could say anything, Homer said, "Are you hungry?"

"Yes," replied Horr.

"Come with me, I need to eat."

Homer led Horr into a building unfamiliar to Horr. When both men stepped onto the wooden porch, Homer said, 'Wait outside. I will bring your food to you. Have a seat." When Homer returned with the hot food, he handed the tin metal plate to Horr and said, "I will be right back."

Horr gobbled the food down without saying a word. When Homer returned to the porch, he looked at Horr and said, "You were very lucky last night. You must carry a rabbit's foot with you for good luck. I have my orders on what to do with you, but what I want to know is how do you know Red?"

He didn't know how to answer Homer. "Was this a trick question? Was this a joke or prank?" Horr wondered.

"Horr, did you hear me? You look worried. How do you know Red?" Homer demanded.

"Red and I have been good friends for a long time. I helped him a few years back when we were working in Chicago, playing Cops and Robbers. That's about all that I can tell you, Homer," Horr stated apologetically.

"Well you must have done something very important, Horr. Red has never allowed anyone to leave this ranch after someone returns for the second time. That's a standing rule. You are a first," said Homer.

Upon hearing that, Horr's heart almost stopped beating. His hands were damp wet with sweat. Horr stood up so quickly, that the tin plate fell on the porch floor. With high anxiety, Horr asked, "Will I be leaving this ranch soon?"

"Yes," Homer quickly responded.

"What's the plan this time?" wondered Horr.

"You better get some sleep, Horr. You will be leaving here at 4 a.m. tomorrow morning. The plan is for you to ride a freight train to Nashville. You will be picked up by two men, who will take you to the train yard in Louisville. The freight train will be hauling bricks, from our operation in Montezuma. The flatbed train car, you will be riding in, will be loaded with stacks of bricks. The flatbed car you will be looking for will have a secret hideaway, inside the stacked bricks. The two who will be driving you to the train yard tomorrow will help you locate the car. One stack of bricks will be painted white. That's what you are looking for. There will be food and water in the hideaway and a small straw mattress. "Once you are on the freight train, stay inside the hideaway," warned Homer.

"But how will I know when I get to Nashville?" asked Horr.

"The freight train is scheduled to drop off the flatbed cars of bricks in Nashville. When the train cars are put onto a side rail in the train yard, you will know at that time you are in Nashville."

After giving those instructions, Homer asked, "Do you understand the escape plans?"

"Yes," said Horr with certainty. "But who will I look for when I jump off the flatbed," he wondered.

Homer explained, "It will be late afternoon when you arrive in Nashville. Be careful before you leave the train car. You will be looking for the Bulls (Railroad Police) or any other railroad workers. Also, you will be looking for a short, one armed man, wearing a coat with the left arm folded and tied off. His name is Falcona. He will give you instructions on what to do."

"How did Falcona lose his arm?" Horr inquired.

"In a gun fight on the southside of Chicago with me." Homer quickly responded.

With great concern for his future, Horr asked, "Do you know where I will end up living?"

"Maybe," said Homer.

Horr continued to ask more questions. "Can you tell me what you know about my escape plan?"

"I know the Black Hand's have connections in Cuba and Florida," stated Homer.

"My guess would be Jacksonville Florida."

Quickly, Horr asked another question, **<u>Have you been to these two places?</u>**

"Yes," answered Homer. "I have family in Cuba."

Horr wondered, "Why Cuba? Was his family hiding from someone, or was that where Homer was from?" His curiosity pushed him to ask yet another question,

"Homer, I was just wondering; how did you get to this horse ranch from Cuba?"

Homer turned and started walking toward the stable barn, turned to Horr and explained, "I'm not from Cuba, but my family was sent there after I fixed a few things back in Chicago. I was a policeman on the southside of Chicago. When the Black Hand needed information, I would help them out. One day, I came home from work to find my wife and two kids tied up with a note that said: 'next time we will kill them all.' That's when Falcona came to me with information about the note. Falcona was helping me get my family out of Chicago, when he lost his arm. The men that are sent here from Chicago are members of a rival Black Hand Family."

"The paper you pulled out of your pocket when you were talking to those four men, is that the note you found with your family?" Horr inquired.

"Yes," Homer replied.

Horr thought, "Homer is protecting his family. That was his main job in life. Homer was not going to allow anyone to harm his family. Why couldn't I have had a father who would protect me?"

Horr continued asking more questions, "Can I see the note that you are carrying, Homer?" When Homer handed the note to him, Horr, he could not believe his eyes. Surprised at what he saw, Horr expressed, "You told me you had two kids. I see four kids in this picture."

A shadow fell across Horr's head and shoulders as Homer stood up. He looked up at Homer's face; Horr could see tears, running down Homer's wrinkled face. Horr placed his right hand on Homer's back, "This must be a real nightmare."

"There's not a day that I can relax without thinking about my family. Why did my two boys have to die? My money problems started this trouble. On my salary, I could hardly make ends meet." Homer continued to explain, "That's when I decided to take money on the side from the Black Hand Family."

Just then Horr realized that Homer's battle over money was the same as his. So, he expressed, "That's how I got myself into this dilemma, over money."

"No, it's not the same," Homer stated. "I had a good job. You were drinking, placing bets, playing cards. I did none of that corrupt activity."

"Well, Homer," Horr shared, "this is one of those unfortunate, but classic situations, where most people find themselves."

"What situation are you talking about?" asked Homer.

"The Cops and Robbers games people play," Horr answered. "You were a cop now you are a robber. I have been a robber all my life. You played the game for material rewards-money. I play the game for the satisfaction of outwitting others. Sometimes we win and sometimes we lose. You lost part of your family; I lost my mother and father. In the game of Cops and Robbers, some are in it for profit, and others are in it primarily for the game. Take my father-in-law for example. He was a cop; his job was to protect is daughter. But when he took my diamond rings, he became a robber. If he had given the rings back, my wife would not be dead. Old Man Meeker will always be a robber in my eyes. My wife outwitted me. She was a robber," Horr continued to explain, "and it gave her satisfaction that she beat me at my own game of Cops and Robbers."

Somewhat confused over the conversation, Homer interrupted, "I don't understand any of this. I would give anything to have my two boys back."

It was now after six o'clock, the two men had sat and talked for over two hours. "Horr," said Homer, "let me assure you that your curiosity about my life is of secondary importance to me. My primary concern is your comprehension of your trip to Nashville."

CHAPTER TEN

The Message

He went to See his two boys

The next morning, Horr was up and on his way to Louisville. When he arrived at the nearly empty train yard, the driver pointed toward the empty boxcars. Horr waited for the driver to finish his sentence.

"Who is that? It looks like a Hoe-boy (hobo) with his sack of possessions," said the driver. The Hoe-boy was stumbling alongside the boxcars. Then he dropped to the ground.

"I haven't the slightest idea how or why that Hoe-boy is laying on the ground," said the driver as he shook his head. "What is he doing?" Disappointment flickered across the driver's face. Horr didn't say a word. It was strange to hear the two men in the front seat having a discussion.

"I don't know if this is such a good idea," Horr said. It took just a minute of wondering and all three men could see the Bull's (Railroad Police) were running toward the Hoe-Boy, with guns held out in front of them. The driver stopped the car, backed up, and drove off from the rail yard.

"With the police everywhere, how are you two going to get me on that freight train?" questioned Horr.

"We have a backup plan," replied one of the other men in the car.

"UM…" Neither one of them said anything else until the driver stopped.

"Why did you stop here?" Horr asked.

"It's part of the backup plan," explained the man in the front seat. "That Hoe-Boy is a decoy. His job is to tell us if the train yard is clear. "Falling down was not part of the plan. He was to walk the train yard. If he found any Bulls, he was to walk, not run from them."

"As you indicated a few minutes ago, something out there is wrong and I agree. But using any logic would tell you that the Hoe-Boy was in trouble," stated Horr.

"Maybe," said the man in the front seat.

"There is something I would suggest," Horr added, "and mind you, it is just a suggestion. How many Hoe Boys are in this train yard? Could that be a different Hoe Boy then the one you are looking for? I suggest you drive back, take another look, and maybe you will find the Hoe Boy working with you two."

"Why not?"

Each waited for the other to speak. "Before this goes any further," insisted the man in the front seat, "I want to get something straight. We have our instructions. If we do not follow the instructions, you know where we all will end up!"

"Where?" asked Horr.

"Back at Homer's ranch, six feet under," replied the two at the same time.

Home continued to work at solving this problem and suggested, "Let's imagine that the Hoe-Boy that the Bulls were chasing was not our Hoe-Boy."

They said, "Okay." They all shook their heads. From that point on, everything happened fast; the driver drove back to the train yard. All three men were very cautious, looking in every direction for any sign of trouble. They spotted the flatbed train car with the white bricks. Horr jumped out of the car with his bag and climbed into the secret hideaway. That was the last time he was in Louisville.

Late Monday afternoon, on October 23, 1914 Horr arrived in Nashville Tennessee. It had been just 37 days since he had murdered his wife. When the flatbed finally came to a stop, Horr was ready to leave the small hideaway. The sound of the train wheels was deafening. Horr could not sleep because his ears, were ringing from the clanging noise the wheels had made rolling across the rails.

As Horr stuck his head out to see if anyone was around the flatbed car, he could not see anyone. He grabbed his bag and climbed down off of the flatbed car. He then reached into the bag and pulled out his hat and placed it on his head. Not knowing the train yard, Horr did not know which way to start walking. Not remembering what Homer had told him to do, he did not know whether he should remain standing there or should he begin walking? At this point, he was very frustrated and thought, "Where is the one-armed man?" When he passed to the next flatcar, he could see the one-armed standing on the other side of the flatbed railroad car. Horr crawled underneath the flatbed car and stood up to the one-armed man. "You must be Falcona?" Horr brazenly said.

In a very quiet voice, Falcona said to Horr, "Shut up don't ask so many questions."

"I know... I know," Horr said quietly.

"Follow me and keep your mouth shut," ordered Falcona. They walked about 50 yards and got into a Model T. As soon as they were both in the car, Falcona said, "Well, first let me say that you are very lucky. I ask you a favor to please keep confidential what I'm about to tell you. That is very important. Homer is missing!"

"Wh-what? Did you say, Homer is missing?" Horr questioned.

"Yes," replied Falcona. "He never made his daily phone call to the Black Hand Family. Two of the Louisville drivers went to check on Homer at the horse ranch. They found a note in his sleeping quarters. The note informed them he went to see his two boys. I was told that there was a hangman's rope at the bottom of the note."

"What's that mean-there was a hangman's rope at the bottom of the note?" asked Horr.

"That means a rival Black Hand Family has kidnapped Homer and they will kill him," Falcona explained. "We have men looking for Homer. Someone is going to get hurt!"

Horr wondered about Homer and asked, "Do you think Homer is still alive? What did the note say? Can you repeat that?"

"I was told the note read: 'He went to see his two boys'," Falcona replied.

"Wait, say that again," insisted Horr.

This time Falcona replied slowly and clearly, "The note said, 'He went to see his two boys.'"

"How many boys are in Homer's family?" Horr wondered out loud.

"Four," replied Falcona. "I should know because I helped Homer's wife and two boys leave Chicago."

Just to be certain, Horr asked, "Did you say earlier that this conversation was confidential?"

"Yes!" emphasized Falcona.

"Then let me ask you a favor," continued Horr. "Please keep confidential what I'm about to tell you. That note could mean two different things. If Homer wrote the note then it could mean that he is going to Cuba to see his family. If the rival Black Hand Family wrote the note, that means they are going to kill him, and he will be with his two boys that are dead."

"What kind of propaganda is that?" asked Falcona.

"Oh, I was just thinking out loud. If Homer wrote the note, he is headed for Cuba, don't you think? Can you tell me the location of Homer's family in Cuba?" inquired Horr.

Falcona immediately responded, "Havana!"

Horr truly liked Homer and was very concerned about him. This might be good news of connecting with his wife and two boys or it might mean that he would be killed. So Horr continued to seek more information. "How did you get his family to Havana?"

"On a boat out of Jacksonville," replied Falcona anxiously. "But I have told you too much already. I need to get you to Billy's place."

As the two men started driving, they could see the burned down buildings on 7th street. Horr inquisitive nature about every aspect of the situation moved him to ask another question, "When did this fire happen?"

"Back in March of this year sparks from Joe Jennings's home set the Seagraves Planting Mill ablaze." Falcona continued, "The fire swept from 1st street to Dew Street, consuming any homes or businesses in its path, destroying over 500 houses and leaving over 2,000 people homeless."

The direction of this conversation was not helping Horr. So, to refocus the conversation, he asked, "Well, tell me more about my time here in Nashville."

Falcona proceeded to give Horr the details. "You will be staying here in Nashville for the next week. When I drop you off, in the back alley, use the side door. Walk upstairs to the third floor, and go to room three. The number three will be hanging upside down. The door will be unlocked; stay in the room until I come see you. Make sure you lock the door; I am your only contact in Nashville. I will slide a note under the door after I knock two times. Look for the note before you open the door. If anyone knocks on the door, and you see no note, do not open the door. Here's a key to unlock the side door. If you choose not to follow my instructions, you are on your own."

"Thank you, my friend," Horr said, less anxiously. I will follow your instructions."

It was now after 7 p.m. Horr reached for his bag with his right hand and stepped out. Horr looked at Falcona and said once again, "Thank you, my friend."

As Falcona pulled away, Horr tossed the key Falcona had given him into the air and caught it with his left hand. Horr was feeling good. He walked up to the side door and unlocked the red door very slowly. He didn't know what to expect as he looked in. He could see an inside door with a light shining under it. As he looked around, he could see the wooden stair case leading up to the second and third floors. There was noise coming from the other side of the inside door. As he closed the side door behind him, he stepped gingerly toward the stair case.

The noise had stopped by the time he had reached the third floor hall way. When he saw the door with the upside down 3, he heard a dog running up the stairs. By the time Horr closed the door, the dog was jumping and barking at the wooden door. Horr stood in the darkness, holding his breath. He thought, "This has not happened to me since I was a small boy being chased by a dog." The memory of that day, when his father just stood by and never helped him flashed in his mind. Horr was now aware of having to walk a fine line. Who would be next to come to the door? He was alarmed. Who owned the dog? When would the owner come and see what the dog is barking about? Did Falcona know about the dog? Horr's mind was racing with question after question.

A voice out of the darkness of the room, "There you are!" Horr jumped, as he heard the voice. He quickly turned to see who it was in the room with him. He could see it was The Italian.

With a surprised look, Horr asked, "What are you doing here?"

"You know someone could have gotten hurt. Red sent me here to give you information on where you will spend the next six months," said the Italian

"Does Falcona know you are here in Nashville?" asked Horr cautiously.

"No. The escape plan must be kept secret; too many Hoe Boys know about Louisville. Homer had to leave the ranch. We got word that a "hit" was put out for Homer. The Hoe Boy we used at the train yard was a tittle-tattle. Remember the Hoe Boy running from the Bull's at the train yard? That was a set up. When the driver dropped you off at the train yard, he made a call to Red, telling him what had happen. Red sent the driver to get Homer and to leave the note," explained the Italian.

With a joyful voice Horr responded, "That the best news I have heard!"

"We don't have much time here in Nashville," The Italian continued, "Red had to change your escape plan. The circus clown plan was the original. But when Sammy was killed, all things changed. Romma was also killed the next night. He started bragging about the two hundred dollars you paid him for the bottle of whiskey. Here, take this money. You will need it later on,"

Horr took the money, counted it, and clarified, "It's all here, what I gave him."

"Like I said, we don't have much time here in Nashville," The Italian reminded Horr. "Let me go over the plan with you."

"Wait," Horr interrupted, "Let me get this right. The Hoe Boy was corrupt, the note was a fake, and Homer is okay, Romma was killed? I have my two hundred dollars, and Falcona doesn't know you are here in Nashville? One more question; was Romma behind the killing of Sammy?"

Anxiously and with great frustration the Italian answered, "Yes! Now stop with the questions! I need to spell out the plan and get out of here." The next thirty minutes the Italian outlined the six-month plan. When the two men finished, they shook hands. **<u>So, you are going to be a Detective?</u>** asked Horr. They both laughed as the Italian stepped out the window and onto the fire escape.

Horr stared out the window over the barren alley and the small bit of Tenth Avenue he could see. Horr noticed a policeman standing on the corner, who seemed to be so unoccupied. The policeman just stood there, watching people as they walked pass him. Horr thought to himself, "How I envy him." It was a subtle reminder of what terrible turns a life could take.

"Ah," Horr sighed, "just two months ago I was feeling like that unoccupied cop. Now, my world has totally changed."

Horr sat down on the side of the bed, began taking off his shoes, and thought, "I must take control of myself. I must remember what the Italian told me, not to lose sight of my escape plan." The night passed slowly, Horr found himself distracted thinking about Homer. "Will I really see him in Cuba?"

The next morning, Falcona came to the room with food. Horr

said nothing about the Italian being in Nashville. After the two finished eating, Falcona went down stairs and made a phone call. Then he returned to Horr's room and assured him, "Everything is ready. I will be here at five o'clock. Be ready and make sure that dog is locked up!"

CHAPTER ELEVEN

A New Day

Horr was sitting on the edge of the bed when he saw the paper appear under the door and heard the two knocks. He collected his bag and walked to the door. "Is that you Falcona?" asked Horr.

"Yes, open the door." answered Falcona. "We have a problem! The police are downstairs."

"Why do you have that number 'three' in your hand?" inquired Horr.

"They are asking about a man who used the fire escape last night. They want to check all the rooms on the second and third floors. Did you go out of this room for any reason last night?" asked Falcona.

"No," Horr responded immediately.

"Remember what I told you? If you choose not to follow my instructions, you are on your own," Falcona insisted.

With a slight panic in his voice, Horr responded, "I looked out the window and saw a police officer standing on the sidewalk. That's all I know."

"We need to find a place to hide you until the police leave. I told them I use this rooming house when I visit Nashville, that I got into town today, and that I was not in the room last night," Falcona explained.

Then Falcona handed Horr a package, "Here's your new name and documents. Look these two papers over later; your new name is Alva Stall."

Horr took the package, examined it and inquired, "Has this package been opened?"

"No!" Falcona assured.

Horr opened the package and began to read what Red had written, When Falcona interrupted and insisted, "We don't have time to discuss what's in the package, I want you to step out into the hallway and start walking toward the back stairs. If the police ask you for your information, tell them you are looking for me, Mr. Shees. I'm a car dealer from Detroit that you have an interview with me, but that you can't find room three."

Making the connection, Horr said, "Ah, so that's why you have the room number in your hand!"

"Yes, dummy." Falcona said in frustration and continued to instruct Horr, if they walk you to this room, act like we've never met. Got it?"

"Yes! Assured Horr, and then continued with yet another scenario, "What if I walk out of the building without being stopped by the police— then what?"

"I will meet you at the corner of Tenth and Woodland Street in thirty minutes. If you do not come back here within ten minutes, just keep on going!" Falcona insisted.

Horr opened the door and stepped out into the hallway. Looking both ways, he turned toward the back steps. He could not see or hear anyone as he walked down the steps to the first floor. When he opened the side door to the alley, he could hear that mad dog starting to bark. Horr hurried and closed the red door behind him. By the time he found Tenth and Woodland, Falcona was in a car, waiting for him.

Horr opened the door and quickly leaped into the seat of the car.

Falcona just shook his head. "Some men have all the luck; you are the luckiest man I know. How did you get away from the police?"

"Well, have you heard the saying 'All my geese are swans?'" asked Horr.

"No," replied Falcona.

Horr continued to take the conversations off track by adding other sayings, "How about 'All my cards are trumps'; or 'good luck will often follow the man who does not include it in his plan'?"

"Stop, just stop, with all this nonsense! Falcona shouted in frustration. "You need to look at that package I gave you. It outlines what your travel plans are to Jacksonville, Florida. I want you to read me the instructions."

Horr pulled out unfolded the two pages, and was about to read, when Falcona interrupted, "Read it word for word before I drop you off at the train depot in Murfreesboro."

"Where's that?" asked Horr.

"South of here," answered Falcona. "We need to get you there by eight o'clock. The train pulls out of the station at 8:05. Look at the road map, for the best way to travel to Murfreesboro."

Falcona started the Model T and pulled from the corner of Tenth Street and Wood-Land. During the ride to Murfreesboro, Horr poured over the escape route to Jacksonville.

"From Murfreesboro I go to Stevenson, Alabama, Chattanooga, Tennessee, on to Atlanta, Georgia; Macon, Georgia, and Savanna, Georgia. From there, I go to Jacksonville. These plans put me in Jacksonville in two days. But I am confused about these getaway plans. How do I get my train tickets?" asked Horr, greatly concerned.

To clarify Horr's confusion and concern, Falcona explained, "When we get to Murfreesboro, you will need a ticket to Chattanooga.

I will buy the ticket for you, with your money. Once you get onto the train, you can pay for the next leg of the trip until you get to Jacksonville. The train conductor will come around asking for your ticket. Stay in the parlor car and have your food delivered to you. Avoid all the passengers. If someone recognizes you, they will inform the police. That's the only way you will get to Jacksonville without having any trouble."

"Do I meet someone at the train station in Jacksonville?" Horr further inquired.

"No," exclaimed Falcona. "Look at the bottom of that paper, see that phone number; use that only if you have a problem."

Horr's concern heightened his anxiety to question, "Why isn't that information spelled out in this letter? How will I know where to stay when I get to Jacksonville?"

Falcona did not reply.

About thirty minutes after they began their journey to Murfreesboro, they came upon an unexpected mishap. A car had stopped to adjust something in the middle of the road. Three hooligans were looking under the car. They had the road blocked; no other cars were in sight. Falcona stopped the car, observed, and said, "This doesn't look good."

Horr did not recognize the problem at first glance. Then the face of Falcona grew red with anger, and he drew his gun; but as swift as the wind, the three opened fire. Horr jumped out and rolled into the side ditch with his hands over his face. Then he stretched out his hands and cried for help. No one came to his aid. Horr could see that Falcona was not moving. His head was hanging over the steering wheel, his one arm holding his gun, as if he was ready to fire a shot. It would not be but a second or two when Horr would see who the three men were. It was the Italian and two other men he did not know. Horr stood up and started walking straight ahead, full of surprise and disbelief.

"What are you doing here? Why did you shoot Falcona?" shouted Horr, standing there stupefied, and confused. Horr seemed as happy and glad to see the Italian as he usually did. Once again, the Italian had rescued him from a bad situation. Standing next to the Italian facing the other two men, Horr still tried to determine why he felt ill at ease. Then he realized he wasn't hearing anything. In the dead silence, he waited for the Italian to say something. Horr reached down to the ground pretending to pick up a rock, hoping the Italian wouldn't see the moisture in his eyes.

Then the Italian started talking. "Did you know that Falcona was going to turn you in at the Murfreesboro train station?"

"No!" shouted Horr.

"What did Falcona tell you at Billy's Place back in Nashville?" inquired the Italian.

Recalling his conversation with Falcona, Horr stated, "He told me that the police were questioning everyone in the rooming house about someone using the fire escape. Was that a lie?" he asked.

"Yes," replied the Italian. "He was going to collect the $200 reward money. These two men told me about Falcon's plan. We need to get you to Murfreesboro before the train gets into the station. You two men take care of Falcona and drive his car back to Nashville. I will see you after I drop off Horr. You, get your bag and ride with me. I will need some money to get your ticket. The police will be looking for a man with one arm. That's the tip Falcona gave the police. By the time the train pulls out of Murfreesboro, the police will still be looking for an armed man."

Trying to understand what had happened, Horr continued, "Okay, I have a question for you. Were you at Billy's place when I walked out the side door?"

"Yes," the Italian clarified.

Reflecting on what he had just learned, Horr thought, "and so that's how I got away, it wasn't any type of luck."

The Italian paid for Horr's train ticket and after telling him to follow the plan, he added, "The next time you see me will be in Virginia."

Horr traveled the next two days by train to Jacksonville. It was now Thursday, October 26, 1916. At the train station in Jacksonville, Horr was on his own for the first time since he left Danville on

September, 17th. It was a new start for him, a new day, a new city. He stepped off the train and just stood, looking around. He could not believe all the phones. He had not seen that many telephones in one place ever.

It was midafternoon, as he marched out of the train station carrying his bag. He could see the blue sky and sun shining as bright as he had ever witnessed. "My day has come," he mumbled to himself. For the next two hours, he wondered up one street and down the next. The warm air blew calmly at his back putting him in a very laid-back mood. It was time to look for a rooming house, someplace out-of-the-way where no one would be looking for him.

After eating, he bought a newspaper, sat down, and he spread it over his knees. He scanned the ads for vacancies. Not knowing the city, or where not to go put Horr at a big disadvantage. Who could he trust? Who could he talk to about a place to sleep that would be safe? Why didn't Red put that information in the package? It was after seven o'clock and the sun had nearly set, yet Horr still had no place to sleep. After checking out five or six rooming houses, he was still not ready to settle down. He had an ill feeling about all the places he had checked. Then he remembered the phone number that was listed at the bottom of the second page Falcona gave him. Horr dropped his bag and opened his inside coat pocket and pulled out the package Falcona had given him.

"Do I call this number? Who will answer my call? Is this a set up? Where will I find a phone to even make the call?" That's when he remembered the train station and all the phones. He hurried to the train station which was a five-block walk. He had decided to call the number listed and take his chances. Horr had to come up with a plan to protect his identity. Whoever answers the phone must know that he was part of Red's group. Horr stood looking at the phone, scratching his head, trying to think of a way to start the conversation. Then it came to him what Smith told him, the code word *Escape*. Horr determined, "That's the way I will start my conversation."

Horr's palms were sweaty when he picked up the phone's ear piece to place the call. Tears slipped from his eyes and rolled down under his full-face beard. He could not make the call. He walked away from the phone, stopped, and shuffled his feet a few times, glared around the train station, and thought to himself, "What would you rather be doing? Sleeping outside or in a rooming house? Make the phone call!" He turned and walked back inside to the train station and made the phone call. After dialing the number, the phone rang six times before he heard a voice on the other end say, "Ciao."

Still not certain of his response Horr simply said, "Escape."

The person on the other end did not reply at first. Then Horr could hear people talking in the background; the next thing Horr heard, "Is that you Alva?"

"Yes," answered Horr, "who is this?"

"Red."

"This is unbelievable!" exclaimed Horr.

"Make this fast," Red urged.

"I need a safe place to sleep tonight," requested Horr.

With wonder Red shared, "That information was in the package I sent with Falcona to give you in Nashville. How many pages did Falcona give you?"

"Two pages," answered Horr. "The last page had the phone number written on it."

"There should have been three pages, not two pages," Red explained. "The third page had information about where you would meet Homer."

"Homer? Is Homer here in Jacksonville?" wondered Horr.

"Yes." Red instructed him further, "You should meet him at 900 W. Adams Street. He has a room for you. Homer will explain page three to you, when you see him."

With a big smile on his face, Horr replied, "Great! How are things going in Danville?"

"I have the police chasing down one lead after another. Both the city and county officers are looking for you in all parts of the county," answered Red.

"What about old man Meeker?" Horr wondered. "Is he running his mouth about how he will capture me?"

"No," answered Red. "I haven't heard any reports from my men about old man Meeker. Don't worry about who is talking about you. Keep to the plan and you will be back in Danville a free man. What I want from you to do now, Horr, is to find Homer and follow what he tells you to do. Got it?"

"Yes," answered Horr boldly.

"Then, goodbye," said Red with further instructions. "Call this number only if you need help, only in an emergency. That's the only time I want you to call this number."

"Goodbye," replied Horr.

When the phone went dead, Horr knew he had a new lease on life. He was going to see Homer. Everything was working out for him. He was feeling that it was a new day.

Horr did not have to walk far before he saw a familiar face. "Hey there, how are you doing, Homer?" greeted Horr.

"I'm doing fine. What about you?" Homer greeted Horr.

"Better, now that I have a friend on whom I can depend on. I need a place to sleep," requested Horr.

<u>All but one of my rooms are filled with boarders</u> right now, but I've saved that room for you. I thought you would be here before now. I was starting to worry about you," Homer said anxiously.

"Worry about me? What about you?" Horr added. "I heard that you were missing and a note was found at the ranch."

"Who told you that?" Homer demanded.

"Falcona told me," Horr immediately responded. "That was one of the first things out of his mouth at the train yard in Nashville. He told me it was confidential information about you."

"I bet!" exclaimed Homer. "Falcona was behind the plan to kill me. He sent two boys to do a man's job."

"Where are the two men that tried to kill you?" inquired Horr.

"You can find them 6 feet under on the third turn on the racetrack at the ranch," Homer stated boldly.

Horr, still interested in learning of Homer's story, asked, "Did you get hurt when the two men came after you?"

"No," said Homer and continued to give Horr the details. "It was a good fight until I broke both of their arms. Before I buried them alive, I made them talk. They gave me all the details about Falcona. He was working for the rival group of the Black Hand Family. He was there when my two boys were killed. He then came to my rescue, telling me all about the note that I found with my family."

"I thought he helped you get your wife and kids out of Chicago?" questioned Horr.

"He did. But that was all a con," explained Homer.

"Are your wife and kids still in Cuba?" Horr continued to ask.

"Yes. The Black Hand Family from Chicago is protecting them," stated Homer.

"Red is working on getting me to Cuba so I can be with my family. This rooming house is owned by the Black Hand Family. I'm just looking after it until I get a phone call from Red letting me know I can go to Cuba."

"I understand," said Horr, rubbing is beard. There was a short pause, "If you don't mind, I would like to go to Cuba with you. But I don't know all the plans that Red has made for me. Falcona didn't give me all the papers in Nashville. The package I received only had two pages. It was missing the third page with the information about who I was to see in Jacksonville. I called Red from the train station and found out you were my contact here in Jacksonville. Red said you could fill me in on the plans."

"Yes, but wait until morning and I will go over all the details with you at that time," said Homer then directed him further. "Your room is on the first floor in the back of the rooming house. You have a private entrance, where you can come and go without anyone seeing you. I will bring your food to your room each day. You will need to give me some money each week for food. Here's the key for the side door, just keep to yourself and no one will bother you."

Horr shifted his weight from one foot to the other, cleared his throat, and said, "I... uh... want to thank you for all your help. Without you, I surely would be dead.

"You're right!" exclaimed Homer. "But that was before you'd made the decision to stop drinking."

Horr grinned at Homer, as he bent down to pick up his bag, stepped back, turned, and walked down the hallway to his room.

Is this the man you are looking for?

CHAPTER TWELVE

The Farmer's Market

The next morning, Horr woke and found his food had been dropped off in his room. After eating, he counted his money, took two hundred dollars out, and placed it between the box springs and mattress. Then he put the bag out of sight, stepped out the backside door and took a deep breath. He could see the Farmer's Market from where he was standing. The morning sun slid from behind a cloud, as he walked out to the street. It was a bit chilly out, but the day held the promise of sunshine and blue skies. "I've not been fishing in a long time," he thought as he gave his beard a couple of yanks. "I'm going fishing." he walked down to the dock by the St. Johns River where a man was already fishing. Horr walked up to him and said, "You don't know me, but I think you owe me some money!"

The fisherman turned and looked at Horr and said, "Are you talking to me? If you are, you have the wrong guy."

Horr started laughing, "What your name?"

"What did you say?" asked the fisherman for clarification. "Did you ask for my name? I cannot understand you. You need to talk to people so they can understand what you are saying."

"Yes, I'm asking for your name," clarified Horr.

"Yes."

"Eddi James. They call me Eddi," replied the fisherman.

Like a true con artist trying to get something from someone else, Horr started a new conversation. "Do you know the real reason Robin Hood robbed only the rich?"

"No, why?"

"Because the poor had no money," answered Horr.

"Well, Robin Hood has not tried to rob me," stated Eddie to note his economic state.

"It looks like you could use some money, Eddie. Would you sell me one of those fishing poles and some bait?"

"Yes, indeed," said Eddie. "Which pole do you want?"

"The one that's caught the most fish, Horr responded with great cunning. I have no use for a fishing pole that's not caught a single fish."

"Sounds like a fish story to me," replied the fisherman.

Horr gave the man a dollar for a fishing pole, purchased half of his bait for two dollars and walked out to the pier.

As he sat with his fishing line dangling in the water, he watched several small boats on the water. No one else was on the dock, except the man he bought the fishing gear from. By noon, Horr had caught only four fish. It was time to go. He gave the fish and the pole to Eddi. Horr lingered for most of the day, enjoying the blue skies and warm wind blowing. As he made his way back to the rooming house, he stopped at the Farmers' Market to get some fruit. That's when he observed two men he thought he knew from Westville, Illinois. They were talking and did not see him looking at them. The closer Horr got to the two men, he could see their faces and the handcuffs hanging from their belts. One man had horn rimmed glasses. It was two of his best customers that came into the café in Danville, Matt Russell and Jack Hilman. Horr turned and walked across the street and watched them until they walked out of sight.

It was now after six o'clock and Horr had returned to the rooming house. When he opened his door, he found a note someone had placed under his door. When he finished reading the note, there was a knock on the door. Startled, he turned and stepped away from the door. Horr knew it was over, and yet he could not move. He stood speechless; his hands curled around the brass bed frame. Quickly, he looked across the room, and then, again he heard the knock. It was as if the door was between two worlds. Inside the room he was safe. If he opened the door, he would be completely unprotected. His memory danced before his eyes. Horr did not know what to do. Whoever was standing outside his room knew who he was, and the note, provided the evidence.

"Where is Homer?" Horr wondered. Then another note was pushed under the door. Horr stood still looking down at the floor. He could hear footsteps fading away; then the sound of someone falling to the floor.

"Open the door. Hurry!" a voice said.

"Hurry!" shouted a different voice.

Horr didn't know what to do. Then, he heard Homer's voice,

"Open the door." Horr rushed to the door and pulled it open. His head sagged forward, his breath stopped. Homer had a gun pointed at his head, and his hands behind him in handcuffs. It was the two men from Westville, Matt and Jack, the ones he had seen at the Farmers Market. Horr stepped back as the two men forced their way into the room, and kicked the door closed.

"Do you know who this is?" asked Matt.

"Of course, I know who this is," replied Jack. "He's the stupid drunk from Danville who killed his wife, and didn't pay us for the bets we made. I told you that at the Farmers' Market, that he was Tenil." Turning to directly face Horr, Jack said, "Tenil, you know us. We have been in your café and placed bets with you on sporting events. So, don't act like we are strangers."

"What should we do now that we have found him?" asked Matt.

"As I see it," advised Jack, "we have two choices. Call the police and get the two hundred dollars reward money or steal the money that Red gave him and kill both of them."

Surprised that they knew about the money he was given, Horr quickly asked, "How do you know Red?"

Hi

"We've been watching him for a long time," note Jack. "All the newspaper reports lead back to Lyons," This is the last time you were seen, Tenil, as reported by Red. We know that Red controls the gambling in the Danville area."

"So, you two work for Red?" Horr inquired.

"No, we have some problems with Red," answered Jack. "He runs corrupt card games. My brother was shot in his place over a card game," said Jack.

"Did he die?" wondered Horr.

"Talk so we can understand you," said Jack.

"Did he die?" Horr said again.

"No," answered Jack abruptly.

"How much money did he lose?" Horr asked.

"A week's wages," responded Jack.

Trying to figure a way out of the situation, Horr kept questioning, "Where does he work?"

"For the Wabash Railroad," stated Jack.

From that conversation Horr thought of a possible way out. He proposed, "If we paid you what your brother lost in the card game, plus the two hundred dollars reward money, would you call it even and let us go?"

"Make it an even four hundred dollars and we will go away," said Jack.

The sandy-haired man with horn rimmed glasses stuck out his hand and said, "Deal," as he shook Horr's hand.

The second gunman, Matt, stepped back and lowered his gun, a smiled, and said, "I told you we could get the money without any one getting hurt."

Still thinking of a strategy to get out of this situation, Horr asked, "How much time do we have to get the money to you?"

"We need it now!" bellowed Jack.

"Look you two shameless characters, I will need a stretch of time to come up with that kind of money," Horr demanded.

"What kind of time do you need?" asked Matt.

"A day or two," replied Horr.

Both gunmen looked at each other, with resentment in their eyes. Jack spoke out, "Matt, do you have any idea what's going on here? They want us to let them go, so they can get the money! Like we are going to let them walk out! If we let them walk out of here, how will we know we will get our money? No. The way I see it, we need to hold one of these fools until the other bring us the money."

Looking at Homer, Jack said, "We will keep Horr until you come back with the money. If you are not back in here by 6 p.m. tomorrow, we will take Horr to the police and collect our two-hundred-dollar reward money," declared Jack.

Disagreeing, "No," said Matt. 'We need to get the money now, and get out of Jacksonville tonight! Let's search them and see how much money they have, and then kill them."

The situation was getting more intense. Homer looked Horr. He knew that Horr had the money, but he did not know where.

"Wait!" Horr shouted. "You two said if we gave you the money, you would let us walk out of here unharmed."

"Do you have the four hundred dollars?" asked Jack.

"I have two hundred," stated Horr. "How much do you have, Homer?"

Homer calmly responded, "Reach into my front right pocket and pull out his money. I don't know how much I have, but you can have it all."

Matt reached for the money, and began to count it. When finished counting the money, the total was two hundred and thirty dollars.

"Where did you get that kind of money?" asked Matt.

"I just collected the rent money today for each room. That's where I got the money," Homer explained.

"So, where's your two hundred dollars, Horr?" asked Jack.

"It's all the money I have," pleaded Horr. "Look under my mattress and you will find the money hidden there."

Matt walked over to the bed, pulled off the mattress, and found the two hundred dollars Horr had hidden there earlier that morning. With the money in his hand he looked at Horr and asked, "Are you sure this is all the money you have?"

"Yes, that's all the money I have," assured Horr.

It was almost time for Homer to call the Black Hand Family and check in for the day. If he didn't make the call on time, someone would come and check on him. Home thought, "If the two out-of-control, small time criminals would just stay here until the Black Hand Family sends someone to check-up on me, maybe we could keep our money and take care of these guys."

"Count the money again," exclaimed Matt, "and give me my two hundred dollars! You can keep what's left over, Jack. I just want out of here before someone turn up. Let's tie them up and get out of here."

"No, I have a better idea," suggested Jack. "Let's put the big guy on the floor, face down under the bed. We will put Horr on face up the box springs and then handcuff them together."

Then the two men from Westville made their getaway.

"How are we going to get out of this mess?" asked Horr.

"The Black Hand Family will send someone if I fail to make my regular phone call on time. It will be a matter of time before they will be here. Until then, we need to try to get me out from under this box springs. Can you move down to the bottom of the bed?" asked Homer, "Maybe," Horr answered while struggling to move his body down to the end of the bed.

"Take it slow," Homer warned and then directed further, "you move first, and then I will follow you." Both men struggled moving down the box springs together. It was now after 9 p.m. And Homer and Horr were sitting on the floor, handcuffed back to back. Both men were exhausted from the effort they had put forth. Homer was wiggling his fingers from side to side when he wondered, "Where men from the Black Hand Family? They are never late on checking and following up when a member of the family fails to call in on time."

"Ain't much dignity being handcuffed," noted Horr.

For the next ten minutes, both men tried standing up. Each time they tried, they would fall back to the floor. Homer took a deep breath, reared back one more time, and pulled Horr off his feet. As Homer moved forward, lowering his head, Horr let out a scream, "Stop, you're pulling my guts out!"

Homer stood back up, dropped his arms, and Horr's feet hit the floor with a giant thump. "What are trying to do, kill me? You, big oaf?" cried Horr. Both men started laughing. "You are one strong mule," exclaimed Horr. I weigh over two hundred pounds and you pulled me up like damn mule puling a boat up the Wabash and Erie Canal."

"Can you walk backwards?" asked Homer.

"It all depends," replied Horr, how far? If you mean across the room to the door? Well maybe. But if you think I'm going to walk backwards out into the hallway and let someone see us, you are wrong. They will call the police and both of us will be finished."

"My room is just down the hallway. I have some tools in my room that can cut these handcuffs off of us. Whether you like it or not, you are coming with me, if I have to drag you down the hall way! So, follow me, and keep your mouth shut!" insisted Homer.

As the two men moved slowly toward the door, they could hear people out in the hallway. Then the noise stopped, as if someone was waiting for them to open the door. Homer stepped sideways, pulling

Horr with him. Just then two bullets came through the door. Both dropped to the floor. "Are you okay?" asked Homer.

"Yes," replied Horr. "Who could be shooting at us?"

"I don't know who is shooting at us," said Homer. "But I know that everyone in the rooming house is up and awake now. The Black Hand Family boys better be the first folks to get here. I can assure you they will take control of this mess."

Suddenly, it was very quiet in the hallway. Horr spoke quietly to Homer, "Do you think the gunman has left?"

"Well, at least the shooting has stopped," replied Homer. "That's one good thing."

Then came knock on the door. They looked at each other and wondered who it might be. Homer's eyes flashed furiously.

Somehow Horr understood what Homer was feelings. Then they heard a voice, seeming to be a safe voice to Homer, "Are you in there, Homer?"

Both men shouted, "Yes! Come and get us!"

The man entered the room with his gun held out in front of his body. "How did you get those handcuffs on like that?" he wondered.

Horr looked at Homer and said, "Let me answer this question." Looking at the man, don't ask so many questions.

What's your name?"

"Lufitig, Gab Lufitig. Call me Gab."

"Just help us get these cuffs off Gab," said Homer and directed him, "I have some tools in my room that can cut them off. Go to my room and bring back the tools." By the time the gunman returned and cut the cuffs off from both men, the police had already arrived. Horr grabbed his bag, and the three men disappeared out the back, side door. When they were safely down the street from the rooming house, they all stopped and turned and watched the police inspect the building.

Horr looked at the gunman and asked his name again. Frustrated the gunman responded, "I already told you my name. Call me Gab! Now shut up and don't ask so many questions."

The three men looked at each other and started laughing. "Well, can I shake your hand?" asked Horr. The gunman held out his hand and Horr shook it. "Thanks for getting us out of that room just in time!" Then he thought, "This gunman is a little weak wristed for a man who could fire a gun."

"Don't mention it. Glad to help," Gab declared.

"What's next? Where are we going to stay tonight?" asked Horr.

"Well, I need to get my things out of my room before we go anywhere," said Homer. "The plan was for you to stay here in Jacksonville and work, until I called for you to come to Cuba."

"When were you going to Cuba, Homer?" asked Horr.

"I planned to take the train to Key West, Florida next week," explained Homer, then jump a boat to Cuba. But that's all changed now. We need a place to sleep tonight."

Then Gab looked at both of them and said, "You two can sleep with me tonight. I have a room not far from here. We can party all night and tomorrow we can decide what to do."

Horr looked at Homer with a surprised look on his face and said, "We need to talk this over."

"What's to talk over? I have a place to keep you safe until tomorrow. What's the problem?" wondered Gab.

Horr was still looking at Homer and didn't act as if he had heard a word the gunmen had said. "Homer, we need to think about this. The police will be gone in a little while, and we can wait this out, and be back in the rooming house in a few hours."

All Horr could think about was the handshake and the way the Gab said, "sleep with me." Horr did not want any part of that arrangement.

"We need to create a diversion," suggested Homer.

"What kind of diversion are you talking about?" asked the gunman. "Something that will get the police out of the rooming house. All I need is ten minutes to get my clothes and tools. Do you two have any suggestions," asked Homer.

"If I were you, I would not go back and get your personal items," suggested Gab.

"You don't know what I have in my room," replied Homer. "My suggestion, for what it's worth, is to stay away from the

rooming house for a few days until the police have completed their work," said Gab.

"When you have a problem with the police, and you need to lead the police in the wrong direction, you give them a reason to look somewhere that will take the pressure off of the real problem," said Homer.

"Well if you need a diversion so you can get your things, I can make a phone call and have the other Family members start some trouble across town," suggested Gab.

"No! What I need is for someone else to go to the rooming house and get my personal items. Horr, give me five dollars!" demanded Homer.

"Why?" Horr wondered.

"I need to pay someone to go get my things," explained Homer.

"Money talks, but it doesn't always talk sense," responded Horr. "That is a dumb idea, Homer. Where are you going to find someone you can trust?"

"Let me worry about that. Just give me the five dollars," Homer demanded again. Horr looked directly at Gab and asked, "Do you have five dollars you can give, Homer?"

"No, do you think I would be associated with you two if I had five dollars? Rather, I would be having a good time with my friends," replied Gab.

No amount of arguing could have influenced Homer.

"Get your money out. We are done talking about this."

Reluctantly, Horr handed the money to Homer and said, "Well, I hope you won't get into much of a hassle asking a stranger to get your clothes and tools."

Homer took the money and walked across the street.

Gab and Horr waited until Homer returned. "Did you find someone to get your things?" asked Horr immediately.

"Yes," replied Homer.

"Did you get his name?" wondered Horr.

"Yes, Mit Patwell," answered Homer, somewhat irritated.

"How long do we wait for this character to bring you your clothes and tools, Homer?" continued Horr.

"The plan is for him to drop my two bags at the back of the saloon at the end of the street," explained Homer.

Within thirty minutes Homer had the two bags and the three men went to Gab's rooming house for the night.

"Listen, Gab, I don't want you to take this hard. I'm not gonna be here come morning. We will be gone before you wake up. All we need is a good night's sleep. We are not here to party. We have a lot of work to do before I get on the train to Key West at six o'clock tomorrow night. The less you know about our plans, the better off you will be."

"That's right!" said Horr. "We just want to get some sleep; we are not here to party. It's after midnight now."

Homer found a blanket lying next to the one chair in the room. Horr found a dirty towel on the floor that he could use to cover himself. Both men fell asleep immediately.

Gab didn't argue with them. He had different plans. He wanted the money Horr was carrying in his bag. He waited for Homer to fall into a deep sleep and then moved to take Horr's bag. Just then Homer rolled over and pulled himself up from the floor and warned, "Gab the last person that tried to steal Horr's money did not get to spend it— not one nickel! I suggest you go to sleep or leave, and stay away until tomorrow."

Gab thought for a minute, and then decided to take a walk. That was the last time they saw him.

The next day, Homer made plans to go by train from Jacksonville to Key West, Florida. He then would board a ship to Cuba and sail to Havana.

Red helped Horr find a place to live in Jacksonville and a job working as a cowboy in the movies, riding horses for a short period of time. Working with the horses on Homer's ranch helped Horr considerably in this job. His job was to make it look like he was in the wild-west circling the wagon train, waiting to be attack by Indians.

Horr decided not to continue working in the movies. He thought someone would recognize him if they saw the movie back in Danville.

It was now April, 1915. Homer sent for Horr to come to Cuba. Horr didn't waste time in making travel plans. He took the same train from Jacksonville, to Key West, Florida, then boarded the ship that Homer used and sailed to Havana. He was met at the shipyard by Homer. He spent the next two months with Homer's family.

During that time, Horr, attended the Johnson/ Willard fight, which was the first heavyweight fight between a black contender and a white contender. In June, 1915, Horr returned to Florida and traveled up the eastern coast by train to Richmond, Virginia. There the Black Hand Family helped him hide out. The plan was for Horr to work at the hotel in Hopewell, Virginia as a cook.

Horr never talked to Homer after he left Cuba. **The Italian was Horr's contact after leaving Havana.**

CHAPTER THIRTEEN

Double Identity

It was July 14, 1915. The Italian and Horr met at the hotel where Horr was working as a chef. It was the largest hotel in Prince George County, Virginia. Both men reviewed the plans that Red had arranged for Horr to be arrested. "Remember follow the plan, be on the street in Hopewell on Saturday August 7th and **you will be a free man in less than five years,**" instructed The Italian.

"Do you really think this plan will work?" questioned Horr. "I'm tired of running from the police."

"Yes," assured the Italian. "The Black Hand Family have connections. They will keep you out of prison. If you are sentenced for killing your wife, you will be out back on the streets in no time."

"What if they sentence me to death? Nowhere in these plans have I read anything about that possibility," fearfully wondered Horr.

Horr stood up and walked to the other side of the room, then turned, and said, "I sure hope you are right!" Worried about the worst scenario, Horr rubbed the back of his sweaty neck, further asked, "What if they hang me?" It's not your neck!"

"Trust the plan that Red has laid out for your escape," the Italian assured Horr. He further instructed him, "Do your part and everything will work out for you. This will be the last time I will talk with you for a while. Remember, **I will see you on the Mississippi River.** How much money are you holding?"

"I have less than five hundred dollars left from the money Red gave me, when I left Danville," stated Horr.

The Italian instructed Horr, "When you are arrested on Saturday, August 7th, make sure you have very little money in your pockets. I will talk to Red about the money you are holding. He will advise me what to do."

"I would like to give some money to a blind piano player, who has helped me considerably," noted Horr.

"Why a blind man?" wondered the Italian.

"First, he can't identify me. Secondly, I like the way he plays the piano. But most of all, he has a sick wife, who needs medical help. I have taken things away from people, and never focused on helping others. I have always helped myself only. Think about this, there are two critical periods in a man's life: when his voice changes and when his choices change. I'm ready to make different choices in my life," explained Horr.

Wondering how this might play out, the Italian asked, "Are you asking me not to say anything to Red about the money you are holding?"

"In a way, I guess I am asking for that. Can we agree not to say anything to him?"

"Yes," replied the Italian and then noted, "But that's going to cost you something the next time I see you."

The following day, Thursday July 15, 1915, the Italian started the 900-mile trip by train back to Danville, Illinois. The four day train ride gave the Italian time to think about the escape plan, to study the locations he was going to report to Chief Walker about Horr's travels. He also decided not to convey to Red, anything about the money Horr was holding. All he could think about was the $300.00 he had been cheated out of by Horr, and getting his money back. He would deal with Horr and the money at a later date. On Monday, July 19th, the Italian met with Red at his saloon on Lyon's Road. Everything was arranged; the plan was in place. Horr knew he had to be on the street in Hopewell, Virginia, August 7th. The Italian was ready for his part of the escape plan, meeting with the Danville Police Department.

The Danville Police received information almost on a weekly basis about Horr. A person by the name of Thomas Andrews made claims to have been following Horr for over ten months. Andrews gave accounts to the Danville Police Department that he had come across a person that looked like Horr on more than one occasion. Andrews requested a meeting with the Danville Chief of Police. Andrews wanted to work as a detective for the Danville Police Department. The Police Department had no job openings for a new detective at that time. Andrews attempted to bargain with Police Chief Walker. "If I show you my ability as a detective, and locate Alva C Horr, will you then make me a Danville Police detective? I would even consider a job as a street cop for starters."

"I can't make any promises to you about a job with the Danville Police Department," stated the Police Chief.

"How about if I track down Horr, can we have another meeting to discuss my opportunities with your police force and a job?" pleaded Andrews.

"Maybe, the Chief responded. Let's find Horr first, then we can talk. If you have any information on Horr's whereabouts, you need to give me that information. I have two detectives working full-time on Horr's case."

"Okay," informed Andrews. "Here's what I know about Horr. He's traveling with a woman; she is a front for him. She buys all his food and whisky. When Horr gets into a card game, she aids him in cheating the other card players. I was playing cards with him and lost all my money. That's why I'm looking for him. I want the money back that he cheated me out of. The two-hundred-dollar reward money will be more than enough to fix the debt Horr owes me."

"Where and when was that card game?" asked the chief.

"In Decatur, Illinois, last September," answered Andrews.

"Tell me more about this card game, Andrews. You say was in Decatur?" questioned the chief.

"No," said Andrews, as he remembered, "The card game was in Mattoon."

Frustrated, the chief asked, "Which is it--Decatur or Mattoon?"

"It was Mattoon," Andrews answered with certainty and continued with more details. "We were at a farm house, south of the city. There were six men and this woman, who was with a man with an injured right hand. No, it was the left hand."

"Well, which hand was injured?" interrupted the chief. "You need to get your facts right, Andrews."

"It definitely was his left hand," assured Andrews. "That information is on the wanted posted."

"How much money did Horr win in the card game?" asked the chief.

"I really don't know," said Andrews, "because I dropped out of the game after I lost all my money."

The chief kept questioning, "Then, do you know the amount of money this man you say is Horr had at the beginning of the game?"

"No," answered Andrews. "I was the last person to get into the card game. When I sat down at the table, the injured man had over a dollar in change showing on the table."

"Well, can you tell me the day of this card game?" asked the chief with a sigh.

"No, I'm not sure what day it was," stated Andrews. "I think it was in the middle of the week, but I cannot tell you for sure. If I was to guess, I would say it was Wednesday."

Fully frustrated with the lack of any helpful information, the chief raised the volume of his voice and advised Andrews, "If you get the opportunity to be a detective for me, you better understand one thing. I need facts stated correctly. Not 'I'm not sure' statements that I have witnessed today. That's your first lesson in police work; get that right the first time. We got a report about Horr being in a card game in Mattoon. That was right after Horr shot his wife. I would have to look at the report to give you the day of the week. We didn't give out any of that information to the newspapers. What other information do you have on Mr. Horr?"

"I saw Horr in Chicago about three months ago, when I was there on a business trip. I followed him down Rush Street, but I lost him, when a woman with a suitcase stepped in front of me and blocked my view. Horr disappeared into the night crowd," reported Andrews.

Still searching for any information on Horr, the Chief asked, "Did you report this to the Chicago police?"

"No, I had no proof," said Andrews and continued reporting, But I know it was Horr, the killer being searched by everyone. I have this flyer with Horr's picture printed on it. I have shown this wanted poster to everyone. I picked up Horr's trail in Indianapolis and followed him to Columbus Ohio. He escaped and I lost his trail. "Then I decided to go to Cleveland, Ohio, but on the way, I stopped in Milltown, Ohio. While I was there, I saw a man that looked like him, but I lost him, when he boarded a train headed east. I boarded the next train out of Milltown and got off the train and stayed overnight in Altoona, Pennsylvania. When I showed the wanted poster of Horr at the railroad station in Altoona, Pennsylvania, the ticket operator told me the same man purchased a ticket to Harrisburg, Pennsylvania."

"Why didn't you notify the local police this time? You had the proof?" wondered Chief Walker.

"I didn't think the police would believe me. Anyway, Horr had a two-hour head start on me at this point. I dismissed that thought of telling the police because I would have wasted my time talking to them. By the time I reached Harrisburg, Pennsylvania, Horr had hopped the next train to Newark, New Jersey. After spending two weeks in the Newark area looking for Horr, I decided to return to Danville," reported Thomas Andrews.

"Look," stated the Chief, directly at Andrews, "I understand you want to play the role of a detective in order to receive the reward money for your work in tracking down Horr."

"That's right; I want to collect the two-hundred-dollar reward money for my detective work and get a job with the Danville Police Department," clarified Andrews.

Looking grimly at Andrews, the chief instructed him, "If you ever do locate Horr in your travels, from now on report your information to the local police before you do anything else. They have the manpower to follow up on your details. Let the police do their job. That would help you land a job with the D.P.D."

"Well, that's all I know about Horr at this time," I'm leaving next week for the East Coast, I know Horr is hiding in that area of the country."

"Before you leave, Andrews," said Chief Walker, "I have some additional circulars regarding Horr's description. This information came from his penitentiary records. Take these circulars with you."

To keep frustrating the chief, Andrews asked, "Why was Horr in prison?"

Tired of Andrews' reporting, the chief said, "Detective Spangler has that file on Horr. You can have all that information the next time we meet. That is, if you track down Horr, and your efforts bring him to the authorities."

To keep frustrating the Chief even more, Andrews asked, "Do

we have an agreement that you will consider me for a job with your police department?"

"As I told you before," said the chief in a very strong-toned voice, "I cannot make any promises to you about a job."

Andrews continued, "If I track down Horr, can we have another meeting to discuss my opportunities with your police force and a job?"

"Maybe, let's find Horr first, then, we can talk. I need to go back to work. If you find Horr or think you know where he is hiding, get the police involved. Now get out of my office!" demanded Chief Walker.

Immediately, Chief Walker turned his chair toward the detectives and called out, "Detective White and Garrard, come in here and have a seat."

"Yes, boss!" they both replied immediately.

"I was just talking with Mr. Andrews. He gave me some information that only a person could know, if they were in the same place as Mr. Horr. Remember the trip we took to Mattoon on a lead given to us about a card game where Horr won over thirty dollars?" the chief questioned.

"Yes," recalled White.

"Well, Mr. Andrews knows something, but his facts are a little sketchy. I played down the fact that Mattoon was our only real lead. He said he was in that card game. Do you two remember anything about a person by this man's name in our investigation?" inquired Chief Walker.

"No," answered Garrard.

Reviewing in his mind all the details he was told by Andrews, the chief asked, "Do either of you remember anyone saying that a female was at the card game?"

"No," said Detective White. "I would have remembered that."

"That's my thinking also," stated Chief Walker. Mr. Andrews's facts are sketchy. "What do you two think? Joe, give me your opinion."

"Maybe he has a different angle in wanting to be part of capturing Horr," expressed Joe.

"What about you George?" asked the chief.

"Did Andrews ask for anything in return for his offering this information to you?" wondered George.

"The two of you two have answered my questions," replied the chief. "So now, I will answer both of your questions with a 'Yes'. His angle, as he told me, was the reward money. Horr cheated him in the card game and he wants his money back. He also wants a job as a detective, working for me."

"Will you employ him, Chief?" wondered George.

"A lot of things will need to happen before I consider Mr. Andrews for a job," said the chief, assuring the other two detectives. "Hey, thanks for helping out on Mr. Andrews."

Before Andrews left Danville, he had one last meeting with Red. Red was happy with the report Andrews gave him about the meeting with Chief Walker. It was on Thursday, July 29, 1915 that Andrews left Danville, Illinois by train, heading for the East Coast. Tuesday, August 3, 1915 Andrews was in Richmond, Virginia, displaying to people the picture of Horr on the wanted poster. Andrews's travels took him to Petersburg, Virginia where it was reported Horr had been seen in Hopewell, Virginia. Friday, August 6, 1915, Andrews traveled to Hopewell. The next day Andrews continued looking for Horr. "What a con; this plan surpassed anything Red has organized," Andrews thought to himself. **Thomas Andrews was part of the escape plan.**

Is this the man you are looking for?

CHAPTER FOURTEEN

You found me

Thursday July 15, 1915, Horr decided to count the money he was holding. With the money he had earned working as a chef, he had six hundred twenty-one dollars and thirty-five cents. Everyone who realized Horr had money schemed to take his cash. Horr was at a point that he did not trust anyone that talked to him about the cash he was holding. The story he gave to **Thomas Adrianople, better known as Thomas Andrews, and even better known to Horr as "The Italian"** was a lie. Horr did know about a blind piano player. But he didn't know if he was married. This gave Horr the chance to hide the money from everyone. If the plans that Red made worked out, Horr would need funds to live on.

For the next two days, Horr struggled thinking about how he could obtain the money back after he shipped it away. He even discussed the subject with different individuals, not giving them the real reason or the information about the money he was holding. Most of the suggestions he was given were "ship it to a friend by train."

The last person who spoke to Horr gave him answer that was most helpful— "Use a transfer service to ship a trunk." When he heard the words, "transfer service", Horr immediately remembered his friend, Smith, James Smith, owner of Smith Transfer Company. Horr made some inquires on how to ship a trunk by transfer service. All his questions were answered by Tucker Green, the clerk working at the local transfer service company in Hopewell. The clerk gave Horr the address for Smith Transfer Company as 21 East North Street Danville, Illinois. Horr had one more important question to ask of Tucker Green, "How long will a transfer company hold the item shipped?"

"Until the item is picked up by the person holding the ticket," replied Tucker.

"Is there a time limit on holding items?" Horr asked for clarification.

"No. You can store it for years at a time. The ticket holder would be responsible for the cost of storage. I have items that have been here for over five years."

With a joyful smile, Horr looked at Tucker and said, "Thanks for the great information." Horr walked out of the transfer office. Suddenly, before the door had closed behind him, Horr had another question. He turned around and walked back inside and asked Tucker, "What if the ticket is lost? How would you deal with that?"

This time Tucker smiled at Horr and replied, "That would depend on how well you knew the owner of the transfer company."

"Thanks again, you have been very helpful," stated Horr, as he left the transfer office.

Now, all Horr needed was a traveling trunk. Horr compensated a bartender, Willie Gilmore, an acquaintance in Hopewell, for purchasing a traveling trunk and having the trunk delivered to his rooming house, located in City Point, Virginia. Horr remembered what Sammy from the circus had told him about putting a false bottom in a trunk. Horr worked three days designing a false lid that fit the bottom of the trunk. By Tuesday afternoon July 20, 1915, Horr was ready to ship the trunk with the six hundred dollars concealed in the bottom. He packed the trunk with newspapers, old clothes and the hat given to him the day he was chauffeured to the West Montezuma, Indiana train station.

Horr continued working at the hotel until Saturday July 31, 1915. This gave Horr seven days until he would be taken into custody. During this time, he spent time listening to the blind piano player.

The day before his arrest, Friday August 6, 1915, Horr injured his left hand and wrist to make it look like he had difficulty using his hand.

Saturday morning, August 7, 1915, Horr awoke from a bad night of trying to sleep. All he could think about was the plans for his escape. The questions that raced through his mind, "What if this…?" "What if that…?" kept Horr from getting a goodnight's rest. His lower legs hurt and he could not stop scratching and rubbing them.

It was now after 8 a.m. The trunk had been shipped the day before to Smith Transfer Company. Horr had $11.35. After paying four dollars for his room and one dollar for lunch, he decided to go to the saloon and listen to the blind piano player one more time. He gave the blind piano player six dollars, walked over and sat down at a table until he was identified and taken into custody. Horr made no effort to escape. When Chief Ferguson of the Hopewell police department stepped up and called his name, Horr said, "You found me."

Horr was taken to the city jail and locked up. Chief Ferguson placed a phone call to the Danville Police Department notifying Chief Walker of the arrest. During the conversation between the two police departments, Chief Walker asked how Horr was arrested.

Ferguson responded, "From a flyer that was given to me by a person going by the name of Thomas Andrews."

Surprised at hearing the name, Chief Walker questioned, "Did you say Andrews?"

"Yes, Thomas Andrews," assured Ferguson.

"Thanks," said Walker and continued sharing his plans. "I will be on the next train to Petersburg. Please have Alva C. Horr ready for me to transport him back to Danville. I should be in the Petersburg area no later than Tuesday, August 10. I will phone you with my arrival time when I have that information. I will be traveling with one other police officer."

Chief Walker phoned the state attorney office and gave them the news. He then called a meeting with all of his detectives and staff, and informed them of the arrest. The newspapers were told of the arrest, also. Then Chief Walker and Detective Spangler went to Clark and Margaret Meeker's home to inform them. During this meeting with Clark and Margaret, both of them thanked the chief for all the effort his office had made in tracking down Alva. The newspapers reported the story of Horr's arrest in the Sunday, August 8, 1915, newspaper with the following accounts.

Alva C. Tinnil Harr, also known as Alva Stall, was arrested Saturday afternoon, August 7, 1915 at Hopewell, Virginia, a small town near Petersburg, Virginia. Horr was charged with brutally shooting down his wife in Danville last September. Horr had been at large almost a year when recognized at Hopewell, Virginia by a Danville, Illinois man.

Horr who was sought by police for almost a year for the murder of his wife is now under arrest. This news and information that Horr was arrested reached chief of police Walker late Saturday evening, in a message from Chief Ferguson of Petersburg, Virginia.

The arrest of Horr came about when he was recognized by Thomas Adrianopolis a traveling man, formerly of Danville, Illinois. Adrianopolis is said to have promised the police in Danville several months ago that he would find Horr during his travels and that he would bring him to be booked. Adrianopolis is said to have had a personal interest in the case.

After recognizing Horr, Adrianopolis called on the authorities, gave them an accurate description of the man wanted, together with a card bearing his picture and description. Horr was then placed under arrest and the Illinois authorities were notified.

Horr, confined in the Petersburg city jail, was about to be moved to the county jail of Dinwiddie County, or to the city jail in Richmond, Virginia, 20 miles north.

When advised that he would be taken to one or the other place for safekeeping, in the event he declined to return, without extradition papers, the much-wanted man advised the chief of police that he would waive rights to extradition and return quietly with Chief Walker and Detectives Spangler.

The 900-mile trip was started by the officers at midnight Saturday; they arrived at Cincinnati at 7:00 a.m. Sunday morning, 445 miles of the journey behind them. They were due to reach Petersburg at 9:45 p.m., Monday. Because of the long trip, which was wearing on the officers, it was not known whether or not they would make an effort to leave Petersburg, Virginia on the return trip at 4:00 p.m., or whether they would wait until the midnight train.

The arrest of Horr, if this man really is the wife-slayer, ends a long and discouraging search. Every state in the union was searching with circulars detailing the fugitive's picture.

Mrs. Horr's murder ended a long feud between her and her husband. She was seeking a divorce for the third time, each time her husband attempted to kill her. He was successful when he followed her and shot her down on West Williams Street on September 16, 1914.

Horr owned a restaurant on Hazel Street until a short time before he shot his wife. He sold the restaurant after he learned that he was being sued for divorce. The divorce was filed on the grounds of drunkenness and cruelty treatment. Mr. and Mrs. Horr had been having trouble for months previous to the filing of the suit.

The murder of Mrs. Horr was probably one of the most sensational in the history of the city. For days after the tragedy it was the chief topic of conversation in the Danville area.

It is possible that Horr will be tried at the circuit court level. He has already been charged with the murder and in spite of the late start the business of the court is being cleared, in a very satisfactory manner. There will be time, it is said, to try Horr before adjournment. If not, trial is held during this term, the case will likely be heard early in the October term.

On Tuesday, August 10, 1915 Horr demanded requisition papers from Chief Walker causing Walker to change his plans in returning to Danville. Walker was hoping that requisition papers from Governor Dunne office would be received in time to return to Danville on Wednesday.

It had at first been supposed that Horr would accompany the officers without requisition papers and that the start home would be made late Monday afternoon, but at the last minute he demanded the necessary documents.

After nearly a year of eluding police officers, and accompanied by worry and mental strain, together with little hard labor, which became necessary to hide his identity, Horr appeared thinner. His general appearance is much the same, but he is lighter. Much of the puffiness above the eyes has disappeared, leaving him with a slight sunken appearance, though not markedly changed. However, he had few traits consistent with a hunted man. Worry had taken its toll. Officers were surprised that he borne up so well. He apparently was in good spirits despite the grave charges he is to face on his return to the scene of the crime.

Nearly three months of liberty have been given Horr because of the fact that Thomas Adrianopolis, the man who brought about his arrest, was slowed by a suitcase in Chicago. Thomas Adrianopolis saw Horr in a crowd. He made a rush for Tenil, but the suitcase distracted him and Horr was lost in the crowd. Thomas Adrianopolis did not give up the chase however. He came to Danville, reported the incident to the police and left again, armed with circulars and the description of the wanted man.

Thomas Adrianopole had a good reason and desire for revenge and justice. It is said that just a short time prior to the slaying of Mrs. Horr, Tenil had beaten Adrianopole out of over $300 in a dice game. It was generally understood that Tenil used crooked dice. At any rate, Thomas Adrianopole believed he had been cheated by Horr. He swore he would get his money back. He gave his word to Chief Walker months before that he would find Horr sometime during his travels and that he would cause him to be arrested. And now, after nearly a year, a spirit of renewal and justice were both about to be satisfied.

Horr had been in and about Petersburg, Virginia, for more than two months. For the past six weeks he had been employed at the E.I. DuPont power manufacturing facility, just outside of the village of Hopewell, Virginia. **He boarded at City Point, another suburb** of Petersburg, Virginia.

A circular sent out regarding Horr gave his description as follows:

37 years old looks younger
5'6" tall
Weighs about 200 pounds
Brown wavy hair
Brown eyes
Reddish complexion
Left hand and wrist crippled

Officers were further advised by the circular that Horr was a gambler and crap shooter and associated with gamblers or may be found working in a lunchroom, if employed. Horr probably knew the officers would look for him in a lunchroom, and avoided obtaining employment in a restaurant.

Horr's measurements that were taken at the age of 22, when he was a prisoner for burglary and robbery, were also given. Bertillon Measurements never changed except slightly as to height and as to weight.

Bertillon Measurements
Height 661
Out's 680

Trunk 906
Head Length 183
Head Width 148
Left Foot 249
Mid Foot 116
Lit F 85
Fore Arm 437
Rear Length 62

There was a story afloat on the street, Tuesday, that Horr's defense would be unique, that he would insist the killing of his wife was an accident. It was said he would set up a defense that he was shooting at his father-in-law, Clark Meeker, who he feared and that a stray bullet struck Mrs. Horr and killed her. It was further stated that Horr would state that Meeker had threatened to kill him, that Mr. Meeker ran toward him when he walked forward to meet his wife, when she was with relatives who were returning from the Modern Woodman Picnic and that Horr shot only in self-defense and that he could not have prevented the bullet going astray.

The firm of Clayton and Boyle was retained by relatives of the prisoner. Knowing nothing of this rumored defense, speaking for both members of the firm, J.M. Boyle gave a statement Tuesday morning:

"We have not gone into the matter of the defense. We cannot say anything until we have talked with Horr. No one else here has talked with him, so far as we know. We cannot conceive how such a report was started. That might be the defense. It might be something else, but until I have talked with Mr. Horr and get his side of the story, what our plea and planned defense will be."

Wednesday, August 11, 1915, this afternoon, Virginia Governor Stuart honored the requisition of Governor Dunne of Illinois, for Alva C. Horr, wanted in Danville, Illinois, for the murder of his wife on September 14, 1916. Wesley G. Walker Chief of Police of Danville, who came to Petersburg Sunday morning to return Horr to Danville, was expected to leave Richmond today with his prisoner.

It was rumored on Wednesday that the authorities were

investigating a report that Horr had been in constant communication with his relatives in Danville. It was said that the evidence, if confirmed that help was given to Horr, by Danville relatives, charges of accessory after the fact could be filed.

Thomas Adrianopolis, the man who led authorities to the arrest of Horr, arrived in Danville Tuesday night from Petersburg, Virginia. Adrianopolis, also known as Thomas Andrews, as he had Americanized his name, was tired of the months of sleuthing. When interviewed by reporters, he stated that he was tired of searching for Horr. He had won out and he was ready to move on with his life. He was tired after a long ride home, but happy the incident was over. His desire for revenge was satisfied. He had shown the Danville police that his story of having seen Horr at various places was true. The "shadow" was ready for a rest, but not too tired to talk.

"If I had not caught Horr," stated Andrews, "I would have died. I had promised Chief Walker I would find him. Many times after missing him by only a few minutes, I had been almost ready to quit. Twice, I almost had my hands on him, but he got away. That made me so sick. Two, maybe three hours of sleep, and then on again, always on his trail. Every place I went, I heard of him. But only three times our trails crossed. In Dallas, Texas I almost had him; at Chicago, two months ago I almost had him, but a suitcase interfered with my movements and Horr escaped into the crowd. He got away and left town. He went to Springfield, Illinois. He was in a card game there. He was in Decatur, Illinois for two days. Some of his relatives he visited in Decatur gave him money. He went to Cairo, Illinois. He was in Kentucky, Tennessee, Ohio, West Virginia, and Virginia, and Newark, New Jersey."

Andrews said Horr had been in Petersburg, Virginia, a little more than a week, when he moved to City Point. There he became employed at the E.I. DuPont Power Company near Hopewell, another suburb. The trail was not easy to follow, but Andrews persisted and, late Friday night, he learned that Horr had eyes on a young woman musician, at a questionable resort in City Point and spent much time there.

Andrews seated himself and placed his order. Within an hour, Horr came in. He sat at a table not 10 feet distant. The girl came in. She sat on Horr's knee. Horr looked closely at Andrews, but if he recognized any familiar features, he made no move. Andrews left the place, called another gentleman, and gave the man a dollar to go to Petersburg to find a police officer, because City Point had no police force. "When the officer came, Horr started to run, and I caught him. The officer asked him his name and Horr replied, "Alva C. Tenil Horr, you found me!" He was taken to Hopewell, locked up, and Danville police notified.

Monday morning, Andrews said that Chief Walker, Detective Spangler and two others traveled by automobile from Petersburg to Hopewell. Chief Walker gave Andrews a portion of the reward money. Andrews gave the reporters this statement:

"All I ask is a place on the police force in Danville. I think I have shown that I will make a good officer."

Andrews said that but for assistance given Horr by relatives and friends in Danville, he would have been taken long ago. He made the statement that there has never been a night since Horr shot down his wife that he did not know all that was going on in Danville, how the search for him was progressing, where they were searching, and other points which would aid him in eluding the officers. Andrews stated he believed he knew the accomplices of Horr, but he declined to make public the names. He also verified a story that Horr had taken more than $300 from him in a dice game some time prior to the killing of Mrs. Horr, but denied that this caused him to pursue Tenil. It may have had the effect of keeping him closer to the trail, but he said the main idea was to show his ability as a detective and secure himself a position as a patrolman in Danville.

Believing that Horr would arrive on a Big Four Train Number 3 at 7:05, Tuesday evening, August the 10th., there was a large crowd on hand at the Vermillion Street Station to greet the returning officers and their prisoner. The station platform was crowded. As the train pulled in, there was a shifting forward of the crowd, all eager for a first look at the prisoner. There was much disappointment shown, when it was learned the officers and Horr were not aboard. At the Union Station, in Indianapolis, Indiana, half a dozen former acquaintances and a family of four were scanning the incoming Cincinnati trains all of Tuesday afternoon, hoping for a look at him.

Thursday, August 12, 1915 with Horr in custody, Chief Walker and Detective Spangler were now en route home. They would arrive in Danville on Thursday night according to a message from Walker to the Danville Police Department. It was believed that the parties would not arrive before Friday morning because of the train connections causing delays.

The party would be returning over the Norfolk & Western Rail Lines. If they were returning by that route, it would be impossible for them to reach Cincinnati before 6:20, Thursday evening. Taking fast train 43, of the Big Four out of Cincinnati, the expected arrival time in Danville would be 3:25 a.m., Friday morning. An earlier arrival could have been possible, but not probable, had another train line been chosen.

Horr, according to the Richmond newspaper, declined to discuss the murder of his wife though he was quite willing to enter into a conversation on other subjects.

The State's Attorney's office was preparing for a big legal battle. John Lawman expected the attorney for the defendant to wage a stubborn fight and for several days had been busy gathering bits of evidence which he might need in the case. The state's attorney said that he would ask for the most extreme penalty provided by law and made the statement that the state will be prepared to show that Horr made numerous assaults on his wife and that the murder was premeditated in months prior to the murder. Chief Walker was said to have twice taken pistols from Horr. Chief Walker was expected to be important witness for the state. The taxi driver, who hauled Horr to a point near the Meeker's home several days preceding the murder, would be summoned to tell of Horr's threats against his wife and also would testify that on that particular occasion Horr carried a gun.

Despite numerous stories currently circulating concerning the plans of the defense, counsel for Horr said they had outlined no campaign, and that they could not arrange for the defense until they had talked with their client.

Meanwhile, interest was centered on the return of the prisoner to Danville. Clark Meeker, father of Mrs. Ida Horr was satisfied that he no longer needed a revolver nor a permit to carry one. He turned the gun over to the new Sheriff, Douglas Williams, and stated that he could rest, now that Horr was under arrest.

Meeker told his fears to Sheriff Shepherd at the time of the shooting and had gained permission to carry a revolver. Besides the revolver, Meeker had a shotgun and a rifle and stated that he would protect his household against any attempt on the part of Horr to kill him or any member of the Meeker family.

"I am not seeking to kill anyone," assured Clark Meeker, "but I am not going to stand by and allow anyone to shoot at me without me shooting back. I do not want trouble and never did. I am a peaceful man and want to get along with those around me, but I fear that Horr may come back and try to harm me or some member of the family."

No one in Danville was any more relieved that Horr had been captured, than the father of the murdered woman.

CHAPTER FIFTEEN

Count Them 1 2 3 4 5 6 7

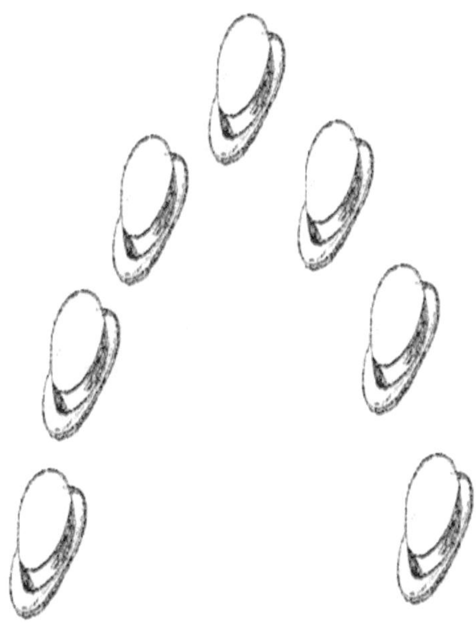

W hen Chief Walker stepped off the Big Four Train Number 43 at the Vermillion Street Train Station in Danville at 3:23 a.m., Friday morning, fifty or more persons were present at the train station. With Horr in his custody, Walker did not anticipate the crowd that had been waiting for over an hour in the early hours on Friday. The newspaper reporters were climbing over each other to get a statement from Horr. Chief Walker and Detectives Spangler were met by Captain Walters, Detective Moore, and Smith and patrolman Harley Diffenderfer. Before the party boarded the police automobile, Horr was allowed to shake hands with a few friends among the fifty or more persons present. Horr could not believe who was standing in the crowd. He counted seven different men wearing the familiar hat that he was given to wear.

Among the innocent bystanders Horr observed: (1) Frank the Bartender, (2) the taxi driver, Vogt, (3) James Smith, owner of the Transfer Service, (4) the big chap he talked with at the West Montezuma Train Station, Ferrell, (5) the gentleman he met at the train station in Evansville, Spinuzzi, (6) and (7) the two jailbirds who drove him to Louisville, Kentucky. No relatives of Horr were at the train station.

After shaking hand with Frank and Spinuzzi, Horr climbed into the police automobile. Chief Walker started discussing his trip back to Danville with the other officers. Walker let it be known that Alva was a model prisoner. "At no time did Alva try to make any attempt to escape. We had a long talk about where he has been for the past year. This man needs to write a book, or make a moving picture. I know he has not told me everything but what he has told me is unbelievable. He was in Cuba when they had that big fight."

Horr just sat there with a smile on his face in the back seat between the two detectives, listening to Chief Walker.

He was thinking, "If they only knew what Red's plan calls for over the next few years."

"Chief, I would like to talk to the reporters when we get to the jail. Could that be arranged?" inquired Horr.

"What do you want to talk about?" wondered the chief.

"I want to set the record straight about where I have been over the last year. I don't want to be tried in the press. I want to make a statement about the facts of the case. I was asked to make a statement to the Richmond Newspapers but I told them, 'No!' I know that Andrews called the newspapers reporters in Richmond. I read the report and I just want to clear up some things Andrews said," clarified Horr.

"Are you telling me that Andrews's facts are wrong?" wondered Walker.

Still manipulating, Horr answered, "Maybe. Set up the press conference and you can hear my side of the story."

"Well, I know that Andrews has trouble getting the facts right sometime," stated Chief Walker. "But before I grant you a meeting with the press, I want my detectives to take a statement from you. Give them your side of the story," directed the chief, showing he was still in control.

"I will talk to your detectives as long as you allow me to give a statement to the newspapers," replied Horr.

"Do we have a deal?" pleaded Horr.

"Yes," declared Chief Walker. "You can talk with the reporters after you give us your statement."

At the County Jail Horr gave the Detective's his side of the story.

"Andrews is mistaken! Andrews, who claims to have been following me for months and to have had an encounter or two with me, is mistaken. I have been told that Thomas Andrews is seeking a position on the Danville Police Force. He probably wants to show his ability as a detective but has failed to stick to the facts. I never was in Springfield, Illinois. I have not been in Decatur, since I left Danville nearly a year ago. I did not visit Columbus, Milltown, Newark, Altoona, Harrisburg, and other sites mentioned by him. He was correct when he said I had been in Richmond, Petersburg, and Hopewell, Virginia and he was right when he said I was arrested at City Point, but only those parts of his story were correct. I never have been accompanied by a woman. I was not in company of a woman when arrested, and I was not employed in the DuPont power mill. For more than two months, I was employed as chef at the largest hotel in Prince George County, Virginia. I was off last Friday afternoon. I was visiting at the place where I was arrested; going over there to see a bartender I knew and stopped to talk to the piano player, a blind man of my acquaintance. I did not see Thomas

Andrews, as he says. I think all he knows about the case is that he was called in to identify me. I understand they were looking for me because of a circular sent out. I was not in Chicago, nor was I in any other northern town during my absence. I only saw one or two persons from Danville. I never was in constant communication with anyone in this city. I made no special effort to avoid people because, by doing so, I would have attracted attention to myself. I went to Virginia because there is more money there than any other place in the country that I know of. The powder companies have millions of dollars. People are working all the time with all the over time they want. I could not work in the mill because of my crippled hand. And I made no effort to escape. When Chief Ferguson stepped up and said they wanted me. I made no denial of my identity. We walked over to the city jail and there I remained until moved to Petersburg. I was afforded nice treatment all the time. I could not have asked for better. I will not say that I particularly wanted to return, but at least I made no effort to escape. I did not go west when I left Danville. I went east. A little later I will tell you what you care to know about getting away from the Danville area from the officers in the river bottom, where I went, and how I went, but just now I would much appreciate it if you would allow me to get some sleep," finished Horr, nearly exhausted.

He slept from about four o'clock, until he went for breakfast. He had just retired again when J. M. Boyle, counsel for the defendant, came for a conference that lasted until 9:00 a.m.

Horr then consented to see a representative of the Commercial News and talked to him for about three quarters of an hour. He was scarcely able to keep awake during the talk and was sleeping soundly within 5 minutes after being returned to his cell.

Horr stated there were a variety of viewpoints concerning his case. He asked that the public withhold judgment until he presented his evidence. Other than that, he declined to discuss the charges brought against him.

"I have no desire to be tried by the public press," said Horr, while in the office at the County jail. "When the proper time comes, action will be taken in court. The state has legal representation that will gather and present the evidence on behalf of the people. I will have counsel to look after my interest; these men are familiar with court proceedings. They will present the case to the judge and jury for judgment. Whatever statement I have to make and whatever evidence I have to present will be given at that time and in the proper form. Until that time, I feel that I should not discuss the charges and I ask that the public suspend judgment until it has heard all of the evidence connected with the case. That's all I have to say at this time," declared Horr.

Horr asked Sheriff Williams and jailer Pratt Taylor to kindly keep out all curious people. Horr requested that only his relatives and his attorneys be admitted to see him. Sheriff Williams informed Horr that his request would be granted. He was taken back to his cell on the first floor of the jail.

Shortly after Horr returned to his cell, a local man by the name of Johnny O'Dell, who worked for Red, was lock up for disorderly conduct and forgery. The Danville Police picked up O'Dell on Logan Avenue for being intoxicated in public. When O'Dell was asked his name, he gave an erroneous name and signed the police reports with the name of John Hillard and the address of Johnny O'Dell. John Hillard was booked early that day and was being held in the county jail. O'Dell was booked and locked up in the same cell block as Horr. O'Dell offered Horr some information about changes in Red's escape plan. O'Dell tapped the message to Horr with a needle. The code was simple, a tap for each letter of the alphabet: 'A' was one tap, followed by a pause; the 'B' was two taps, and so on. It took time, but Horr had more than enough time on his hands. Horr had been coached in this jailhouse code when he was in prison the first time at the Pontiac Correctional Central in 1898. There he learned to read and write at a very low level. The original escape plan was for Horr to escape from the Vermilion County Jail before the trial started. Red had paid the jailer, Russ Weaver, to have Horr placed in a cell on the second floor. This jailer was as big a crook as the inmates. This is where the plan failed; Sheriff Williams placed Horr in a cell on the first floor of the jail. Horr needed to be on the upper floor; a solid oak door on the first floor prevented him from reaching the second floor. If he succeeded in breaking through the door, he would have to climb up to the porthole leading to the roof, creep across the roof and down to the courtyard, climb on top of another jail brick building and back down, then sneak over the outer fence of the jail yard. At any stage, he could be shot on sight. He didn't think the plan to escape from the Vermilion County Jail was a safe plan. All he could think about was climbing out onto the roof of the jail and jumping a fence. Horr didn't think he was capable of that. He was beside himself; the message that he received from O'Dell was short and to the point. "Halt escape plans go to back up plan, more later on."

When his brother-in-law, David Collier, from Tilton, came to see him, Horr asked him to give a message to his old friend Red, but to Horr's surprise, **his brother-in-law had the information he needed.** This gave Horr a fresh outlook. The back-up plan was for him to go to prison. Now he knew what was necessary for him to be a free man. Horr was removed from his jail cell at 1:00 P.M. and taken to the Vermilion County Court House for a pre trial hearing.

CHAPTER SIXTEEN

On Cross-Examination

The actual events that followed are given as historical evidence of the trial.

FIFTY FIFTH DAY OF MAY TERM, A. D. 1915. Friday, August 13th, 1915

Court convened pursuant to adjournment at 9 a.m. All the officers of said court present as herein fore and set forth. Whereupon certain proceedings were had and entered of record in said court in words and figures following, to-wit: -

No. 11274 Murder

The people of the state of Illinois

vs

Alva C. Horr alias Tenil Horr

Now, come the people by the State's Attorney and the said defendant in his own proper person also comes and he being now duly presented with a list of jurors and witnesses herein is arraigned for a plea and for a plea herein said defendant says he is not guilty as charged.

N. 11275 Assault with intent to Murder
The people of the state of Illinois
vs
Alva C. Horr alias Tenil Horr

Now, come the people by the State's Attorney and the said defendant in his own proper person also comes and he, being now duly presented with a list of jurors and witnesses herein, is arraigned for a plea and for a plea herein said defendant says he is not guilty as charged.

Friday, August 13, 1915

Ten hours after he arrived in Danville, Horr was arraigned in the Circuit Court at 1:30 before Justice Judge Augustine A. Partlow. About 150 people were in the courthouse at the time of the arraignment, many of those present being old cronies of the prisoner. He was represented by Attorney John M Boyle. A date was set for the grand jury. Horr was asked as to whether he desired to plead guilty or not guilty. Horr replied "not guilty" in a nervous voice that could barely be heard 10 feet away.

The date of the trial was set for Monday, September 20, although Judge Partlow stated to attorney Boyle that if grounds could be shown for an extension, he would grant. The State's attorney wanted to go ahead with the case right away.

"You will have names for a jury by August 30 and the state will be ready then," said Mr. Lawman

"Your honor, I need more time to prepare my case," argued Boyle. He wanted several weeks to prepare the case. He wanted to wait until his law partner, Crayton, returned to the city.

The Judge did not grant an extension, Monday, September, 20, 1915, was the date set for the trial.

Case number 11274 charged Horr with murder.

Case 11275 charged Horr with assault with intent to commit murder, referring to the attack made upon Clark Meeker, his father-in-law.

The next twenty-eight days, Horr was lock up in his cell until the judge ordered no more delays in the murder case.

Friday, September 10, 1915

Judge Partlow in the Circuit Court Friday morning ordered Sheriff Williams to summon special venire to special jurors for the trial of Horr, on Monday, September 20. The action meant the case against the former restaurant owner would be tried on that day, unless some good excuse was offered for a continuance. When the case was called in court, it would be exactly a year and a day since the burial of Horr's wife and just four days past the first anniversary the tragedy that occurred on West Williams Street.

Due to the shocking murder and the interest taken in the case when Horr made his getaway, it was doubtful if any group of 100 men will yield 12 men, who had not heard of the crime, expressed an opinion, or discussed the case. The only reason so far for requesting a continuance of the case, was the unpreparedness of the attorney for Horr.

Horr continued to spend his time at the County Jail, refusing all visitors except relatives or his counsel. No other visitors were allowed to see Horr.

Friday, September 17, 1915

The stage was being set for the Horr murder trial, the last case to be heard in the Circuit Court during the May term and probably the biggest trial of its kind in the city in a number of years.

The escape used by Horr could have been staged for a moving picture. The case has attracted more than usual interest and there was going to be big crowds present at every session of the court.

With the trial set to start at nine o'clock Monday morning, rumors were afloat that important evidence was uncovered, at the 11th hour, but these rumors were denied at the office of the State's attorney.

Counsel for the accused declined to say what new evidence was uncovered or what the line of defense would be, but from inquiries directed by investigators for them, it was believed it would be self-defense. Three men, who visited the Meeker's home just a few days prior to the shooting, would be summoned by the defense. These men would be asked to testify that two of them, accompanied by a deputy sheriff, went to the Meeker home to retrieve some diamonds bought by Horr, not entirely paid for, and held by Mrs. Horr. Horr went with them in an automobile to show them where the Meeker family lived.

They would testify that at the time Meeker made threats against Horr, stating Meeker said he would kill Horr onsite and that he would kill him, if they ever met again. An investigator for the defense claimed to have a witness who would testify that Horr fired over the head of Meeker during the encounter before Mrs. Horr was killed. The defense would attempt to show that Horr feared Meeker, that Meeker came toward Horr with a knife, and that Horr fired several shots, and a stray bullet killed Mrs. Horr.

And the State, on the other hand, would attempt to show that Horr threatened his wife many times prior to the shooting, that he drove to the scene of the slaying, met the family returning from a picnic, and started toward his wife, that he had a pistol, and commenced firing. An effort would be made by the State to show that the murder was premeditated.

The sheriff's office completed the work of serving notice on the first special venire of 100.

Saturday, September 18, 1915

About all that could be heard around the Vermilion County Courthouse these days is the murder trial when Horr would be placed on trial for killing his wife.

The States Attorney's forces were ready to go ahead with the trial. All of the evidence that was needed was in their hands and there would be a vigorous objection to any suggestion of a continuation in the case. There have been rumors that attorneys Clayton and Boyle would ask for a continuation, but they would say nothing in advance as to what they proposed to do.

Monday, September 20, 1915

"Order in the court, order in the court," shouted Judge Partlow. The court room was filled to the limit. "Everyone, remove your hats, please!" ordered the judge.

SEVENTY FIFTH DAY OF MAY TERM, A. D. 1915

Monday, September 20th 1915

Court convened pursuant to adjournment at 9 a.m. All the officers of said court present as hereinto and set forth. Whereupon certain proceedings were had and entered of record in said court in words and figures following, to-wit: -

No. 11274 Murder
The people of the state of Illinois
vs
Alva C. Horr alias Tenil Horr

Now, the people by the States Attorney and the said defendant as well in his own proper person as by his counsel also comes and the parties hereto bring now ready for trial comes a jury of 12 good men and true who have been duly elected, tried, and swore accordingly to law and there upon statements of both the prosecution and defense is now made to the jury and officers are sworn to take charge of the jury.

Every seat in the court room was taken. Many of the seats were occupied by the men who had been summoned for jury in the case, and by the afternoon many had been weeded out, but the seats were quickly filled as fast as a man was excused. Several of those who did not fill the requirement for jurors were interested in the hearing, enough to remain after having been excused.

Late in the afternoon, the gallery of the courtroom was thrown open to accommodate the crowd. In the audience were large numbers of the sporting elements of the city, many of those present having been personal friends of the defendant.

By three o'clock, a number of jurors had been excused:

Court adjourned until 8:30 A.M. September 21, 1915

SEVENTY SIXTH OF MAY TERM, A.D. 1915

Tuesday, September 21th, 1915

Bailiff proceed Court convened pursuant to adjournment at 9 a.m. All the officers of said court present as hereinto and set forth. Whereupon certain proceedings were had and entered of record in said court in words and figures following, to-wit: -

No. 11274 Murder

The people of the state of Illinois

vs

Alva C. Horr alias Tenil Horr

Now again, come the people by the State's Attorney and the said defendant as well and his own proper person as by his counsel also comes and comes also the jury hereto impaneled herein and thereupon the jury hears evidence herein.

Court convened promptly at 8:30 a.m., but there were several other matters up for discussion before the trial could be called. They were dispensed within about twenty minutes.

"Gentlemen of the jury you have been summoned to hear this case. This court is now in session. My name is Judge Augustine Partlow. You are the jury and the trial is set to begin. You have a serious responsibility. Will the innocent be sent to jail or the guilty go free? Your job is to make sure that justice is served. Both sides of the case will be presented to you. The person being accused his Alva C. Tenil Horr, the defendant. Remember, each side will try to convince you that his version is what actually happened. But you must make the final decision. The courtroom bailiff, Mr. Modre, will provide security for the courtroom, for me, the staff, and those in attendance. He will assist in the administration of court functions as directed by me and the clerk of the court. Most importantly, he will escort the defendant to and from the court room and prevent escape. He will also escort you, the jury, to and from the court room. Mr. Modre, would you escort the defendant Alva C. Tenil Horr into the courtroom?"

Horr entered the courtroom in the custody of Sheriff Williams and was placed in the prisoner's dock until Judge Pardow called the case, which was at 9:21 a.m. Horr was then moved to a chair immediately to the rear of his counsel, and within a dozen feet of his father-in-law, Clark Meeker.

By the side of Clark Meeker sat the mother of the murdered woman. On the same bench were Mrs. Horr brothers: Art, Charles, Frank, John, and Eli, and sisters: Minney, Flora, Martha, and Alice.

Horr was in a blue suit with a green four-in-hand tie and outing shirt. Despite being twenty pounds lighter than the time of the killing, he appeared to be in good health and showed no signs of nervousness. He spent his idle moments drumming on the seat of his chair with his fingers. It was like he was talking to someone in a secret language.

Little time was lost in summoning twelve candidates for jurors. Clerk Wellman read the names from a big stack of cards until he had filled the box with twelve men. Frank Lee, Lewis Nolan, John Reynolds, E.G. Greenwood, Harry Phillips, William Watkins, A.L. Legates, Carl Claypool, Sam Alexander, R.E. Trimble, C.U. Noble, and Carl Walker were the first twelve names called.

Frank Lee, a real estate dealer and an insurance agent, was the first man questioned. He had lived in Hoopeston 15 years. He admitted knowing attorney Boyle of the defense, and belonged to the same secret order, but said that he had no regrets, religious or otherwise, that would prevent him from invoking the death penalty. It was that final question which gave the first indication that hanging could be recommended by the State.

Among the man challenged for cause were: Lewis Nolan, who stated that he had formed an opinion; John Reynolds, a paper maker of Danville, who had formed an opinion; E.G. Greenwood, a machinist at the Malleable Iron works, who had pronounced views on the subject of capital punishment; Harry Phillips, a clerk at Bismarck, who was opposed to capital punishment and could not vote for hanging a man, even if they were convicted of murder; and William Watkins, of Fithian, who said that he had formed an opinion that would require evidence to change his mind.

A.L. Legates, of Muncie, whose wife was a cousin of State's Attorney Lawman, was excused by the defense.

From the questions posed by the defense, there was little doubt that a plea of self-defense would be made. Prospective jurors were asked if they believed in self-defense. What if it could be shown that the fatal shooting took place because the man on trial felt his life was in danger? If perspective jurors wavered on self-defense issues, they were challenged, or excused by the attorneys.

Carl Claypool, an auctioneer residing in Bismarck, formerly in the grain business and the proprietor of a livery stables, was the fifth juror to be quizzed. He knew Horr slightly, having patronized his restaurant on several occasions. He was not opposed to capital punishment but was excused.

Sam Alexander, a clerk employed at Potomac, Illinois, was also excused because of his opinion against capital punishment.

R.E. Trimble, a grocery clerk employed at Oakwood, was finally excused because he had known Horr as one of his customers, while Trimble had been employed as a food salesman for several years.

C.U. Noble, employed in the restaurant business in Catlin and also employed as an agent for the Illinois Traction Company there, was accepted by both sides, but had not been formally put on the list as approved by both sides. Noble was at one time a city salesman for a tea company of the city and in that way had come in contact with Horr.

Carl Walker was excused for cause by the State. He was opposed to capital punishment.

Henry Strindberg, a prominent farmer in the vicinity of Snider in Belmont Township, looked like he was going to be accepted as a juror, but at the last minute was not due to his health.

It was then 12 o'clock and court adjourned. State's Attorney Lawman, and the defense held a conference with the judge to decide the list of jurors accepted and the potential impact.

Bailiffs Williams North and Will Modre, who were sworn in to look after the jurors, were not only to be together, but must abide by the judge's requests. By noon four jurors were selected, three who may yet be refused and the fourth that had not been decided upon. They were all taken out for dinner and instructed against speaking to any outside parties. No one would be permitted to speak to them and they were to abstain from reading any newspapers.

It was evident early in the afternoon that many people were opposed to the death penalty. Shortly after the court resumed, seven men had been challenged by the State's Attorney on this issue. By two o'clock, potential jurors had to decide their view on the question of capital punishment. Those who were excused by the Judge for this reason were: Dan O'Connell, former West Williams grocery, L.C. Flat, a clerk of Danville; Fred N. Sheets, a farmer, of Grape Creek; J.D. Brown, a farmer living near Hoopeston; C.K. Lane, a grocer, from Danville; and William Cooper, a miner Georgetown.

George J. Gray, proprietor and manager of the Aetna House, was called, but after a short series of questions, it was decided that he was opposed to capital punishment and he was challenged for cause by the State.

George J. Gibson, farmer residing in Catlin, appeared to be acceptable to the defense, but his final selection remained uncertain.

John Giddings and John J. Higgins, both veteran blacksmiths at the Chicago and Eastern Illinois Railway, were excused because they had heard a lot of stories in regard to the murder.

J.J. Smith, a former stationary engineer from Vicksburg, Mississippi, who had recently returned to Illinois and gone to farming, near McKendree, was still being questioned.

James Megarry, grocer, but better remembered as a funeral director, took ill and he, too, was excused from service.

The following jurors were accepted by both sides: Ed Fisher, Frank Lee, John Gulogly, Joe Knight, John Graham, Thomas Sailor, S.W. McGuire, John Barnett, W. H. Mock, R. K. Barney, W.A. Ramey, and Will Irvin.

The twelve jurors had been seated. State's Attorneys Lawman called his first witness, Norman Timmons. Timmons, a patrolman, testified to answering the phone at the police station and going to the scene in the patrol wagon. He said that the body of Mrs. Horr was found lying on the ground where she had fallen.

Detective Joe White testified going with Detective George Germannet to the Horr apartment.

Nellie Museriman, who had been employed in the Horr's restaurant, testified that during June 1914, the defendant struck his wife, kicked her to the floor, and then kicked her in the side. She said the trouble arose over money matters, and that Mrs. Horr had said, "I have turned away the cigar man and the furniture man and you cannot have the remaining money or the rings." On cross-examination she testified that she quit her job at the café.

Mandy Adams, another employee of the restaurant, testified that on one occasion she saw Mrs. Horr exit from the kitchen of the establishment holding her hand out over her face. Horr was following behind her and said, "I will knock your block off." Then demanded the rings from Ida.

Coroner Cole was called to the stand to testify about holding the inquest on the body of Mrs. Horr. He was followed by Dr. E.L. Winslow, who at that time was county physician. Dr. Winslow testified to holding the autopsy and stated that he found the bullet in a muscle in the back of her body and that it had entered the chest, penetrating the heart and lodging where he found it.

Mrs. Clark Meeker, mother, of the murdered woman, was one of the last witnesses on Tuesday afternoon. It was about 3:30 p.m. when she took the stand. The moment that her name was called, there was a stir throughout the audience as those who were interested in the trial realized that one of the star witnesses for the State, probably one whose testimony might result in sending her son-in-law to the gallows, was about to tell of the tragedy. There was a subdued murmur throughout the big crowd and the judge had to rap for order.

Mrs. Meeker's testimony was clear and not until the cross-examination did she show any unusual emotion. Her answers in the cross-examination were unusually sharp. She stated that she was the mother of the murdered woman and that she had known Horr for about 12 years or since he married her daughter. She was a resident of Morin's Addition, which skirts the west bank of the North Fork River, southward from the Sutherland Ford Bridge.

Mrs. Meeker related several quarrels that the couple had had, particularly the one on November 23, 1913, when Horr came to the house and sought to gain entrance after his wife had left him. He tried the kitchen door and found it locked, went around to the east, and kicked in the door. She stated that she was not at home when this happened, but she was sent for at a sick neighbor's house, and arrived before Horr had departed. She claimed that Horr had threatened to kill Ida and to kill himself, and that three years ago, they had gone through a similar quarrel.

Counsel for Horr objected, but the objection was overruled by the Judge. Coming to the tragedy of September 16th, Mrs. Meeker told of the trip that her husband, her daughter, Mrs. Della Hawes, and she had made to Lincoln Park in the afternoon, where the Woodman Associate were holding a great country picnic. She told of getting a glimpse of Horr at the park and then related the circumstances of their return to their home. Mrs. Hawes was with them and the two Hawes children were in the lead Della and Ida were a few paces behind and she and her husband were about the same distance behind their daughter. They walked through the grass at Lincoln Park until they came to Logan Avenue and had reached the street. There they saw Horr in an automobile that sped north along the avenue.

They crossed to the west side of Logan Avenue and walked to Williams Street, and turned west on that street, crossing to the south side. As they neared the Children's Home, Horr passed them, again.

This time the taxi was going south and traveling at a high rate of speed. At Williams Street the car turned west and kept up its high speed. The car threw up a tremendous cloud of dust after getting off the paved street at Logan Avenue. They walked westward along the South side of Williams Street, stopped at the Hetherington Grocery Store, where Mr. Meeker obtained some tobacco."

Court adjourned until 8:30 a.m., September 22, 1915 the jury was sequestered and became accustomed to their cots in the white walled dormitory on the top floor of the courthouse. The bailiffs saw that they had plenty of exercise. There was a long walk after supper on Tuesday evening. Bright and early Wednesday the twelve men were taken out on North Street through Ellsworth Park, and up to the site of the new concrete bridge, now nearing completion. Various points of interest were explained to them before they were taken to the courthouse.

SEVENTY SEVENTH OF MAY TERM, A. D. 1915

Wednesday, September 22th, 1915

Court convened pursuant to adjournment at nine o'clock A. M. All the officers of said court present as hereinfore and set forth. Whereupon certain proceedings were had and entered of record in said court in words and figures following, to-wit: -

No. 11274 Murder
The people of the state of Illinois
vs
Alva C. Horr alias Tenil Horr

Now again, come the people by the State's Attorney and the said defendant as well and his own proper person as by his counsel also comes and comes also the jury heretofore impaneled herein and thereupon the jury hears evidence herein.

The court room, the crowd was not as large as on previous days, but there were still a number who were compelled to stand around the side and back walls.

Margaret Meeker was called to the stand again Wednesday morning. She identified the umbrella used by her daughter in her fight for life on the afternoon of September 16th. The umbrella was then offered as evidence. There was an objection, but it was overruled. Clark Meeker was then called to the witness stand. He testified about threats made against Mrs. Horr. Counsel for the defense objected to evidence being introduced, which extended back two years before the shooting, stating there had been reconciliation after the quarrels in question. The judge asked for more details on the subject. Attorney Clayton read a lengthy decision handed down by a higher court, but the judge ruled that the cases were nothing alike, and that the evidence was admissible.

Meeker testified that in October 1913, Horr came to his home and asked for Ida. Being told that he did not know where she was, Horr stated, "You better tell me where she is. I am going to kill her and then myself." Meeker testified that he had demanded Horr to quit making threats. He did not want any trouble, and was not going to have any such behavior on his place. Asked if he had ever seen Horr in the vicinity of his home prior to the trouble, Clark Meeker replied, "I saw him lurking in the vicinity of my home a number of times in October and November, 1913, and a number of times during the few weeks before the shooting. I could see his head above the weeds and grass in front of my house and I also saw him a number of times in the bushes, along the North Fork River. Sometimes I saw him walking across the open space between the house and the river. I did not see him have a gun."

A motion was made by the defense to exclude the testimony and to have the jury disregarded it. The evidence was admitted by the judge. Meeker stated that on one occasion he had seen Horr draw a revolver on one of the Meeker boys. Upon cross examination, Meeker testified that Horr had stated he would kill the Meeker family. The defense attempted to question Meeker on threats he had made against Horr but an objection was raised by the State's Attorney.

Frank Meeker, a brother of the dead woman, testified that he had seen Horr in the vicinity of the Meeker home a number of times prior to the shooting and that he was close enough to see that Horr was carrying a revolver.

Mrs. Ruth Meeker, daughter-in-law of Clark and Margaret Meeker, testified that she had heard Horr made threats against his wife at her home about ten months before the shooting. She said that Horr had started that he would kill Ida or anyone that interfered in the matter, and that he would kill himself. She stated she had told Horr that he should not feel that way about it. Horr asked her to go to Ida and persuade her to come back and live with him.

"Her mother went to Ida," the witness stated, "but she said there was nothing doing that she would not live with him again."

On cross-examination she admitted that Horr and his wife had made up a few days after this conversation.

Mark Cooper, a brother-in-law of Horr who lived in Georgetown, testified that on any number of occasions he had heard Horr make threats. "We met one day at Lyons, when my wife and I were returning home from the Meeker's. Horr asked me if I had been to see the old folks, and when I told him I had, he asked how they were and also asked me to take him in my car because that he wanted to see Ida and makeup with her. I told him I did not want to mix in their trouble, but when he insisted, we started back to the Meeker home. When we got to the bridge over the North Fork River, he got out and told me Clark Meeker had forbidden him going on his property and for me to go and get Ida. I told him that if he caused any trouble over the visit, I would get a wrench and knock him in the head. He said it would be justified, if I did. Ida refused to have anything to do with him and we took him back to Lyons. When he got out of the automobile, my wife told him that Frank Meeker had asked that he keep away from the Meeker's home and not causes any more trouble. Horr said, "You tell Frank that someday I will get full on booze and come to the Meeker home and the undertaker will have three or four to look after."

George W. Woolsey, a friend of Horr and editor of the Illinois

Banner, testified that Horr had come to his office and asked him to go to the Meeker home and try to persuade his wife to live with him. At first, the witness refused to have anything to do in the matter, but finally agreed to see Mrs. Horr. He saw Mrs. Horr and she stated that she would not live with Horr, that when he was drinking, he was brutal to her and that she feared trouble. She could not live with him.

Chief of Police Walker, Detectives Wash Smith and Lou Spangler, told of being called to the Meeker home and of the search for Horr. Walker told of finding Horr in Virginia, where he had been arrested by officers. The defendant had told him all the way to Danville that he was going to enter a plea of self-defense, and he stated that he was shooting at Meeker when he killed his wife. Horr also told Walker of his travels in the south, to Cuba and of his coming to Virginia.

Sheriff Williams was called to testify about the search made for Horr, but this was objected and little of the testimony was entered into the record.

Mrs. May Sutton, a pastry cook, was called to testify about trouble at the Hazel Street restaurant, when Horr knocked his wife down. She told of the fight and of Horr knocking his wife to the floor and kicking her. She testified that she did not see Mrs. Horr at the restaurant after that had occurred.

Mrs. Rachael Mobaker, who lived near the Meeker's at the time of the trouble, told of Horr calling her on the telephone and asking her to go to the Meeker home and deliver a message to Ida. "Tell her to come to Justice Hall's office tomorrow at nine o'clock; she'll know what it is for," the witness stated. He asked her if she thought Clark Meeker had anything to do with his wife staying away from him. The witness stated she had told him that she did not believe Mr. Meeker had anything to do with Ida's decision that she had heard Mr. Meeker tell Ida she could do as she pleased. In a conversation with Mrs. Horr, the witness said Ida had told her she would die before she would go back to Horr. This statement was ruled out of order.

Mrs. Lucile Phillips of Detroit Michigan, who formerly lived at 1315 West Williams Street, testified that she saw Ms. Horr attempt to get in her house when the shooting occurred. Mrs. Horr tried to get in, but the screen door was latched and Ida had pulled so hard, the witness could not unlatch the door. The witness said Horr came up on the porch and she heard Mrs. Meeker say, "Oh, no, don't shoot her." Horr replied, "I am going to shoot her." Mrs. Horr then begged her husband not to shoot and he replied, "I am going to shoot you." He had a bright looking revolver in his hand, but did not shoot at that time. The two backed off the porch into the street.

On cross-examination witnesses testified that Horr carried the gun in his right hand and that, as he advanced, Ida was forced off the porch. Mrs. Phillips could not identify any of the family except Mr. Horr, knew him only by sight.

Don Sheppard, 1320 West Williams Street, the first house east of the Phillips' home, was at home on the afternoon in question. He was in a shed at his home. He heard the shots fired and ran into the street where he saw Tenil Horr and his wife. Mr. Sheppard stated he saw the fatal shot fired and saw Ida fall to the street. She had been striking Horr with an umbrella. Horr then started running west with the revolver in his hand, and disappeared. When last seen, he was going toward the river. The defendant disappeared over the hill into the brush and timber along the river.

Dick Hatfield, who was working down the street from the Phillips home, testified he heard three shots, and arrived at the scene in time to see Horr pull his wife off the Phillip's porch, and saw her start to run. Horr followed and after they had run a short distance Horr fired the fatal shot. Hatfield stated he saw Mrs. Horr sink to the ground. Bennett English, another young man who was with Hatfield and some other boys, testified to much the same.

Vegnie Shepherd, 1320 West Williams Street was setting on the porch at the home of Don Sheppard, testified to the same. Mrs. Alice Taylor of Indianapolis, Indiana, was visiting her parents, Mr. and Mrs. Don Sheppard, was about 600 feet behind the meeker party, as they returned from the picnic at Lincoln Park. She saw Horr get out of the automobile and began firing. She heard the shots and saw Mrs. Horr fall.

A carpenter was working on a house on McKinley Avenue directly to the rear of the Phillips' home. He and Frank Donelley came to see what the shooting was all about and saw a hatless man running west. The man he saw was Horr. He came to within forty feet of them and disappeared over brow of the hill, reloading as he ran.

Additional witnesses, who had heard the shots and rushed to the scene, testified during the afternoon. The witness list included: Mrs. Samantha Phillips, mother-in-law of Mrs. Phillips, at whose home Ida tried to enter, when pursued by her husband; Bert Gray, who was at Don Sheppard home, who ran to the street, when he heard shots fired; John shepherd, who was coming from his work, and saw Horr running westbound with Meeker in pursuit. John shepherd reported hearing Mr. Meeker was yelling, "You killed my daughter!" The witness stated that Horr continued westward and that Meeker picked up a rock or brick and struck him.

Another witness, George Cummings, a cook, testified that while he was working at the lunch stand in Lincoln Park, owned by John Buser, he saw Horr and shouted to him, "Hey, Tenil, I just saw Ida go by."

Cummings continued to testify that Horr replied, "She is a nice little girl. She has sued me for a divorce and I gave her $10 last week." He stated that Horr asked if a taxicab had come for him. Just then, a taxi showed up and Horr got in and let the park.

The divorce papers that were filed in court and afterward withdrawn, were produced as evidence but were not admitted. The State then rested its case.

A ten-minute recess was taken. When court resumed, Henry Vogt, the taxi driver, who drove Horr about the streets in Danville on the afternoon of the shooting, was the first witness for the defense. Apparently, from a list of witnesses whose names were called, he was the only eyewitness to the incident. The rest of those who spoke for Horr were character witnesses and businessman that knew him from the cafe.

Vogt, in his testimony, placed all of the altercation out in the middle of the street. All of the previous witnesses placed it on the sidewalk or on the lawn, south of the sidewalk. "He also claimed that Clark Meeker was the aggressor and that the aged man picked up two rocks and threw them at Horr before Horr even made an effort to draw his revolver," stated the taxi driver. That Clark Meeker provoked the situation. Horr did not fire until after Meeker had drawn his bowie knife and opened the blade. I am positive that four or five minutes elapsed before Horr even made an effort to draw his revolver." Stated the taxi driver Vogt continued his testimony by telling of having his taxicab at the park and of starting toward the city, when Horr hailed him near the refreshment booth and ask him where he was going. Horr said that he wanted to go downtown. They drove out of the park to Fairchild Street, then to Vermillion, down Vermillion to North, and then east to Hazel where they stopped at the Dock and Bert saloon. Five minutes later, they were going west on North Street to Logan Avenue and then north to English Street. At the park, they turned back and went south to Williams, when Horr said that he wanted to take a drive in the country. They turned west on Williams Street, traveling northwest, crossing over the North Fork River Bridge, and to a point about a quarter of a mile further on the Hungry Hollow Road, when Horr said that they would have to turn back because it was almost time for him to go to work. He said that he had a gambling place at Lyons.

Returning to Williams Street and turning east, Vogt testified that he saw some persons on the sidewalk, going west and that Horr told him to turn forward to the edge of the street because there was a party with whom he wanted to talk. Vogt turned in toward the ditch and Horr started to get out of the cab before it stopped. The taxi still moved about ten feet after Horr had stepped out.

Here is where the testimony varied from the others. Vogt said that the first thing that was done was Meeker stooped over and picked up two rocks, which he hurled at Horr. After a minute or so, Horr reached in his hip pocket and Meeker did the same. Horr then drew a gun cland Meeker drew a Bowie knife, which he opened. Vogt said he saw the knife was definitely open. Several minutes passed before either man made a move. Then Meeker advanced toward Horr and Horr fired the first shot. He shot in the air, apparently not aiming to hit Meeker. Seconds afterwards the second shot fired and it also went into the air. Shortly after came the third shot.

The gun misfired. Horr turned and ran toward the auto, breaking the gun to loaded new cartridges. Vogt said Mrs. Horr was hitting her husband with her umbrella and, after the third was fired, Ida nearly knocked the gun from his grip. When Horr had replaced new cartridges, he was within eight feet of the car. He then turned and started back. Vogt said that at this moment he started his car and drove slowly away toward Logan Avenue.

On cross-examination, State's Attorney, Lawman attempted to trip the witness up on several points. He produced evidence given at the coroner's inquest, where Vogt said that as they went north on Logan Avenue, Horr remarked, "There's the party I think I know." Vogt denied ever having said it. He also denied several other important points in the coroner's "inquest" or "version".

"How can the jury believe any of the statements you have made? No further questions," declared Lawman.

Other witnesses for the defense, who followed Vogt were: John Emerson, Frank Barnett, James Battle, Clint Tilton, Al Franks, J.H. Tarpley, Charles McCord, Ralph Tilton, L.E. Schario, Gene Ryan, and Robert Dickson. All these men were character witnesses for Horr. None of them could testify to what happen on September 16, 1914. One by one each witness on cross-examination was stymie, when asked how long they knew Mr. Horr. Most could not answer the question.

Horr was called to the witness stand. He stated he had lived in Danville 37 years and had been in the restaurant business for 9 of those years, four years ago on Van Buren Street and two years on Hazel Street. Horr testified that he married Ida Meeker about 12 years ago and that he knew Clark and Margaret Meeker and the family. He continued sharing that he was in Danville on September 16, 1914 and that at that time he was separated from his wife. He went to Lincoln Park about 3:00 p.m. and saw Vogt, the taxi driver.

He entered the taxicab about 4:00 p.m. and drove to town to Dock and Bert's Saloon. He bought a half pint of whiskey, got a drink of beer, went on North Street to Ellsworth Park and then on to Lincoln Park. After arriving near Lincoln Park, they turned around and headed east. He saw his wife, Ida, her father, Clark, and other members of the family. On Williams Street, near a vacant lot he passed the party with whom he wanted to speak.

He stated he wanted to speak with his wife in the hope of reconciliation. He had received a letter from a sister asking him and his wife to come to Washington and he wanted to show his wife the letter. Mr. Meeker was standing nearby, about 15 feet away. He admitted to walking around the cab and asking Meeker to let him see Ida. Meeker told him to go away and picked up a rock and threw it at him. After throwing a second rock, he could see Meeker's hand go into his pocket, so Horr started toward him.

Horr admitted shooting at Meeker, after Meeker had pulled out his knife. He fired the shot in a southwest direction to scare Meeker away. Horr expressed that he was afraid of Meeker. He fired a second shot in a northwestern direction. Horr recalled that he fired three shots. After the third shot was fired, Horr started walking east on Williams Street. It was tense. Ida was fighting him and Clark Meeker was coming toward him with the knife.

Horr continued testifying that he heard Margaret Meeker crying loudly, "Kill him!" and Horr told her that he was not going to shoot her. From Phillip's porch, Horr traveled northward. But all the time he was watching Clark Meeker.

As Horr was leaving, Ida hit his right hand very hard with the umbrella discharging the gun. Horr insisted in his testimony that he had told Ida that he was not going to hurt her.

The first he knew that Ida had been hit by the bullet was when he arrived at Lyons. The saloonkeeper told him that the police were looking for him because he shot his wife. He told the saloonkeeper that he did not intend to kill his wife. He only shot to frighten his father-in-law.

Some other witnesses testified on behalf of the defense stating that at an earlier date, in July of 1914, Clark Meeker threatened to cut Horr's throat. Upon hearing that threat, Horr left the scene immediately. When these witnesses were asked about where this alleged event took place, they could not answer. Yet another witness testified that on another occasion, in the Harter Saloon, Meeker stated that he would kill Horr. Frank Barnett Testified that, on one day, Meeker stood outside the Harter Saloon with a knife in his hand, waiting for Horr. Fred Jahnke went out to confront him and asked him to leave the area.

Court was adjourned until 8:30 a.m. September 23, 1915

SEVENTY-EIGHT OF MAY TERM, A. D. 1915

Thursday, September 23th, 1915

Court convened pursuant to adjournment at nine o'clock A. M. All the officers of said court present as hereinto and set forth. Whereupon certain proceedings were had and entered of record in said court in words and figures following, to-wit: -

No. 11274 Murder

The people of the state of Illinois

vs

Alva C. Horr alias Tenil Horr

Now again, come the people by the State's Attorney and the said defendant as well and his own proper person as by his counsel also comes and comes also the jury hereto impaneled herein and thereupon the jury hears arguments herein.

When T.J. Cutler (Red) took the stand, it was the first time Red and Horr were in the same room for over a year. Horr wanted to jump over the table, where he was sitting, and give Red a big hug and thank him for being a true friend. Red didn't show any emotion during the time he was testifying.

When T.J. Cutler, who operated a saloon on Lyons Road, told that Horr came to his saloon on the morning of the day of the hooting, following the shooting, and asked for whiskey. Cutler stated that he placed a shot of whiskey on the rear step and Horr asked him what he had done wrong. Cutler told him that he had killed his wife. Not having anything to say, Horr drank the shot of whisky and went away. Cutler did not see him again.

No other witnesses were called to the witness stand that day. Mr. Cutler had an answer for all questions asked of him. On cross-examination, State's Attorney, Lawmen, attempted to trap the witness with different questions, but could not get the witness to waver from his testimony. As soon as Red finished answering the questions from both lawyers, he stood up and walked out of the court room without looking at Horr.

Then State's Attorney, Lawmen, said, "Your honor I would ask the court to adjourn until tomorrow. I have additional questions for Mr. Cutler."

Court adjourned until 8:30 o'clock A. M. September 24, 1915.

CHAPTER SEVENTEEN

What You Say

SEVENTY NINTH OF MAY TERM, A. D. 1915

Friday, September 24th, 1915

Court convened pursuant to adjournment at 9:00 a.m. All the officers of said court present as hereinto and set forth. Whereupon certain proceedings were had and entered of record in said court in words and figures following, to-wit: -

No. 11274 Murder

The people of the state of Illinois

vs

Alva C. Horr alias Tenil Horr

When T. J. Cutler was called back to the witness stand by the State's Attorney for more questioning, Horr could not relax, "What additional questions would be asked?" he wondered.

State's Attorney Lawman began, "Mr. Cutler, you testified yesterday that you were the last person who spoke to Mr. Horr. Is that your testimony today?"

"No!" assured Cutler and calmly explained, "I testified that on the morning following the shooting, Horr showed up at my saloon on Lyons Road. Mr. Horr asked for a whiskey. I placed a whiskey on the rear door step and then he asked me what he had done. I told him he had killed his wife. He didn't have anything to say. He walked away and I did not see him again. That was my testimony yesterday and today."

"Is it true that Mr. Horr and you are very good friends?" asked Lawman.

"Yes," replied Cutler.

Lawman continued questioning, "Would you lie to your good friend, Mr. Horr?"

"No," uttered Cutler.

"Your Honor, would you have the court reporter read back the testimony given yesterday by Mr. Cutler?" requested Attorney Lawman.

The judge then had the testimony read to the court:

"Horr came to my saloon on the morning following the shooting and asked for a whiskey. I placed a whiskey on the rear door step, and then Horr asked me what he had done. I told him he had killed his wife. He did not have anything to say, but went away and I did not see him again."

"Gentleman of the jury, you have just heard this witness a very good friend of Mr. Horr, state not once, but twice, that and I quote, 'I told him he had killed his wife.' What more proof do you need that Alva C. Tenil Horr murdered his wife, Ida Horr on September 16 1914?" urged Attorney Lawman.

Mr. Cutler didn't show any emotion during the time he was testifying. Horr's attorney, John Boyle, didn't cross-examine Cutler. As soon as Red finished answering the questions, he stood up and walked out of the courtroom without looking at Horr again. State's Attorney, John Lawman then called the only eyewitness, Mrs. Shepherd. And ask the final question, "Can you tell this court exactly who you saw kill Ida Horr on September 16, 1914?"

"Yes," Mrs. Sheppard boldly stated. She pointed at Horr and continued speaking, "the man sitting at the table next to his attorney, Mr. Horr." Attorney, John Boyle, didn't cross-examine Mrs. Shepherd. Court was adjourned for lunch.

When the judge called the court to order at two o'clock both lawyers made their final statements. Horr's attorney, John Boyle, argued that Horr was defending himself again the knife that Clark Meeker pulled out of his pocket and that he had accidently shot his wife. The State's Attorney, John Lawman, argued that Horr murdered his wife, Ida, for the action she took in filing court papers to divorce him. Horr should receive the maximum sentence allowed, which was to be hanged.

The Judge then gave final instructions to the jury. Judge Partlow read the fifty-three pages of instructions to the jury, which took the greater part of an hour. According to the instructions, which had been submitted to the judge by the attorneys, there was little or no hope of receiving a short term in the penitentiary. All efforts were directed toward saving Horr's neck or getting a sentence of less than life.

"Gentlemen of the jury, you have just heard the case for Alva C. Tenil Horr. You must decide on the merits of the case. Be sure to carefully examine only the evidence given in this court of law. Do you the jury have any questions?"

Frank Lee, the jury foreman, responded, "No, your honor."

The judge then ordered the bailiff to move the jury from the courtroom, then adjourned court. Horr knew that he would be found guilty of murder. The only question now was how much time he would be sentenced to serve, or would he be sentence to death by hanging?

Four ballots were taken by the jury in deciding the guilt or innocence of Horr. On the first ballot, eleven were for guilty on the charge of murder and the second ballot was unanimous. Two more ballots were taken to determine the punishment. A number of the jurors were for the death penalty, but they were not forceful enough and a compromise was soon made for the twenty-five-year sentence.

The only mitigating circumstance in favor of Horr, was the fact that Clark Meeker had made threats against him, and this, the jury believed, was sufficient to show that there were ill feelings on the part of the father-in-law. This the jury believed could have contributed to Horr's action.

Precisely forty minutes after receiving the instructions of the court, the bailiff was summoned and advised that a decision had been reached. The twelve men asked that they be taken into court and the verdict given to the judge. Spectators scurried back toward the courtroom. Because it was not expected that there would be a decision short of midafternoon, most of those interested had gone to lunch.

There was a death-like stillness in the room when the jurors re-entered and the judge asked for the verdict to be handed to him. As Judge Partlow looked out over the crowd, he asked the foreman whether a verdict had been reached.

'We have, your honor," clarified Frank Lee.

"What say you?" asked the judge.

"Guilty of murder," declared the foreman, Frank Lee.

Horr turned pale when the verdict was read. For the first time since he returned from Virginia in the hands of the officers, was his face anything but a blood red color. He turned to a light pink in an effort to control his feelings, he tried to swallow the lump in his throat and for the first time since the trial began, he showed his feelings.

Neither the defendant nor his counsel said anything further. No comments were made about the verdict. Therefore, it was ordered by the court that Alva C. Horr, alias Tenil Horr, be taken from the courtroom and returned to the Vermilion County Jail. The sheriff of Vermilion County was ordered to transfer Horr to the penitentiary at Chester, Illinois, where he would be held for a term of twenty-five years, less the credit for the time served in the Vermilion County Jail.

None of the members of the Meeker family were present when the verdict was read. Alva's father and mother were in the court room seated in the back row. They said nothing to their son.

"I have prevailed to carry on with the plan," Horr thought to himself.

He was immediately sentenced to the state prison, and it was reported that counsel for Horr would attempt to get a retrial, but neither Boyle nor Crayton would indicate what they intended to do.

From the very first they realized what they were up against the toughest proposition that ever fell to criminal lawyers. There was not the slightest chance for a defense. The testimony which they had relied upon was totally dependent on the words of one man, Henry Vogt, the taxi driver, who drove the auto to the scene of the murder. The ploy had quickly been knocked from under the guise of self- defense and the entire defense collapsed. From then until the end of the trial, the attorneys devoted their entire energy toward saving the neck of their client.

Horr returned to the county jail, went to bed, and tried to sleep, but he had a strange itching and crawling sensations with in both legs. He was restless and, at times, he would pace the floor. In his jail cell bunk he would toss and turn. He could not stop rubbing his lower legs. "That liniment Homer gave him was for horses only, not people. That's why his legs were itching," he told himself.

As soon as the jurors had eaten their dinner, a number of them went to West Williams Street, to see for themselves the scene of the fatal shooting.

One of the jurors was asked after the trial, if there had been any evidence introduced by the defense to show that Horr was trying to get his wife from the Phillip's home and into the automobile, and if the fact that she had struck him over the arm, causing the revolver to be discharged, would have indicated an accidental shooting.

According to a number of jurors, the closing arguments by the attorneys in the case were not needed. The jurors had made up their minds, as the evidence had been presented. The attorneys talked longer to the jurors than to any jury in recent years. Both the State and the defense attorneys took up just five-and-a-half hours reviewing case.

Soon after the trial, Clark Meeker stated that, while there were people who would not be satisfied with the verdict, he, for one, was content with the punishment fixed by the twelve men. The following names were the members of the Horr jury:

Ed Fisher from Butler Township
Frank Lee from Hoopeston, works Real Estate
John Gulogly from Sidell, a Farmer
Joe Knight from Muncie, a Sanitation Engineer
John Graham from Rossville, a Carpenter
Thomas Sailor from Oakwood, a Ticket Agent
S. W. McGuire from Rossville, an Insurance Agent
John Barnett from Indianola, in the elevator Business
W. H. Mock from Danville, worked at the Danville Brick Company
R. K. Barrley from Catlin, a Grain Buyer
W. A. Ramey, Georgetown, a Farmer
Will Irvin, Roseville, and a Farmer

Although many people sought admission to the courtroom, there was perfect order. There was a crowd all week. There wasn't any outburst at any time and little difficulty was experienced in maintaining order. As soon as the courtroom and the gallery were occupied, no one else was permitted unless they could show they had business in court. The circuit court room was never intended for a large crowd. The circuit courtroom was large enough for most ordinary purposes, but when it came to a murder trial, such as was conducted this week, it proved to be insufficient.

Following their visit to the scene of the fatal shooting on West Williams Street, members of the jury expressed themselves as having misunderstood the setting. They had believed that the view of the street, where Horr and his wife met on that fatal afternoon, was obstructed to such a degree that it would have been impossible for anyone to see clearly all that had happened. When they saw the area for themselves, they found that there was no obstruction and that a good view could be observed.

Members of the jury really thought that they were giving Horr a life sentence, when they fixed his punishment to 25 years. One or two of the men on the jury were in the insurance business, and they figured that a man at the age of 38 would be released at age 63. The jurors failed to take into consideration, Horr would be able to cut that sentence down to about 14 years and could be out of prison in 1929 at the age of 54, given time for good behavior.

CHAPTER EIGHTEEN

Alive and Well, Safe and Sound

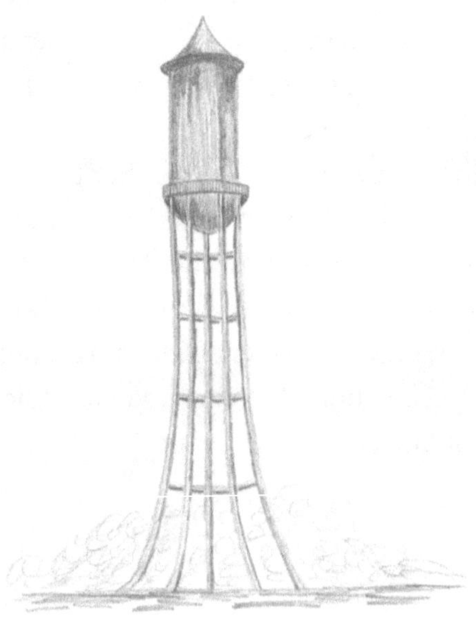

Saturday, September 25, 1915, not more than fifteen hours after the sentencing, Alva was awakened in the early morning hours and told to get ready for the long train ride to Chester, Illinois. Sheriff Williams along with Chief Walker, had made plans to move Horr in the middle of the night. The sheriff was anxious to get away as quietly as possible, to avoid any crowd who might want to be present, if Horr was taken away in the daytime. Horr was escorted to the police automobile which was parked in the back of the county jail. He was tired from not sleeping and had a lot of questions on his mind. Horr kept asking himself, "Will everything Red planned work?"

Horr assured Sheriff Williams and Chief Walker that he would make every effort to obey the rules of the institution and that he would try and make as good a record as possible. Sheriff Williams left with Horr on the Wabash train at 3:15 a.m., Saturday morning, for Chester, Illinois.

Both Alva and Sheriff Williams found empty seats in the rear of the train car, sitting with their backs to the wall. This gave the sheriff a confident feeling, knowing that no one could be seated behind them. Alva was handcuffed and seated next to the window. Williams was sitting to the left of Alva, talking to other passengers on the train. He held a cigar in his hand and from time to time, took a puff and blew out a small cloud of smoke.

Then the sheriff began to laugh. Alva began to laugh also. "What's so funny?" asked the sheriff.

<u>"You government men, when you come looking for answers,</u> you develop a big ego, that's what so funny. The look on your face tells me that you are very happy," declared Alva.

"How do you know that?" wondered Sheriff Williams.

Confidently, Horr replied, "From playing cards and watching people's faces when they look at the hand they have been dealt, that's how. You have fulfilled your goal as sheriff, being part of the biggest murder trial in Danville, and then escorting me to the penitentiary. That's what so funny. You know that I am right."

"Ah... you don't know what you are talking about, Horr," declared Sheriff Williams. "I'm just doing my job." Then he took another puff on his cigar and continued, "I will grant you that your murder trial has been the biggest event in my time as a sheriff."

"What's next for you after you return to Danville, being a detective?" Horr laughed.

There was a period of silence, as if the sheriff had nothing else to say. He moved forward in his seat, holding the cigar in his left hand. "Before we leave this subject about my ego," said the sheriff, "you are right. I do have a great feeling of accomplishment. Thank you for bringing that to my attention. Now go to sleep."

Alva just smiled and laid his head on the window glass and said, "Wake me when breakfast is served."

By the time the train had pulled into the Decatur Depot, both men had dozed off for about three hours. The news about Alva traveling to Chester, Illinois, to serve his sentence had reached the citizens of Decatur. Huddled outside the depot were folks eagerly anticipating the arrival of the train, carrying the convicted murderer. The iron wheels rolling over the steel tracks and the puffing of the locomotive could be heard before the rumble and roar of the engine slowed down to stop at the depot. When the train finally came to a complete stop and the porters opened the train doors, the crowd rushed to the side of the train. The newspaper reporters from the Decatur Herald rushed into the train cars.

"This is serious," uttered the sheriff to Alva, "I wasn't expecting any trouble like this during the trip to Chester."

"How's your ego now?" chided Horr.

"Don't worry about my ego," rebuked Sheriff Williams.

"But you are so young, so impulsive. I am afraid you will expose your true self to the newspaper reporters. Try not to be too modest about your sense of duty," harassed Horr.

By this time some of the reporters had located Alva and the sheriff. One reporter shouted, "Over there! Get a picture of him."

The sheriff stood up, tried to stop the crazed group of reporters, saying, "No pictures; no pictures please." Alva could only laugh.

"I suppose I am being rude, but I repeat no pictures!" ordered Sheriff Williams.

"What about a few words on your trip to the State Penitentiary?" shouted one of the reporters, as he took out his pencil and note pad from his coat pocket.

Just then Alva got a glimpse of a man in the crowd wearing the grand hat. It was like time had stopped. Alva didn't hear what the sheriff said to the reporters. His eyes were focused on the gentleman standing on the depot platform. Folks gathered on the platform blocked Alva's view of the man's face at first. Then the man moved to where Alva could see him. It was James Smith standing on the platform. Alva knew he could not show any interest in the man. Smith tipped his hat and walked away. "My friends are still looking after me," thought Horr with a smile on his face.

Alva turned his head away from the window just in time to hear the porter shout, "All aboard!" and the train conductor blew the whistle. The curious crowd stepped back away from the train. Slowly, the train started moving and in no time the train was out of sight and up to speed.

Alva sank back into his seat and let out a long sigh, he tried to relax. He told himself that the plan that Red had made for him would work out. Then his legs started itching again and the same crawling sensations began to bother him in both legs as it did at the Vermilion County Jail the day before. The more he rubbed his legs, the more they itched. At each scheduled train stop, crowds of people would be waiting to see if they could get a look at the murderer. Sheriff Williams was talking to every reporter that would listen to him. His ego was in full bloom.

Alva and Sheriff Williams didn't talk much during the next eight hours. When they did talk, it was about the small towns and cities they were passing through in Central Illinois. Passengers knew when they were coming to a new town by the name on the water tower. Every water tower had the name of the town painted in large letters.

This was a statement from the people of the town saying, "You are here; you have found us; welcome to our part of the world." Some towers were constructed of wood and supported by large oak timber logs; others were built with bricks. They came in different shapes, but most were circular or oval in design. A few looked like a long cylindrical, tube-like structure, standing tall above the trees and buildings, serving as a land mark for travelers. Some towers had American flags painted on them, or a well-known logo of the local area. Where folks could see their home town water tower, they knew they were with friends and family-at towns like Blue Mound, Stonington, and Taylorville. By the time they arrived in East St. Louis, the train had stopped at ten different small towns along the way. At the train depot in East St Louis, Alva and Sheriff Williams switched trains. As soon as the train had loaded on wood and fresh water, they boarded the southbound train to Chester at eleven o'clock. The train moved slowly at first, then pick up speed gliding fast and smooth past freight yards, past tenements with washing strung on lines, past warehouses on the edge of town.

Alva dozed off as soon as the train left the train depot. It helped him forget the irritation in his legs. They arrived at Chester at about two o'clock Saturday afternoon. Horr was processed into the penitentiary during the afternoon and began his sentence as a regular inmate of the Southern Illinois Penitentiary. The minute Horr was placed in his cell, he began plotting his escape. At first the escape seemed almost impossible because he was on the upper floor of the prison. He worked in the kitchen as a cook. Shortly after Horr arrived at Chester penitentiary, a fellow prisoner offered him a glimmer of hope, by giving him a sketch of the prison farmland. At that time, the Southern Illinois Penitentiary inmates were responsible for harvesting all food for themselves.

Walls enclosed the eleven and a half acres of the prison grounds. The rear wall ran over the top of the prison's rock quarries. The original buildings were all built by inmates' labor. The north and south cell houses each contained 400 cells on four tiers. Inmates lived two to a cell. None of the cells had plumbing; buckets were used instead.

The first year Horr began planning his escape by making a detailed study of the guard's routines and prison security. During that time, Horr was a model prisoner. He was rated under the Progressive Merit System and given a rating of "A", the highest rating for an inmate. This rating allowed inmates to write two letters a week, but did not include any act of kindness from the prison guards. The only time Horr was given any favorable consideration was when the prison warden, James White, would meet with him to talk about his journeys during the year he was on the run. The warden was anxious to hear him explain, in detail how he survived without any help. Alva never gave away any of the escape plans or any names of associates who helped him. Horr distrusted the warden. The warden would always ask for more details each time they met. These discussions with the warden opened the door for him to be given better treatment by the prison guards. By the end of 1917, Horr had been in prison for 28 months. The warden had stopped meeting with him but always made sure Horr was **alive and well, safe and sound.**

Basically, being ignored by the warden offended Horr. But in June of 1918, six months later, when the warden made him a trustee prisoner, he was no longer offended. This gave him new status within the prison. Trustee prisoners had authority over other prisoners. Prisoners who were not trustees were sub-ranked as "do-pops".

At night, trustees helped keep order along with two prison guards. All other guards were off duty. Trustee prisoners were responsible for the institution's perimeter security; this was the last part of Red's plan. During the day, the prison barracks were empty, since most prisoners worked in the fields. At night, the two guards made their rounds in the central corridor, but did not volunteer to go into the barrack units. Trustees were assigned to keep the order at night in the barrack cells.

In January of 1919, Horr was assigned to the prison chicken farm during the day. As a trustee, he was allowed to leave and reenter to the prison. Late Wednesday night or early Thursday morning, March 6, 1919, Horr escaped from the prison, never to be seen again.

Word of the escape came to Danville on Thursday morning in a telegram from Warden James White to Sheriff Williams. The telegram contained no particulars as to how the escape was made. Horr spent just three years and seven months in prison before the escape.

On Friday March 7, 1919, Illinois Governor Edward Lowden offered a reward of $50.00 for the capture of Alva C Tenil Horr. The reward announcement was sent to every sheriff and chief of police in the state. Having been a trustee, it was believed that after making his last security check of the perimeter on the morning of September 6, 1919, he just walked away.

No trace was found of the escaped convict by the local sheriff's office.

After March 6, 1919, Alva C. Tenil Horr was never found. He was never again in trouble with the law. He had ten years and eleven months remaining on his twenty-five-year sentence. Horr's sentence was reduced to fourteen years for good behavior. There are no records or documents of any efforts to search for Horr after March 1920. The following chapter outlines Alva C. Tenil Horr's life after March 1919. Do you know what happened to Mr. Horr? The tips that I have given you in this book will lead you to Mr. Horr's whereabouts until his death. It is now time for you to use your detective skills to solve the whereabouts of Alva C. Tenil Horr before reading the next chapter. If you would like to send me your best guess as to the where about of Mr. Horr, you may send it to www.bookspreferred. com, click on the Guestbook tab and add your comments.

Tips and Hints as to where Alva C. Tenil Horr is located

Chapter 1

Do-Pop

Red
Adrianoplis
Your corrupt, no-good friends
Smith Transfer Company

Chapter 2

Tilton
I would change my name
Something like Meeker
You're soft and unable to stand hardship
His brother-in-Law sent him here
I have given two years of my life for you
A day when my debt will be paid in full
All Red needed to do is say the word, and things
happen

Chapter 3

Friends that will help me, whenever I need help!

Chapter 4

You need to pay attention to the questions asked of you
Taxi driver returned to the scene

Chapter 5

If Horr is not found in the next day or two

Chapter 6

Find the trail back to Danville, and I will find Horr

Chapter 7

Left by train
East side of the river, disappearing
No trace of the body was found
Still alive
I must have something that he wants
Seeks out a friend
But no trace of Horr could be found

Chapter 8

Make sure you wear this hat at all times
What do you think you are, a trustee?

That's my family now, they will take care of me until
I die. That's That's what they call me in these parts
Talk to no one
I was told never to use that name

Chapter 9

Have you been to these two places?

Chapter 10

So, you are going to be a Detective

Chapter 11

All but one of my rooms are filled with boarders

Chapter 12

The Italian was Horr's contact after leaving Havana

Chapter 13

You will be a free man in less than five years
I will see you on the Mississippi River
Thomas Adrianoplis was part of the escape plan

Chapter 14

Thomas Adrianoplis, better known as Thomas
Andrews, and even better known to Horr as "The
Italian"
His brother-in-law had the information he needed
He boarded at City Point, another suburb

Chapter 15

Count Them 1 2 3 4 5 6 7

Chapter 18

Alive and well, safe and sound
You, government men, when you come looking for
answers

These are your clues for finding him. Hopefully, you now know
where Alva C. Tenil Horr's life ended.

CHAPTER NINETEEN

Truth Be Told

It's been quite a journey for Alva since shooting his wife, Ida, on Wednesday afternoon, September 16, 1914. Since jumping into that vehicle on the morning of September 17, 1914, near Hooton cemetery, he encountered more danger than he could have possibly imagined. Life is a story and we all have a story to tell. Alva's and Ida's story unfolded like a drama— from the diamond rings to the shooting on Williams Street, then the path Alva traveled for the next eleven months before the trial, the trial itself, the conviction and imprisonment, and finally his escape from prison in March of 1919.

Truth be told, we need to know the rest of the story. Stories are how we figure things out. Look at our fixation with the news. Every day, in all part of the world people read papers, or use computers, mobile devise, or TV's, and radios to be informed by the news. It because we humans have this craving for meaning for the rest of the story. Though Alva's and Ida's eyes we saw what their life story entailed, the courage of Ida, and the grief of her family. We hope to find in someone else's story something that will help us understand our own. The journey that Alva traveled for most of his adult life was a hard life. The insurmountable odds that he faced in his journey led to his downfall and things fell apart all around him. This is why, if you want to get to know someone, you need to know their story.

Let me bring this story a little closer to home. What better escape is there than traveling back in time with a compelling historical mystery? One of the reasons many people read is to escape. It's nice to step out of our own world for a while. Life is not always easy, and even when things are going somewhat smoothly, readers enjoy the chance to take a break from their own lives.

While this mystery novel offers plenty of escapism, it also addresses some serious real-life issues then and now:

Question and Issues

1. Alva was a good kid but not a smart one. Loved sports but did not like to work. That was the conflict between Alva and his father. How real is that statement, then and now, between parents and their children? The key word in this statement is "smart". Alva acknowledged his difficulties in reading and writing and was always challenged by his lack of education. Education enhances lives. It ends generational cycles of poverty and disease, and provides a foundation for sustainable development. A quality, basic education better equips individuals with the knowledge and skills necessary to adopt healthy lifestyles.

2. What poor choices did Ida make that contributed to her unhealthy relationship with Alva? If we had a crystal ball that would tell us the future, then no one might make a mistake.

3. "Do you want us to call the police?" May, the café employee asked. "No!" Ida said. How many times will you say, "No" before you say "Yes" in your personal matters before the matter becomes public?

4. I just have to convince my father that I mean what I say. How many opportunities should you have?

5. Alva drank excessively at times. Did his problems go away the next day after a night of drinking? No! What about your problems? Make a plan and follow the plan. You don't plan to fail, rather, the problem is if you fail to plan.

6. Horr's father, Allen, refused to talk with Alva. If you cannot communicate, how will you restore your relationship with family and friends?

7. Horr had been coached in jailhouse jargon when he was in prison the first time. That's when he learned to read and write at a very low level. The only reason he developed these skills at that point in his life was because he was motivated. How motivated are you in developing a skill, and for what reason? Get busy!

8. "You need to pay attention to the questions asked of you. Think before you answer someone," said Clark. Too many people listen with their mouths and fail to use their eyes and ears. Do you look at the person with whom you are talking and do you listen carefully?

9. It was said that the only time our family gets together these days is when someone passes. Can you relate to that statement?

10. "Don't ask so many questions." The most important question is the one that you never ask. If you are afraid to ask a question, you have a greater chance to fail.

11. "This is my job today." Ida's father was always speaking about what his job was in taking care of Ida. This reminds me of a song, "That's My Job" written by Hap Hall and recorded by Conway Twitty. The words to the song are as follows. You can listen to the song on the internet.

THAT'S MY JOB
Recorded by Conway Twitty
Writer: Hap Hall.
I woke up cryin' late at night – when I was very young
I had dreamed my father – had passed away and gone
My world revolved around him – I couldn't lie there anymore
So, I made my way down the mirrowed hall and tapped upon his door.

And I said, "Daddy, I'm so afraid!
How would I go on, with you gone that way? Don't wanna cry anymore
So, may I stay with you?"

And he said,
"That's my job, that's what I do
Everything I do is because of you
To keep you safe with me...
That's my job, you see."

Later we barely got along – this teenage boy and he Most of the
fights it seems – were over different dreams. We each held for me...

He wanted knowledge and learning – I wanted to fly out west
"Said I could make it out there – if I just had the fare
I got have will you loan me the rest?"

And I said, "Daddy, I'm so afraid
There's no guarantee in the plans I've made
And if I should fail, who will pay my way back home?"

And he said,
"That's my job, that's what I do Ev'olthing
I do is because of you to keep you safe with me ...
That's my job, you see."

Every person carves his .pot – and fills the hole with life And I pray
someday I might – light as blight as he.

Woke up early one blight fall day – read the tragic news After all
my travels, I settled down – within a mile or two
I make my livin' with words and times – and all the tragedies Should
go into my head and out instead – as bits of poetry.

But I say, "Daddy I'm so afraid
How will I go on – with you gone this way?
How can I come up – with a song to say, "I love you?"

"That's my job, that's what I do
Ev'orthing I do is because of you
To keep you safe with me...
That's my job, you see."

"Ev'rything I do is because of you
To keep you safe with me."

In every escape, one thing counts more than anything else: "luck", no matter how carefully the escape was planned. Alva C. Tenil Horr was a very street-smart individual, a person who could see the big picture and was disciplined in staying focused on the problems that faced him. This was nothing new to him. He had to manage his whole life this way. From the day Horr left Danville, until his escape from the Chester Illinois State Penitentiary, Red had protected Horr with a written plan. The outside help that Horr received from the Black Hand Family was the cornerstone of his escape. Without their help, Horr would not have safely gotten out of Vermilion County, Illinois.

Now, let's focus on the question, "what happened to Alva C. Tenil Horr?" Based on my investigation and documents of records the following facts are known.

Alva did not attend school and could not read or write very well, nor could he speak with a good quality of sound. His local dialect voice was hard to understand, which was very common in those days. When he had to give someone detailed information about himself, that person would write down what they thought Alva was saying. Many of the documents that I have discovered are written by different people. The single signature on record that I have located was found on the marriage license.

Have you heard the statement, "Dead men tell no tales, but their handwriting does?" Your writing tells a compelling tale about yourself and your secrets. The analysis of the strokes of letters written by a person can reveal very specific traits in a person's character; strokes of letters can be interpreted to find out more about your personality. Here is the analysis of Alva C. Tenil Horr.

This signature is the only non-counterfeit signature I found. Alva's hand writing was embellished. He lacked cultural refinement, has low intelligence, is vain, selfish, immature, and dishonest. The letter "A" is unfinished, "no cross in the middle," shows he was extremely diplomatic. He was often timid, lied, and dissimulated (hides true feelings) due to inner anxiety and anguish. He was vulnerable (at risk), and susceptible (having a tendency). Alva's handwriting showed evidence of deliberateness (to consider something carefully and in detail) with possible procrastination (postpone doing something lazy). Alva was deceitful and dishonest, high strung, won't take criticism, and was stubborn. He was a mean, moody person, who sometimes lacked emotional stability. Alva would, nearly always, take a chance when confronted with danger (gambling). Alva was habitually rebellious, whether the pressure be good or bad.

This one single document brought the story of Alva Horr full circle because one's handwriting expresses who the person really is.

Alva's father, Allen HARR (not Horr), who did not have a good quality sounding voice, was also hard to understand. The last name on the marriage license for Alva and Ida was listed as Horr. The person completing the marriage license document entered the name as they understood or heard it. (Reference 1902 Marriage License) From that point forward, the family officially went by the last name of Horr. From 1906 to 1910 the Danville, Illinois City phone directories listed Alva and his father Allen under the last name Horr. (Reference Danville City phone Directories)

Alva C. Tenil Horr was born Alvin C. Harr. (Reference 1880 United States Federal Census)

Alva C. Horr used the alias Tenil Horr, Not Tennil (check the spelling) (Reference official Criminal Court Records Fifty Fifth day of May Term A.D. 1915, Friday, August 13th, 1915)

Alva Horr escaped from the Southern Illinois State Penitentiary on March 6, 1919. The Illinois State archives records, from the office of the Secretary of State, reveal that the investigation was discharged, March 26, 1920, one year after Alva escaped. No other records show that a search was continued after that.

No police documents were obtained by my investigation. The Danville Police Department records unit has no documents on file for any criminal activity for Alva C. Tenil Horr. Very few documents were found in the Illinois State Archives Department of Corrections.

James Smith and Thomas Andrew helped Alva escape from the Southern Illinois State Penitentiary. This was all part of the plan that Red had organized. After his escape Alva went by the alias of William Kincanon and lived in Tilton Illinois, (Danville area) with is sister, Minnie Laura Collier, and brother-in-law, David Collier, reference (Fourteenth Census of the United States 1920 Population) until his death. Remember the tip in chapter seventeen **"his brother-in-law had the information Horr needed" He** did not own any property and worked in pool halls, getting paid cash for the work he performed. He did not have a Social Security Number and no tax returns. Clark Meeker, Ida's father, did not look for Alva after he escaped from the Southern Illinois State Penitentiary. He was 76 years old and in poor health.

Both Ida's parents died without knowing what happened to Alva. Alva would have been released from prison in 1929 and would have been a free man until his death. There is no certification of death records in Vermilion County, Illinois, with the name of William Kincanon, Bill Kincanon, Billy Kincanon, or Kincanon from 1900 to 1988. Alvin C. Harr, AKA, Alva C. Tenil Horr, Alva Stall, Tennil Horr, William Kincanon, Bill Kincanon, Billy Kincanon died a pauper. His cadaver (body) remained unidentified for an extended period in the Danville City Morgue and his funeral services were paid for by the local government funds. No grave marker was placed at the grave.

The following documents assisted me in uncovering the whereabouts of Alva C. Tenil Horr.

1. Alva C. Horr's real name (Alvin C. Harr) source <u>Ancestry. com</u> web page
2. Lila Harr Allen Horr's real name (Allen Harr) mother source <u>Ancestry.com</u> web page
3. Allen Harr and family members source 1880 U.S. Census Official Document
4. Marriage license for Alva and Ida September 1, 1902 source Vermilion County Clerk's office
5. 1906 Danville, Illinois City Directory with Clark Meeker's listing source Vermilion County Museum
6. 1906 Danville, Illinois City Directory with Allen and Alva Horr's listing source Vermilion County Museum
7. 1907 Danville, Illinois City Directory with Allen and Alva Horr's listing source Vermilion County Museum
8. 1907 Danville, Illinois City Directory Smith Transfer Company listing source Vermilion County Museum
9. Danville, Illinois City Directory Alva and Ida Horr listing source Vermilion County Museum
10. The Danville Commercial News Paper dated Thursday Sept. 17, 1914 "Slays His Wife" article
11. Ida Horr Certification of Death Record source Vermilion County Clerk's office
12. Danville, Illinois City Government 1914 source Vermilion County Museum
13. Danville Street Directory (Williams Street) 1312 Wm. Drucker, 1316 S. A. Phillips Listings
14. Southern Illinois Penitentiary inmate records 1915 Recorded (Alvie) Horr source Chief Records Officer Office of Inmate Records State of Illinois

15. Southern Illinois Penitentiary inmate records 1920 Recorded (Alvie) Horr source Chief Records Officer, Office of Inmate Records State of Illinois

16. David Collier, Minnie Collier, and William Kin-canon 1920 U.S. Census official document

17. Minnie Collier and spouse David Collier source <u>Ancestry.com</u> web page

18. Last available picture of Alva C. Horr source Danville Commercial News Paper

Name:	**Alvin C. Harr**
Age:	4
Birth Year:	abt 1876
Birthplace:	Illinois
Home in 1880:	Danville, Vermilion, Illinois
Race:	White
Gender:	Male
Relation to Head of House:	Son
Marital Status:	Single
Father's Name:	Allen Harr
Father's Birthplace:	Illinois
Mother's name:	Maggie Harr
Mother's Birthplace:	Indiana
Neighbors:	
Occupation:	At Home
Cannot read/write:	
Blind:	
Deaf and dumb:	
Otherwise disabled:	
Idiotic or insane:	

Household Members:	Name	Age
	Allen Harr	29
	Maggie Harr	28
	Johnny Harr	11
	Louisa Harr	9
	Minnie Harr	7
	Alvin C. Harr	4
	Gracie Harr	10m

Name:	**Lula Tipps** **[Lula Harr]**
Birth Date:	17 May 1871
Birth Place:	Williamsport, Indiana
Death Date:	2 Jul 1933
Death Place:	Danville, Vermilion, Illinois
Burial Date:	4 Jul 1933
Burial Place:	Danville, Vermilion, Illinois
Death Age:	62
Occupation:	Homemaker
Race:	White
Marital Status:	M
Gender:	Female
Residence:	Danville, Vermilion, Illinois
Father Name:	Allen Harr
Father Birth Place:	Indiana
Mother Name:	Margaret Campbell
Mother Birth Place:	Indiana
Spouse Name:	George E. Tipps
FHL Film Number:	1675013

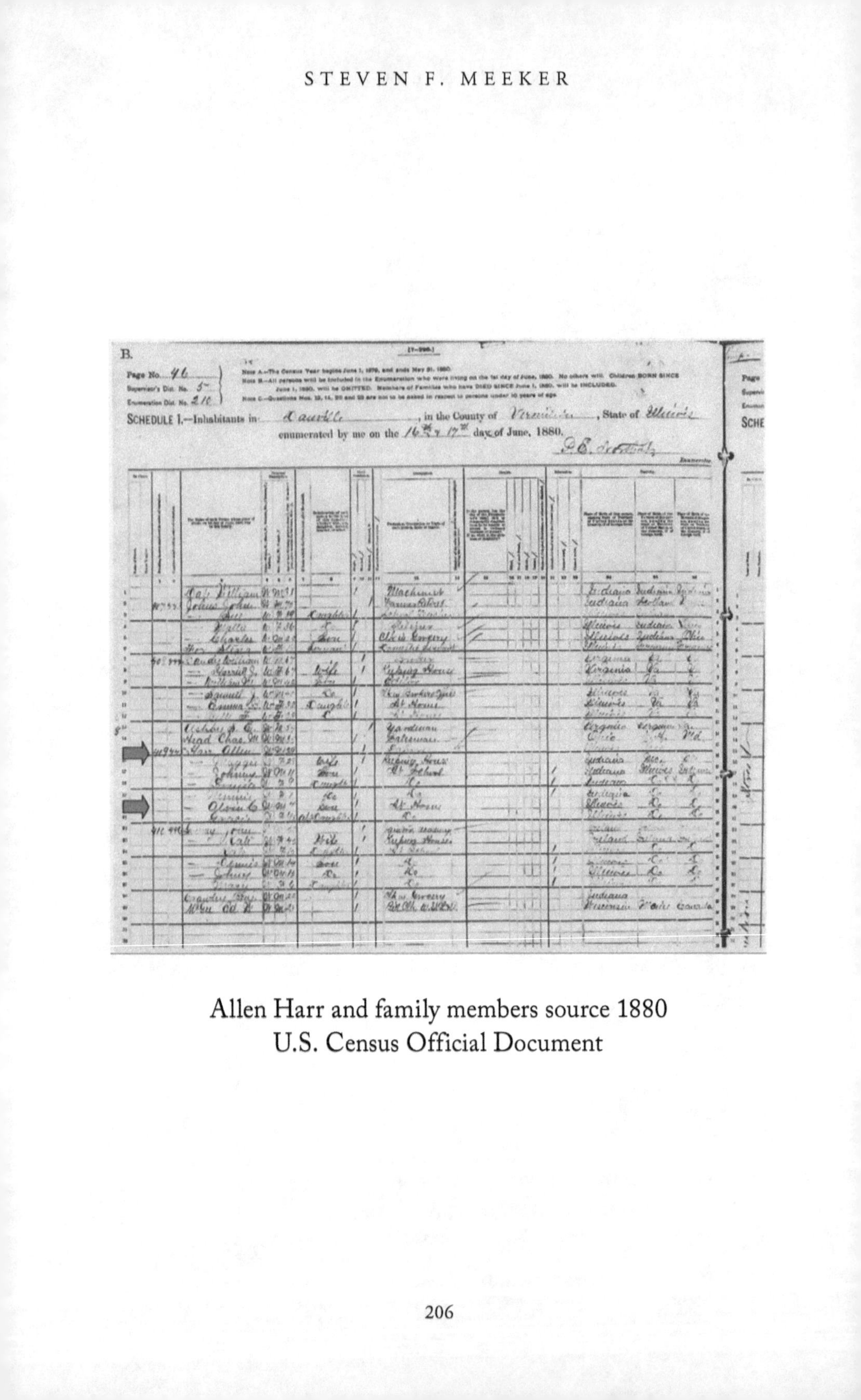

Allen Harr and family members source 1880
U.S. Census Official Document

Marriage License for Alva and Ida September 1, 1902, source Vermilion County Clerk's office

Talking Machines BENJAMIN TEMPLE OF MUSIC 30-32 N. VERMILION

350 ZORN'S CITY DIRECTORY

MAYS JOHN F, restaurant 131 E Main, h 847 E Main. Mrs Senora A.
Mayse Minnie (col), res rear 118 Hays.
Meacham Asa P, student, rms over 117 N Walnut.
Meade Annie, teacher, res 740 Logan ave.
Meade Cyrus, farmer, h 2708 E Main. Mrs Arzella.
Meade David, teacher, h 740 Logan ave. Mrs Lucy.
Meade E E, feed dlr, h 822 E Main. Mrs Nora.
Meade Jessie, insp Gus M G Co, res 740 Logan ave.
Meade Margaret, student, res 740 Logan ave.
Meade Ray, clk Wab R R Tilton, res 740 Logan ave.
Meadows Edgar H, painter, res 310 Franklin. Mrs Jessie.
Meadows James (col), lab, res 342 E Madison. Mrs Anna.
Meadows Thomas (col), res 342 E Madison.
Meagher Frederick, mach C&EI, res 2009 Cannon, Oaklawn.
Mealke Jennie (wid), h 28 Vermont ave.
Meagher John, fireman E&TH, rms 204 Wisconsin ave, Oaklawn.
Meck Joseph, clergyman, res 115 E Seminary. Mrs Matilda.
Medaris Fred, barber 107 E Main, h 303 E Williams. Mrs Ocha.

Vermilion County Abstract Co. IN CONTINUOUS BUSINESS SINCE 1869. 4 E. MAIN ST.

Medrow Chris, res 3020 E Main.
Medrow Fred, miner, h 502 S Bowman ave. Mrs Mary.
Medrow William, butcher 403 South, res 832 Commercial. Mrs Ida.
Meece Scott, carp, res 23 Buchanan.
Meehan John J, foreman 218 W Main.
Meek Carl, barber 7 E Main, res 208 N Jackson. Mrs Anna.
Meek Charles E, carp, h 19 Wisconsin ave, Oaklawn. Mrs Belle
Meek Elijah T, carp, h 2513 Henderson, Oaklawn. Mrs Rachael
Meek Fred, foreman bridge gang, res 442 South. Mrs Dollie.
Meek Isaac, miner, h 11th st, Highland Park.
Meek Jasper N, carp, res 903 May, Germ. Mrs Olive.
Meek Nora E, res 2513 Henderson, Oaklawn.
Meek Perry, painter, res 2513 Henderson, Oaklawn.
Meeker Charles, teamster ,res with Clark Meeker.
Meeker Clark, lab, h Morin's add, near Williams st bridge. Mrs Margaret.
Meeker E M, prop feed stable, res 15 South. Mrs Mary.
Meeker F Scott, feed dlr, res 15 South.
Meeker Lillian, res 206½ E Main.

Force & Booth Co. Carpenters' Tools A SPECIALTY 126 N. VERMILION

Patent Medicines 201 E. MAIN STREET **A. ESSLINGER**

OF DANVILLE, ILLINOIS. 351

Meeker Miles A, foreman 117 N Walnut, h 205 W North. Mrs Grace.
Meeker Minnie, res rear 109 Green.
Meeks A E, lab, 126 N Hazel.
Meeks Claude, electrician, res 205 N 3d, Ver Hts. Mrs Lizzie.
Meeks Esther, res with James Meeks, Morin's add.
Meeks Ida, teacher, res 601 Wayne.
Meeks James, teamster, res Morin's add, near Williams st bridge. Mrs Clara.
MEEKS JAMES A (Rearick & M), master in chancery, office 506 The Temple, h 508 Elizabeth. Mrs Frances P.
Meese Joseph, supt for A. Cruzan, h 1104 Grant. Mrs Gleen.
Meese Richard, driver Am Hom Co, h 16 W Bridge, S D. Mrs Rose.
Mefford Minnie (wid John), res Alma Hotel, Danv June.
Meharry Charles W, barber, h 1004 Myers, Germ. Mrs Clara.
Meharry Clyde, clk 900 E Fairchild, res 912 Maple, Germ. Mrs Millie.
Meharry H F, lab, h 522 Harmon ave. Mrs Martha.
Meharry John, carp C&EI, res 807 Martin. Mrs Mary.

European Plan E. T. BATES, Prop. 9-19 S. Hazel **Saratoga Hotel**

Meharry Wm L, laundry driver, h 428 Harmon ave. Mrs Frances.
Meigroth A J, civ eng, rms 505 W Madison.
Meinke Albert J, watchman Danv Gl Co, res 1509 E Fairchild.
Meinke Christina, res 1509 E Fairchild.
Meinke Frederick, wks C&EI, h 1411 E Fairchild. Mrs Sophia.
Meinke Frederick sr, carp C&EI, h 521 Green. Mrs Caroline.
Meinke Frederick, lab, h 1110 E Main. Mrs Frederica.
Meinke Frederick jr, caller Wab, res 519 Green. Mrs Mary.
Meinke Emily, res 15 Fremont.
Meinke Frederick, lab, h 1337 E Main. Mrs Lena.
Meinke Mary (wid), h 1509 E Fairchild.
MEIS BROS CO (Joseph and Alphonso), dry goods, etc, 102-106 E Main.
Meis Alphonso (Meis Bros), rms 217 W Harrison.
Meis Joseph (Meis Bros), rms 216 Franklin.
Meis Lucian (Meis Bros), rms 126 Franklin.
Meis Milton, clk 102 E Main, rms 126 Franklin.
MEITZLER & CO (J W and Geo P), cigars, tobacco, etc 17 W Main.

GONES & SANDUSKY 37 N. VERMILION ST. **Furniture of Quality**

1906 Danville, Illinois City Directory with Clark
Meeker's listing, source Vermilion County Museum

BENJAMIN TEMPLE OF MUSIC
FOR EVERYTHING IN THE MUSICAL LINE

278   ZORN'S CITY DIRECTORY

Hooton Maud, res 207 Buchanan.
Hooton R Albert (H Bros), h 503 W North.
Hooton Reason, bricklayer, res 628 Oak. Mrs Francis M.
Hooton Roberta, h 207 Buchanan.
Hoppe Louis, barber 119 E Main, h 1344 N Walnut. Mrs Jennie.
Hoppe Millie, teacher, res 1344 N Walnut.
Hopper C L, carp, res 1413 Sherman. Mrs Laura.
Hopper Orville F, life ins agt, h 1003 Robinson. Mrs Grace D.
Hopping Edward, switchman, res 437 Short. Mrs Lucy.
Hopkins D A, fireman C&EI, res 2105 Cannon, Oaklawn.
HOME BLDG ASSOCIATION, J H Phillips secy 110 W Main
Hormig Frank, police officer, h 1001 Collett, Germ. Mrs Sophia.
Horn William, barber 9 W Main, res 7 W Davis. Mrs Parthenia
Hornecker James W, ins agt, rms 16 Hays. Mrs Rose.
Hornbeck Frank W, salesman 23 N Verm, res 609½ Robinson.
    Mrs Emma J.
Horner Jesse (col), lab, res 449 E Williams. Mrs Alice.
Horr Allen, miner, res 518 E North. Mrs Maggie.
Horr Alva, barkpr, res 703 E VanBuren. Mrs Ida.
Horr Lucy, res 608 E Seminary.

Vermilion County Abstract Co.
IN CONTINUOUS BUSINESS SINCE 1869.   4 E. MAIN ST.

Horsley John, lab, res 114 E Madison.
Horsley Lenna, saleslady 119 N Verm, res 114 E Madison.
Hosby Joseph (col), miner, res 924 N Oak. Mrs Josephine.
Hosch August, lab Gas Co, h 909 May, Germ. Mrs Mary.
Hosch Annie (wid John), res 822 E Fairchild.
Hosch Mrs Anna, h 1617 E Fairchild.
Hosford Harry M, timekpr C&EI, res 453 Oak.
Hosford Raleigh M C, P O insp, h 453 Oak.
Hosford Wm H, clk Fed Court, res 453 Oak.
Hoshaw Nathan, blksmith, h 115 Oakwood ave, Ver Hts.
    Mrs Sarah.
Hosick Chauncey L, lab C&EI, h 612 Anderson. Mrs Leah.
Hoskins Earl, res 1432 N Walnut.
Hoskins Ethel, res 1432 N Walnut.
Hoskins Samuel H (col), barber 26 N Hazel, rms 394 Union ave
Hoskins Theodore, farmer, h 1432 N Walnut. Mrs Carrie.
Hoskins W J, mach C&EI, res 34 Virginia ave. Mrs Opal.
Hostin Scott (col), barber, res 212½ South.
Hotel Majestic, M B Skorcz propr 124 Ohio ave, Oaklawn.
Hottle Joseph, eng C&EI, res 519 N Collett. Mrs Hattie.

Force & Booth Co.   YALE & TOWNE
Builders' Hardware
126 N. VERMILION

Everything in the Drug Line   **A. ESSLINGER**
201 E. Main Street.   Tel. 64

OF DANVILLE, ILLINOIS.   279

Hottle Laura, teacher, res 519 N Collett.
Houchin David, boilermkr C&EI, res 18 Iowa ave, Oaklawn.
    Mrs Nellie.
Houchin Huldah (wid), h 18 Iowa ave, Oaklawn.
Houlf Albert, butcher 16 N Jackson, res 612 E Seminary. Mrs
    Catherine.
Houk Martin H, min stock dlr 408 Daniel bldg, res Richland.
House Catherine (wid John), h 1014 E Fairchild, Germ.
Householder E Newton, coal dlr, h 1023 Chandler. Mrs Millie.
Houseley George (col), miner, bds 218 Sidell ave.
Houser James C, carp, res 510 W Fairchild.
Houser Louis, fireman Pawnee mine, h 34 Columbus. Minnie.
Houseman Myles J, lab, bds 326 E Madison.
Housier J H, teamster, res 1016 W Williams. Mrs Mollie.
Houston A J, ticket agt C&EI Danv June.
Houston Edward, miner, res Perrysville ave, near limits. Mrs
    Bessie.
Houston H A, restaurant 20 S Verm, left the city.
Houston Warren W, miner, res 933 Cleveland. Mrs Florence.
Houston, see also Huston.

European Plan **Saratoga Hotel**
E. F. HOTEL, Propr.   8-10 S. Hazel

Howard Charles, butcher, res 409 W Madison.
Howard Charles, mach 213 E North, rms 324 E Seminary.
HOWARD E CO, household specialties, H C Emerson mgr
    429 E Main.
Howard Elizabeth (wid), h 312 Grant.
Howard George W, electrician 14 E North, res 312 Grant.
Howard Harley, waiter, rms 111 E Madison.
Howard James M, mach, res 312 Grant.
HOWARD JOHN B, groceries, provisions, etc 617 W Madi-
    son, res 312 Grant.
Howard John L, painter, res 18 Clark.
Howard Mary, res 312 Grant.
HOWARD M L, physician, office and residence 107 Franklin.
    Mrs E May.
Howard Ora, wks C&EI, res 30 Pennsylvania ave, Oaklawn.
    Mrs Clara.
Howard Preston, foreman, h 604 S Main, S D. Mrs Ella.
Howard Wm T, R R postal clk, res 312 Grant.
Howe Horace, paper hanger, res 1207 W Kimber.
Howe Norris, paper hanger, res 1207 West Kimber. Mrs Laura.

GONES & SANDUSKY Furniture of Quality
37 N. VERMILION ST.

1906 Danville, Illinois City Directory with Allen and
Alva Horr's listing, source Vermilion County Museum

HOOKER HENRY F, wife Nellie M, physician 602 Baum Bldg, tel 185, r 317 Franklin, tel 1480.
Hooker Martha J Miss, wks Soldiers' Home.
Hooper Edward L, wife Cora, mach C & E I, r 14 Illinois av.
Hooton Charles B, wife Olivia M, lumber 601-605 N Gilbert, r 607 W Madison.
Hooton George W, wife Charlotte, r 509 W Madison.
Hooton Kendall, r 607 W Madison.
Hooton Maude Miss, r 207 S Buchanan.
Hooton Reas, wife Frances, mason, r 713 N Walnut.
Hooton Miss Roberta, tchr Lincoln Sch, r 207 S Buchanan.
Hooton Roscoe V, driver Wm Hahne, r 713 N Walnut.
Hooton Walter, r 207 S Buchanan.
Hoover Albert, wife Ethel C, plasterer, r 720 N Vermilion
Hoover Carrie Miss, r 223 S Griffin.
Hoover Ethan, wife Nannie, r 10 Delaware av.
Hoover Frank A, wife Goldie, agt Prudential Ins Co, r 909 N Hazel.
Hoover Fred, r 223 S Griffin.
Hoover Harvey, wife Mary E, r 223 S Griffin.
Hoover Kate, wid Milton, r 206 Illinois av.
Hoover Laura V Miss, tchr Douglas Sch, r 909 N Hazel.
Hope John H, wife Maude, miner, r 217 Sidell av.
Hopkins Thomas P, wife Renie, r 4th, Tilton.

Hoppe Louis, barber, rms 314 N Walnut.
Hopper C Lester, carp, r 1413 Sherman boul.
Hopper Clyde, wife Amanda, elect eng, r 322 Harmon av.
Hopper John, wife Jennie, r 820 Walnut.
Hopper Orvil F, wife Grace D, insurance 412 I O O F Bldg, r 932 N Walnut.
Horming Sophie, wid Frank, r 735 E North.
Horn Olpha A, wife Marie, wks C & E I, r 23 Minnesota av.
Horn Wm, wife Mary, bricklayer, r 202 Oakwood av.
Hornbeck Frank W, wife Emma, clk Straus & Louis, r 609½ Robinson.
Horne Wm, wife Parthena, barber, r 114 N Collet.
Horner Edward J, wife Cora, asst supt trans Dan Ry & L Co, r 113 Payne av.
Horner Effie Miss, stenog Mielke Bros, r 702 Sheridan.
Horner Harriet, wid Luke, r 702 Sheridan.
Horner Nellie Miss, r 702 Sheridan.
Horr Allen, wife Maggie, lab, r 209 E North.
Horr Alva C, wife Ida, restaurant opp Wabash pass depot Delmonico Hotel, r 11 5th av.
Horr Williard, wks Opera House, r 209 E North.
Horsly Lena Miss, clk Golden Rule, r 503 N Hazel.
Hosbey Joseph H (col), wife Josephine, capt Fire Co 2, r 1012 Oak.
Hosch Andrew, wife Emma, farmer, r 1128 N Jackson.
Hosch August, driver H Manteufel, r 908 Jewell.

DANVILLE CITY DIRECTORY   385

Smith Paul (col), porter Dowling-Schultz Hdwe Co, r 301 Cherry.
Smith Pauline H Miss, r 517 N Collett.
Smith Phenious, wife Almeta, wks Dan Brick Co, r 1031 Oak.
Smith Philip, wife Josephine, mine foreman, r 606 Cunningham av.
Smith Philip O, clk Allith-P Co, r 1215 N Vermilion.
Smith Ralph, wife Jeanette, lab, r 208 S Vermilion.
Smith Raphael M, wife Annie, miner, r 121 Vance av.
Smith Raymond D, wife Nina, tire repr 48 N Hazel and plant chf Tel Co, r 14 E Roselawn av.
Smith Rebecca, wife Rhodes, r 820 E Seminary.
Smith Richard, wife Irene, piano tuner, r 1210 Harmon av.
Smith Richard K, blksmith C & E I, r 1313 King (S D).
Smith Robert A, wife Margaret, wks C & E I, r 518 Jewell.
Smith Robert J, wks C & E I, r 507 Jewell.
Smith Rose Miss, rms 111 Hayes.
Smith Russell G, r 202 S Main (S D).
Smith R Curt, wife Myrtle, clk Cavanaugh & Meyer, r 18 Pine.
Smith Samuel J, wife Mattie, carp, r 109 W Roselawn av.
Smith Sarah Miss (col), r 114 Short.
Smith Sarah, wid E C, r 322 N Gilbert.
Smith Sarah, wid John, r 114 Short.
Smith Sarah E, wid John, r 526 E North.

Smith Sibbie Miss, seamstress Emery D G Co, r 22 Pine.
Smith Stella ss, public stenog Aetna House, rms 408 Franklin.
Smith S S   waiter Plaza Hotel.
Smith Theo   wife Mabel, carp, r 1223 Marion.
Smith Thom   wks C & E I, r 517 N Collett.
Smith Ther   wife Ida M, coal opr, r 1309 N Franklin.
Smith Thom   wife Belle, mach C & E I, r 803 Harmon av.
Smith Thomas D, wife Rebecca, carp, r 801 N Gilbert.
SMITH TRANSFER CO (N R and A C Smith), office Plaza Hotel, barn 21 E North.
Smith Vida M Miss, stenog Mielke Bros, r 219 W Harrison.
Smith Walt (col), porter L M Goldman, rms 115 Lemon.
Smith Walter D, wife Eleanor, shop supt C & E I, alderman 5th ward, r 1701 E Main.
Smith Walter H, wife Hope, mngr Morris & Co, r 319 N Walnut.
Smith Walter L, wife Hazel, coll clk American Bank & Trust Co, r 120 Conron av.
Smith Walter R, wks Ill Ptg Co, r 702 Sherman.
Smith Warren C, wife Augusta, eng C I & S, r 716 N Hazel.
Smith Wash C, wife Jennie, detective, r 49 Columbus.
Smith Watt V, wks C & E I, r 33 Bremer av.
Smith Wilbert M, wife Clara, cond C & E I, r 13 S Bowman av.

Knabe and Everett
PIANOS

**Benjamin Temple
of Music** 30-32 North
Vermilion

Holycross Wm, wf Myra, plumber, r 546 Commercial.

Holycross Wm, jr, clk, r 846 Commercial.

Home Baking Co (H E Strader, B S Wade) 405 South.

HOME LOAN CO, W A Rochford mngr, 213 Daniel Bldg.

Homrighous George, wf Hettie, jeweler Weber & Turnell, r 707 N Vermilion.

Hong James (Chinese), wks James Sing, r 105 E North.

HOOKER HENRY F, wf Nellie M, physician and surgeon, 315 Temple Bldg, office hours 11 to 12 a. m., 3 to 4:30 and 7 to 8 p. m.; Sundays by appointment, phone 185, r 206 New York, phone 1480.

Hooker Mrs Martha, r 322 N Logan av.

Hooton Charles B, wf Oliva, lumber 603 N Gilbert and 219 W Main, r 607 W Madison.

Hooton George W, wf Charlotte, r 609 W Madison.

Hooton Miss Maude, r 207 S Buchanan.

Hooton Reese, wf Frances M, bricklayer Western Brick Co, r 713 N Walnut.

Hooton Miss Roberta B, tchr Douglas sch, r 207 Buchanan.

HOOTON SCHOOL, A—— Chapin tchr, southeast of city.

Hooton Walter, printer, r —— 8 Buchanan.

Hooton Wm, wf Gertrude —— —— geon 40 College, r 7 S Buchanan.

Hoover Albert, wf Ethel C, plasterer, r 127 Kentucky av.

Hoover Albert J, bartndr E N Smith, r 405 E Main.

Hoover Miss Carrie, r 1108 Wabash av.

Hoover Fred W, driver Knox Furn Store, r 1212 E Fairchild.

Hoover Harvey W, wf Mary E, r 1212 E Fairchild.

Hoover Kate, wid Milton, r 206 Illinois av.

Hope John, wf Maude F, agt Prudential Ins Co, r 217 Sidell av.

Hopkins James O, clk J C Morehouse, r 321 N Walnut.

Hopkins Thomas P, wf Rena, miner, r Page cor Cherry (Tilton).

Hoppe Louis, wf Jennie D, barber C Willis, r 1344 N Walnut.

Hopper C Lester, wf Laura, carp, r 1413 Sherman.

Hopper John, wf Jennie, r 820 N Walnut.

Hopper Orvil F, wf Grace D, agt N Y Life Ins Co, r 912 N Walnut.

Hopper Rouse L, mach C & E I, rms 210 Indiana av.

Hormig Frank, wf Sophia, r 736 E North.

Horn Olpha, wf Mary, wks C & E I, r 1702 Russell av.

Horn Patrick, tel opr, r 202 Oakwood av (V H).

Horn Wm, wf Mary, bricklyr, r 202 Oakwood av (V M).

HORN WM, wf Parthenia (Shields & Horn), r 114 N Collett.

Hornbeck Frank W, wf Emma, clk Straus & Louis Co, r 408½ Robinson.

Horner Edward J, wf Cora, motorman St Ry, r 9 Lake av.

Horner Miss Effie, bkpr Success Co, r 702 Sheridan.

Horner Mrs Harriet, r 702 Sheridan.

Horner Miss Nellie, r 702 Sheridan.

Horr Allen, wf Margaret A, wks Alva Horr, r 209 E North.

Horr Alva, wf Ida, restaurant 13 McDonald, r 21 College.

Horr John I, r 209 E North.

Horr Wm, janitor Grand Opera House, r 209 E North.

Horsley Miss Lenna, clk W H Goff, rms 121½ N Vermilion.

Danville, Illinois City Directory Alva and Ida Horr listing, source Vermilion County Museum

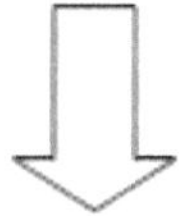

THE COMMERCIAL

VOL. XLVII—NO. 221   DANVILLE, ILL., THURSDAY, SEPT. 17, 1914.

SLAYS HIS WIFE

Tenniel Horr Shoots Woman in Williams Street Battle

STILL AT LARGE

Had Attempted to Kill Woman's Father Before Shooting Her; Caused By Old Feud

---

USE CARE IN ADDRESSING MAIL

(By Associated Press). WASHINGTON, D. C., Sept. 17.—In future, mail addressed to business houses that does not bear the street number of the addressee will not be delivered by the carrier, but will be placed in the general delivery of postoffices, according to an order issued today by First Assistant Postmaster General Roper.

TAKE PERCY BROWN AFTER LONG TIME

ELONGATED SWAIN FROM BAW-BUCK NEIGHBORHOOD, CAPTURED IN DEAD OF NIGHT.

SHOT SCHOOL TEACHER

LARGE CROWD AT LANGLEY HILL

First Hill Climbing Contest is Declared a Success by the Promoters.

GOOD TIME MADE NEGOTIATING HILL

FRED ROBERTS OF WESTVILLE WON THE GREATEST NUMBER OF EVENTS RUN.

WEATHER WAS FINE

Was An Ideal Day For The Sport And The Road Was In Excellent Condition.

HARMONY GIVEN A JOLT BY DEMOCRATS

BIG MEN OF PARTY CONSPICUOUSLY ABSENT FROM O'HAIR ROUNDUP WEDNESDAY.

IT WAS TANTALIZING

Gang Method Men Were in Evidence in Extraordinary Numbers.

FAMOUS LANDM

CERTIFICATION OF DEATH RECORD

CERTIFICATE AND RECORD OF DEATH

VERMILION COUNTY

1. Full Name Ida Horr
2. (a) Sex F. (b) Color W. (c) Single—Married—Widowed—Divorced Married
3. (a) Birthplace Ill. (b) Date of Birth 1882
4. Age 32 Years Months Days Hours
5. Died on the 16 Day of Sept. 1914 at about 5 P.M.
6. Last Occupation (a) Housewife (b)
   From the Year (c) To the Year
7. Former Occupation (a) (b)
   From the Year (c) To the Year
8. Place of Death 1016 W. Will. Danville County of Vermilion.
9. How Long in State Life
10. How Long in U. S. if Foreign Born
11. (a) Name of Father James Meeker
    (b) Birthplace of Father Ill.
12. (a) Maiden Name of Mother
    (b) Birthplace of Mother
The foregoing stated personal particulars are true to the best of my knowledge and belief.
13. Informant J. A. Meeker
    Address Danville, Ill.
14. Place of Burial Farmers Chapel
    Date of Burial Sept. 19" Hour P. M.
15. Undertaker E. Bolton
    Address License No. 113

MEDICAL CERTIFICATE OF CAUSE OF DEATH

(a) Cause of Death Gun Shot Wound (murder)
(b) Contributory (Secondary) Fired by Husband

Witness my hand this 17" Day of Sept. 1914
Signature Ralph M. Cole Coroner
Address Illinois.

Filed for Record this 24" day of Sept. 1914. Thos. J. Dale County Clerk.

July 26, 2011
This is to certify that this is a true and correct copy from the official death record filed with the Illinois Department of Public Health.

Lynn Foster
Vermilion County Clerk

ANY ALTERATION OR ERASURE VOIDS THIS CERTIFICATE

Ida Horr Certification of Death Record, source
Vermilion County Clerk's office

MISCELLANEOUS INFORMATION

CITY GOVERNMENT.

(City Hall, 24 N Walnut.)

Mayor—W C Lewman.
City Clerk—John Torrance.
City Collector—W. J. Parrett.
City Treasurer—Charles T Elliott.
Corporation Counsel—Howard A Swallow.
City Attorney—Buell H Snyder.
City Engineer—W H Martin.
Superintendent of Streets—C. E. Leverenz.
Superintendent of Buildings—L F W Stuebe.
Chief of Police—W G Walker.
Chief of Fire Department—Peter Cessna.
Police Magistrate—W F Heath.
Plumbing Inspector—Wm Connors.
Health Commissioner — Dr S L Landauer.
City Weigher—C A Myers.
City Electrician—Ed Dinsmore.
Board of Local Improvements—W C Lewman, E M Phillips, J W Barger, W D Smith, W H Martin.

Aldermen.

First Ward—Joseph Werner, Frank Schroeder.
Second Ward—J L Bracewell, E M Phillips.
Third Ward—John J Belton, John W Barger.
Fourth Ward—J T Otto, W G Halbert.
Fifth Ward—Walter D Smith, Thomas Reddy.
Sixth Ward—Charles G Swanson, H C Darnall.
Seventh Ward—Walter S Hannum, Edwin Winter.

Committees.

Finance—E Winter, Halbert, Schroeder.
License—J W Barger, Phillips, Werner.
Police—C G Swanson, Belton, Reddy.
Fire and Water—W D Smith, Darnall, Winter.
Public Buildings and Grounds— J T Otto, Phillips, Werner.

Sewerage—W G Halbert, Bracewell, Barger.
Bridges—E M Phillips, Swanson, Schroeder.
Ordinances—J J Belton, Otto, Smith.
Printing—F Schroeder, Hannum, Swanson.
Lighting—Jos. Werner, Halbert, Belton.
Claims—H Darnall, Otto, Bracewell.
Streets and Alleys—W S Hannum, Otto, Reddy.
Health—T J Reddy, Barger, Bracewell.
Markets—J L Bracewell, Darnall, Hannum.
Public Welfare—J L Bracewell, Darnall, Werner.

Board of Election Commissioners.

(City Hall.)

J H Barnhart, pres; W C Brown, sec; Francis M Grimes, chf clerk; Charles G Taylor.

POLICE DEPARTMENT.

(City Hall.)

Chief of Police—W G Walker.
Night Captain—Wm Walters.
Desk Sergeant—Johnson Gammel.
Turnkey—Edward Goulding.
Patrolmen—Ed Vinson, Frank Simpson, Wm Braden, Frank Wrisk, E O Hughbanks, N W Timmons, Frank Coit, John Emerson, Joe Kelly, Frank Flaherty, Mort Phillips, J A Diffenderfer, E A Dyas, William Humble, Irvin Driver, John J Flynn, Charles Saunder, Thomas Rambo, W C Smith, Joseph White, Nelson A Rose, Conley Martin, B Fay Lemon, J M Carpenter, George Garrard, T S Owens, H V Custer, Peter Doocoons, Fred Vutrick.

FIRE DEPARTMENT.

(Headquarters 28 N Walnut.)

Chief—Perry Cessna.
Assistant Chief—Wm Hilga.
City Electrician—Ed Dinsmore.

Fire Co No 1.

(28 N Walnut.)

T E Simmons, capt; Wm Hilton, S B Crewdson, Oscar Fern, drivers; C W

1013	Nathan Weaver.
1014	C C Murphy.*
1015	T R Wright.
1016	S B Parsons.
1017	John M Buser.
1018	David Westwater.*
1019	W A Shepherd.
*	Logan av.
1106	Charles B Myers.
1108	Charles Brady.
1110	Andrew Frederickson.*
*	Romine.
1202	H J Dettman.
1204	J E Smith.
1214	Ernest Ritter.
1218	Union Mission.
*	Meade.
1302	A E Hetherington.
1306	Benj P s.
1308	James Meeks.
1310	Miss M le Crane, Leroy Garretso.
1312	Wm Drucker.
1314	L A Russell.
1316	S A Phillips.*
1318	Vacant.
1320	J H Shepherd.
1324	John F Ridge.*
1330	L W F Stuebe.
1332	John Stuebe.
1348	W E Russell.*
1615	W H Grimes.
1619	W A Cole.*
1628	H H Loutzenhiser,* O E Skelton

WINTER AVENUE—EAST.

(Form 2101 N Vermilion, east to limits.)

402	Mrs Flora Faurot.*
424	Mrs Emma Cummings.*
436	J C Long.

WINTER AVENUE—WEST.

(From 2100 N Vermilion, west to limits.)

100	Thomas Kench.

WISCONSIN AVENUE.

(Form 2501 E Main, north to Cannon.)

5	Ervin Anders.
17	T E Hendricks.
19	W W Hammond.*
27	W D Wood.
28	F E Hervey.*
36	H S Ayling.*

*	Henderson.
101	George Wikle.
102	R S Coffman.
103	Everly Tunis.
105	C E Jackson.
106	P W Dudley.
120	T H Huston.
121	James McDaniel.
145	J F Smock.
146	H C Hill.
147	J R Mahoney.
148	Joseph Kiser.*
149	Mrs Ida Burke.*
150	J F Pierce.
*	Cannon.
201	Joseph Craft.
202	Edward Peterson.
203	E E Hamilton.
204	Mrs M E Swick.
205	J A McWhinney.

WITHMER AVENUE (V H).

(From 1100 Oakwood av, south.)

14	Omar Cripe.
18	Claude Bradford.
102	Vacant.
104	Charles H Pickett.*
108	Ira O Kiger.*
112	C O Randall.*

WOODBURY—EAST.

(From 801 N Vermilion, east to Washington av.)

8	Bert Gardner, Jack Archer.
9	A A Berhalter.*
14	E E White.
*	Hazel
105	W A Barrick.

WOODBURY—WEST.

(From 800 N Vermilion, west to Logan av.)

9	Vacant.
10	J E Tiller.
*	Walnut.
106	Mrs Addie Kane.*
108	Vacant.
110	Pruitt Grocery Co.
110½	C E McGuire, L J Barth.
*	Franklin.
207	Henry Steinway.
209	S J Marshall.
211	Charles Bordolo.
*	Oak.
306	Albert Dickerson.
*	Gilbert.

SOUTHERN ILLINOIS PENITENTIARY

NAME	COUNTY	CRIME	Sentence	When Discharged	REMARKS	
Charles Jackson	Vermilion	aut to murder	P.		[illegible] Leavenworth 1999 / 1 Term Pontiac	
Oscar Jackson	"	Burg			Chester - 1378 / 1 Term Pontiac	
Frank Brown	Williamson	"			[illegible]	
Thomas Buxton	Edgar	Horse Stealing				
James W. Hampion	Champaign	arson / keep				
John Martin	St Clair	to Defraud	P.		alias John Martino	
Benj Franklin	"	B & L	P.			
Jas. Robb	Christian	" " "	P.		Chester # 9366	
Alvie Horr	Vermilion	murder	25 yr		Chester # 6454 / 1 Term Pontiac Escaped	
Wm L Blane	Macoupin	Forgery	P.			
Jas. Hardy	Coles	"				
	"	B & L			alias [illegible]	

Southern Illinois Penitentiary inmate records 1915,
recorded (Alvie) Horr, source Chief Records Officer,
Office of Inmate Records State of Illinois

SOUTHERN ILLINOIS PENITENTIARY.

Vermilion

Received	Reg. No.	Name	Discharged	Sentence	Crime	Re

Southern Illinois Penitentiary inmate records 1920,
recorded (Alvie) Horr, source Chief Records Officer,
Office of Inmate Records State of Illinois.

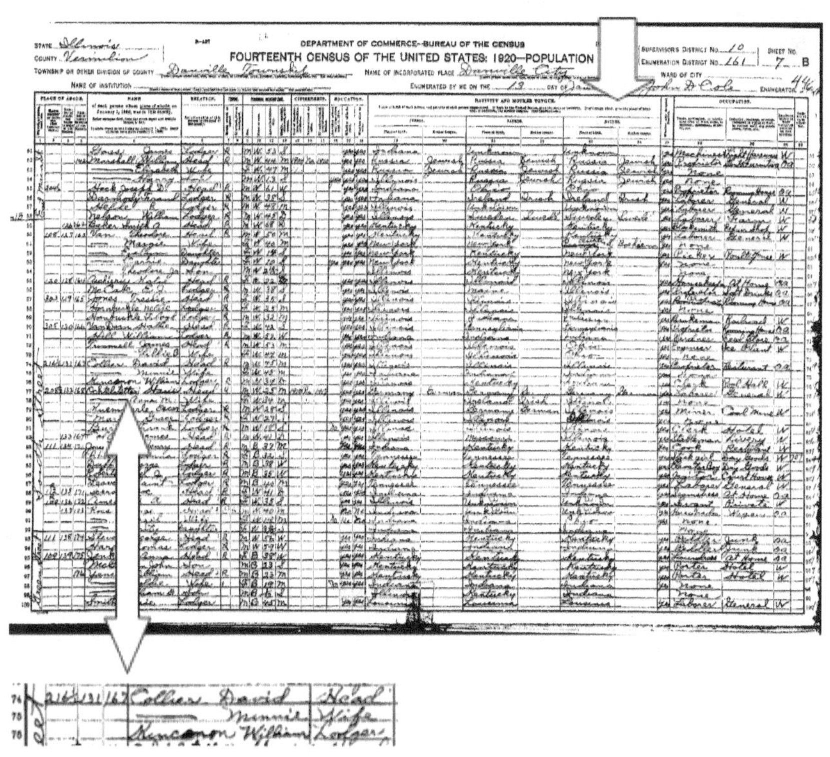

David Collier, Minnie Collier, and William
Kincanon 1920 U.S. Census official document

Name:	**Minnie Laura Collier** **[Minnie Laura Horr]**
Birth Date:	11 Dec 1875
Birth Place:	Attica, Indiana
Death Date:	23 Aug 1936
Death Place:	Tilton, Vermillion Co , Illinois
Burial Date:	25 Aug 1936
Burial Place:	Danville, Vermillion, Illinois
Cemetery Name:	Springhill
Death Age:	60
Occupation:	Housewife
Race:	White
Marital Status:	M
Gender:	Female
Street Address:	903 So. "L" Street
Residence:	Tilton, Danville Twp., Vermillion Co., Illinois
Father Name:	Allen Horr
Father Birth Place:	Frankfort, Indiana
Mother Name:	Margaret Campbell
Mother Birth Place:	Green Castle, Indiana
Spouse Name:	David Collier
FHL Film Number:	1766169

Last available picture of Alvin C. Harr (AKA) Alva C. Tenil Horr